# THE BRIGHT FACE

Geraldi's dandified appearan         air deliberately-bely the steel concealed within. Known as the "Frigate Bird", he is an accomplished card-sharp and dice-cheat, preying upon the sea hawks of unscrupulous gamblers seeking to fleece the unwary. Whilst keeping a very close watch upon Robert Ingall, an Egyptologist accompanied by his daughter Mary, he finds that his old acquaintance Edgar Asprey is also observing the pair. Both men have an eye to stealing Ingall's magnificent golden box, in which is embedded a large emerald, and Asprey proposes that the two join forces to purloin the treasure. But they are not the only ones after it. Five highly skilled thieves are also on the trail of the Egyptologist, and Geraldi finds himself in the position of defending the Ingalls against kidnap in order to preserve the mysterious box for himself . . .

# THE BRIGHT FACE OF DANGER

## MAX BRAND®

SAGEBRUSH
Large Print Westerns

First published in the United States by AmazonEncore

First Isis Edition
published 2017
by arrangement with
Golden West Literary Agency

ISBN 978–1–78541–229–5 (pb)

Published by
F. A. Thorpe (Publishing)
Anstey, Leicestershire

Set by Words & Graphics Ltd.
Anstey, Leicestershire
Printed and bound in Great Britain by
T. J. International Ltd., Padstow, Cornwall

This book is printed on acid-free paper

# Table of Contents

# The Golden Horus

# CHAPTER
# ONE

## "Geraldi Rises Early"

With the dawn, Geraldi rose. He spread a folded blanket on the floor and knelt upon it like an Arab about to pray toward the east. Instead of prayer, Geraldi took out a dice box and fell to work, shaking the dice until they rattled again with a great clatter and then shooting them out upon the blanket, so that they flashed over and over and came to a pause at its end.

It looked like the simplest matter in the world, but the smooth brow of Geraldi was fixed with thought, for the trick was not as simple as it appeared. Try to hold two dice invisibly in the fingers of the same hand that holds the dice box, and yet make those dice rattle prodigiously against each other, and against the leather sides of the box. Do this, then, with an apparent abandon, a careless gesture flinging the dice before one. So Geraldi managed, and sent the dice spinning away, and nine times out of ten he called the turn.

But that was not all. For a half hour he continued this task. Then he varied it, and for a half hour he spun the winking dice down the blanket and made them bounce back from the wall. Enough to destroy all chances of cheating, say the gamblers, but Geraldi knew better. Dice can be made to listen to speech, Negroes believe; if Geraldi did not believe quite so much as that, at least he was willing to trust to manipulation past the point where manipulation was possible. He bounced the dice against the wall, and still two times out of four he won, or three times out of five as luck added to his skill.

Then Geraldi abandoned the dice and sat down cross-legged by the blanket. He took two packs of cards and began to deal poker hands continuously, mixing, dealing, and flicking the hands up for examination. He spoke a few words from time to time: "I win!" "I lose." "He wins." "You win!" And only once did he make a mistake. That time he looked upward with a faint smile, as if to say to the god of gamblers: "Suppose I had put a million on that?" For a whole hour Geraldi worked at this task with perfect patience.

After that, he rolled the blanket, placed it at the foot of the bed, and lay down with his head upon that roll. He was not to rest, however. He produced two revolvers, full-size .45s, heavy and long of barrel, and these he began to spin into the air. He made them cross from hand to hand. He caught them handle down. He made them alight upon one another, handles to handles, or mouth to mouth. Those heavy guns floated from one hand to the other like foolish birds on the wing, graceful and purposeless. Or rather they seemed like bright ghosts more than metal and wood, for the rapid spinning that Geraldi imparted to them made them disappear in mid-air, as though by conjury.

Fast and slow, he kept at his task for a full fifteen minutes. And when at last he stood up, he was perspiring and panting. Then he cleaned and loaded the guns and put them away in cunning slip holsters beneath his armpits.

Still his work was not ended. He had brought up to his room a square of soft, spongy wood a foot across. On this he drew with pencil a black cross, the lines just sufficiently wide to be visible across the room. After that, he opened his pack and took out a folding case of soft, thick chamois that he untied and spread. There appeared a set of eight knives, like hunting knives in a way, and yet with handles that hardly were adequate to accommodate a struggling, straining hand through all the ardors of skinning a deer or a bear. The blades were narrow and only slightly curved.

He laid the knives on the edge of the little table in the center of the room and began to juggle them. The ceiling was not high, and yet before long he had six of those winking bits of steel fluttering and gleaming in the air, twinkling down into his hands to be flicked up again with a spin so violent that they hung aloft as though suspended by invisible wings.

He restored them to the table edge and immediately began to flip them at the penciled cross, holding them in the flat of his palm. Lightly they shot across the room and buried themselves in the target. When all eight were affixed, the outstanding handles rudely fashioned a cross.

He drew them out and examined the marks. Two had alighted fairly upon the lines. The others were a sufficient distance to either side to make Geraldi shake his handsome head. He repeated the attempt, and again and again, but with every repetition his work grew a little more inaccurate. A cloud settled upon that brow, smooth as a child's.

But, abandoning this work, he turned the board and penciled a shaded circle in the center, large as the palm of a hand — a slender hand, like that of Geraldi. At this target he made play in a new fashion, walking about the room at the farther end and, whenever his back was fairly turned upon the goal, spinning and casting. Only one of the eight blades struck the central circle. But the rest were grouped closely around it. And Geraldi actually frowned as he plucked out his handful of steel and recommenced operations. He finally had planted four of the eight knives in the center of the goal, and with this he seemed to rest satisfied.

An oilstone and a few drops of oil, and he proceeded to sharpen the eight at the points, and made sure that all the edges were keen.

Still his morning's work was incomplete.

He began a most strange operation, which was an attempt to climb to the top of the casing that framed his door. This was to be managed with finger holds hardly half an inch deep, and the feet were helpless. By arm power alone he must support himself. Moreover, all must be managed so softly, so delicately, that a sleeper in the room beneath that creaking floor of pine would not be roused when Geraldi's grip slipped and he dropped to the floor again. Light as a bird with stretched wings, he fell. Patient as a spider, he would recommence his climbing until after a half hour he was able to attain to his foolish goal, which was to thrust himself up with one arm above the top of the door frame, and with the other hand catch at the board that rimmed the ceiling. In that manner he was able to support himself for a whole minute, flattened against the wall. Finally he lowered himself to the floor again.

Silent as that work had been, he was breathing hard — yet so controlling every breath that not a sound was heard. His face was flushed, the veins throbbed in his forehead, and perspiration ran down his face like water. He lay for a moment stretched on his back on the floor.

By magic, as it were, all token of fatigue left him. As the stunned, half-beaten boxer sinks helpless on his stool at the end of a round, loose-muscled, weak, and in the single minute of rest recovers himself — his eye clears, the cords of strength stand up again along his legs, his arms, his shoulders, and he can leap like a tiger into the ring at the next tap upon the gong — so rose Geraldi.

Then the hotel bathroom, a thick lather of soap, a cold bath, a strong rub with a towel, and he was ready to dress. This could be an affair of an instant, when occasion demanded. But now there was leisure. For three hours — since four in the morning — he had been constantly at work with hands, wits, or the full play of his muscles. And still he was a shade early for breakfast.

Fine, snowy linen was next to the skin of Geraldi. He wore not socks but golf stockings of thin, English wool that clasped themselves in place through their own elasticity. On his slender feet he fitted low shoes, extremely wide and low of heel, and rather square across the toes. Across the ball of the foot and at the heel were inset corrugated strips of the finest rubber, and the sole leather was so thin, so jointed, that the foot had all the freedom that is given by a tennis shoe. Made after this method, clumsy shoes they would have been except that a master craftsman had fashioned them. They had the look of comfort; they possessed a touch of fashion, also.

Geraldi, as critical of these as a swordsman of another century would have been of a sword blade, moved swiftly and lightly around the room, side-stepping, retreating, like a pugilist shadow-boxing. But at last he was satisfied. He stepped into thin, gray-flannel clothes, the looseness of the trousers and the sleeves accentuating the slenderness of his body and making it appear — what it was not — a trifle weak. The looseness of those sleeves served another purpose — they enabled him to hang that bulky pair of revolvers beneath his armpits. Yet, although a thousand times before he had done this, now he stood and twisted and turned before the mirror, making certain of what movements to the side were apt to reveal the jutting handles or the muzzles of the weapons.

When he had, for this thousandth and first time, reassured himself upon this point, he proceeded to make himself confident upon a still more important subject. He tried the guns singly. He tried them both together, flicking them out with one brief gesture. The warriors of the West had practiced intricate rolls and prepared themselves for shooting from the hip, because, so doing, they did not waste the vital hundredth part of a second necessary to raise the gun to the line of the eye. But the method of Geraldi was better. The very act of drawing flung the weapon into position for an aimed shot. He had no doubt of these guns, or of these movements, but like a general confident in the efficiency of his army he constantly kept himself in review and under inspection.

So when he stepped out from his room with a straw hat in one hand and a narrow Malacca stick in the other, Geraldi looked quite a dandified type — a figure that would bring forth wide grins when he appeared on the street in this rough Western town. But in spite of appearances he was ready for the test, for he was an athlete who had to be forever at the top of his form. He was like a champion who never knew when the supreme test might come and whom the world could challenge when it would. His reward was simply life preserved, but one defeat would be death, to Geraldi.

# CHAPTER
# TWO

## "Two Old Friends Meet"

The dining room of the hotel was proof that San Felice was now a booming town. It had had a treble life — first it was laid out as a sort of mountain metropolis, all the squares blocked out, corner stones laid to mark the streets, and many frame shacks run up. Then San Felice died. The knees of the houses were sprung by wind and neglect and their backs were broken by time. San Felice recovered suddenly on rumor that a railroad was coming that way. There were a few years of frantic life. That ended. Decay set forward once more. But this was the third boom, not a sudden flowering, but a gradual growth. Chance had decided that San Felice was to be turned into a real town because lumber was being felled in the mountains, and someone had found copper ore worth mining. Besides, the cattle business had crept up out of the desert, out of the hills, and now new range was opening to the south of the town.

So Geraldi found the dining room well filled even for breakfast. From the prominent lumberman and the well-to-do tourist down to the professional idler and the hardworking cowpunchers and lumberjacks, all were in the same room, almost elbow to elbow. But

10

even the tourist, who sat at the corner table by the window with his pretty daughter, had made concessions to Western fashions, Western style. And his daughter might have passed as a cowgirl, with a broad-brimmed hat set back on her head, a loose blue blouse, and a silken bandanna knotted at her throat. Only Geraldi made no concessions. As he stood in the door, he was complete to his panama and his thin, chamois gloves. He was a little stooped, it appeared, as though he were inertly relaxed. One would have said that a touch of wind might stagger him; he seemed even a trifle hollow-chested.

Then he saw a small table at the side of the room with two places, one of which was taken by a big lumberjack who attacked his food vigorously, his elbows swinging out at wide angles, his head dipping far down toward his plate of ham and eggs.

Geraldi made the vacant chair through a little silence that had fallen upon the room. The silence was broken by the rumble of the rich lumberman on the farther side: "Now what does a thing like that mean by comin' out here and exposin' himself to the open air?"

"He'll get ate up with rust," said another.

"Leave him be," replied a third, "because the more rich young fools that we get out here, the better it is for us."

These remarks were made in voices that were hardly veiled, yet one would not have thought that they could have carried to the ear of Geraldi. On the contrary, he would have heard every syllable if they had been little more than whispers, and not a whit of his smile diminished — a little, sleepy smile, half politeness, half content with himself, and a spice of satisfaction with the world at large. But in fact it was not all acting. He wanted to make exactly that impression — a rich young man — a rich young fool.

"Is this chair taken?" asked Geraldi.

The lumberjack looked up into his eyes, then slowly surveyed him to the floor.

"I don't see anybody in it," he observed, and turned his attack upon his last slice of ham.

Geraldi sat down, a little gingerly, and turned his smile around the room. He had seen two or three heads go up as he entered, and he knew what that meant. So the fox sticks its nose in the air when it sees the goose. They had seen Geraldi — three cardsharps, he made them out at a glance. Two of them, perhaps, with a great deal of ready cash. The smile of Geraldi grew still brighter, for these were his particular prey. Not in vain was he called the "Frigate Bird." Upon the sea hawks he preyed, leveling tribute.

"Whatcha havin', hey?" the waitress shot at him as she went by with an armful of dishes. "Whatcha havin', hey?"

She did not stop; she merely turned sidewise, and Geraldi raised his head and allowed his smile to grow more marked. Sun-browned and dark of eye, a glorious head was Geraldi's. The waitress blinked and came to an unsteady halt.

"Coffee and toast."

She went on again, still blinking.

"I found a feller . . . ," she began to her chum in the pantry.

"I seen you did," said her irreverent friend. "Go pet him, dearie, and see won't he purr."

"Coffee an' toast," said the lumberjack at the table with Geraldi. "Now what kind of a meal is that, to start a day with?"

"Ah," said Geraldi, "I have an aversion to heavy breakfasts. A light stomach makes a light heart, I feel."

He laughed a little. The laughter was not returned by the lumberjack. The latter paused, one cheek bulging with a wedge of ham; his eyes were glassy with disapproval.

"Huh!" said the lumberjack, and finished his meal with a few broad gestures, the last of which emptied a coffee cup at a mouthful. He rose and went across the room with heavy heels. "Pretty lady, ain't he?" he said, hooking a thumb over his shoulder.

There was more general laughter at this comment, but still Geraldi did not seem to hear it. He put his elbows lightly on the edge of the table, joined the tips of his fingers, and slowly turned his hands so as to admire or criticize the condition of his nails.

Even the tourist, politely inattentive to disagreeable objects, now looked at Geraldi askance, and the lip of his pretty daughter was frankly curling. Then the coffee and toast arrived. The waitress hung a moment over the table. She was rewarded with another smile, and retreated flushed and foolish of face.

But here there was a bit of diversion that took attention from Geraldi. A big cowpuncher, a plump, large man, was riding past the hotel when a dog ran at him barking, and the horse straightway began to perform as though a demon had been wakened in him. It was an artistic exhibition of pitching. With arched back, hard as rock, the pony heaved itself into the air and came down on alternate forelegs. It whirled as though on an oiled pedestal. It snapped itself this way and that, and the enthusiasm of the crowd in the dining room grew enormous. Even the tourist and his daughter left their table and joined the crowd at the windows.

Geraldi, however, did not stir. He went on with his coffee and toast, eating daintily, in smiling content, oblivious to the yells of pleasure.

"Ride him, cowboy!"

"Scratch him fore and aft!"

"Look at him ride straight up. That's a boy!"

Apparently the rider was mastering the horse. Presently the crowd went back to their chairs, and now the hero in person appeared in the doorway.

He seemed far from a Western 'puncher in all but dress. Your ordinary range rider is a leathery, sun-dried fellow. This was a round, soft man, tall, ponderous. He was not greatly darkened by weather, and there was a bright pink in either cheek. He looked around the room for a place.

"That little old son-of-a-gun," said the 'puncher. "He's apt to act up a bit. He gets tired of the look of me and wants to turn me inside out." He spotted the empty chair and came to Geraldi's table. "This free?"

14

"No charge at all," smiled Geraldi, and the other sank into the chair.

He ordered: "Oatmeal, bacon, four eggs, plenty of bread, and don't forget the butter." Then he gave his cheerful attention to his table companion. He seemed to be talking of ordinary commonplaces, but his voice was so skillfully pitched that none of their neighbors could hear the conversation.

"So here we meet again," the fat 'puncher said.

"We meet again, cousin Edgar," Geraldi remarked.

"Not cousin, please," said the other, with a touch of annoyance. "Let the past die. Every day is dead except this one and tomorrow."

"I'll raise no ghosts," Geraldi said. "Have you been having luck?"

"Ah, fair . . . fair," said the man called Edgar Asprey. "I've had my chances, and used them fairly well, here and there. Fortune helps the bold, you know."

"But not always." Geraldi smiled.

"No?" Asprey said, rubbing his soft, thick palms together. "As a matter of fact, I lost a great opportunity. Through you, of course. But I don't mind. I bear no grudges. If only I could understand what was in your mind at the time. What set you on?"

"Why, guess, Edgar."

"The girl, I was sure. You wanted to marry my dear little niece. Was that it? No, because you could have had her for the asking, dear boy. The beautiful and romantic Geraldi made her dizzy."

Geraldi raised his hand, and the other nodded complacently.

"Very well," he said. "I'll drop that theme."

"If you please," Geraldi stated, with just a hint of cold danger in his smile. "But as for motives, Edgar, it was chiefly the pleasure of taking a hand against a very clever fellow . . . a man who had worked out an idea and based it on bedrock."

"Then you saw that I had fish in my claws," said Asprey. "And they call you the Frigate Bird!"

Geraldi made a gesture as foreign as his name. "That's ended," he said.

"And you bear me no malice now, Geraldi."

"No more, at least, than you bear me."

"Come, come. I'm not such a hypocrite. When a man does evil, my dear boy, he has to be prepared to lose . . . and lose gracefully. I did that, I think. Now, Geraldi, let me tell you that I never was gladder to see a man than I am to see you today. If you can work with me, I can put you on the trail of the greatest coup even you have ever had in hand. But the question is . . . can you work with me?"

"Ah," Geraldi said, dropping his forehead in his hand, "let me think it over."

# CHAPTER
# THREE

## "Short History of the Sun"

While Geraldi was lost in thought in this manner, Asprey seemed to pay attention to nothing but his breakfast. He ate hugely, with constant relish. For there was nothing so bad that he failed to find some thread of enjoyment mingled with the evil. The porridge was burned, but still he wrinkled his nose and ate it swiftly. The toast was soggy. He turned up the brown side of each piece and consumed it without hesitation. The coffee was a frightful compound, but he turned it gray with canned milk and swallowed it with avidity.

Still Geraldi thought. "What sort of work may it be?" he asked.

"Good work . . . happy work . . . the very sort of work that you would enjoy, Slim Jim."

At the use of this name, Geraldi looked up with a quizzical lift of his brows. "Frankly" he said, "I've been having a dull time. Only had one thing to interest me lately."

"That?" Asprey said.

"I don't mind telling you. You see the fellow with the pretty daughter? There they get up, now."

"A grand-looking fellow," said Asprey. "And a charming girl. But you're not interested in girls, Geraldi."

"If you don't mind," Geraldi said, "we'll forget that name altogether."

"True, true," Asprey replied. "I forget that you are famous. One murmur of that name, and all your work is hopeless, useless, wasted. The fish fly away from you . . . you starve in a desert of cautious men."

This description made Geraldi chuckle. "It's true," he said. "It's exactly true. I begin to be too well known. My trail has crossed itself too often. Even in London, even in Paris, people begin to know me. The fish are warned off just as they rise to the bait. I am growing lean and evil, Edgar. I am growing cruel with hunger."

"Of course," said Asprey. "But not a thin pocketbook."

"No," Geraldi said. "Crime pays me very well, as usual. I find that there is always money in the bank. But that isn't the point. Why does a man hunt big game? For the heads? For the masks? For the horns or the hides? Or does he hunt to fill the pot?"

"No," Asprey responded. "It's for the sake of seeing the tiger's eyes turn into torches as he charges. Then put out the flame."

"You understand me," Geraldi commented, "like a brother. But I have found that the big game no longer charges. It runs the other way. I've been reduced to perfectly foolish things . . . like watching that gray-headed man and his girl for the last few days."

"What are they?"

18

"He's an Egyptologist. He's done some very neat excavating. His house in Boston is a museum full of prizes. He reads hieroglyphics as fluently as I read the newspaper."

"That doesn't sound exciting," Asprey stated. "It must be the girl, then?"

Geraldi shrugged his shoulders. "Did you look at her?"

"Yes. She's pretty enough to qualify."

"She's a very good girl," said Geraldi. "Very good, modern type. She knows a good deal about life. She's been taught to face it, you see. Cheerful, good-natured, clever, rather witty . . . no dog, no false pride about her, and a devoted daughter."

"Sounds a nice dish," said Asprey.

"But for lack of seasoning . . . ," Geraldi trailed off. "You know how it is?"

"Of course, I do," said the other criminal. "People who live in the underworld grow to like shadows and fire."

"And the underworld women, Edgar, can be seen by their own light."

"No doubt. Still, Geraldi, that's a weakness."

"To prefer them, you mean?"

"Yes. Now, for my part, someday I expect to marry a quiet woman with a pleasant house, a cheerful little garden, perhaps a pasture where the cows graze . . . a modest place, a modest woman . . . then let the years go by like oiled silk."

"The Arab" — Geraldi grinned — "is always thinking of the green oasis. But I know you're right. It's

**19**

the fatal defect in me. Otherwise, I feel strong. Otherwise, I feel like Achilles. I have no partners to betray me . . . dope and drink never could take hold on me. I know my work and how to handle the tools of my trade. But, of course, I was held by the heel before I was dipped in the river. And one of these days some woman who . . . as we've just said . . . can be seen by her own light will . . ." He let the sentence unfinished.

The fat man looked him steadily in the face and then nodded with much gravity. He poured himself another cup of coffee and remarked: "I'm losing a terrible lot of caste by being seen here wasting my time on an effeminate tramp like you, Geraldi."

"You are," admitted Geraldi. "You' better walk back into your role of honest cowpuncher."

"First, I want to find out why you're interested in the Egyptologist."

Geraldi drummed his fingertips lightly on the table, and his keen eyes gleamed at the fat man. "I shouldn't talk," he said, "but I allow you to persuade me, this morning. Well, then, a few days ago when I was out for an early morning stroll . . . before sunup, in fact . . . I saw a man standing on top of that little hill, east of the town. He stood as still as an Indian, with his arms folded, facing the spot where the sun would rise. There's a stretch of poplars at the bottom of that hill, as you know. I slipped along through them until I could get a close view of him. Then I saw that he had a queer headdress on. He had a box folded between his arms and his breast."

"He had a what?" asked Asprey.

20

Geraldi hesitated. "Why are you so interested?" he asked.

"Because," said Asprey, "people don't stand like cranes on the top of a hill before sunup."

This assurance seemed to satisfy Geraldi, but only after he had turned the words back and forth in his mind several times, and had weighed and reweighed them. He took Asprey with the utmost seriousness, as it appeared.

"At any rate," went on Geraldi, "after a time this fellow raised the box in both hands and held it before him and above his head at the end of his straight arms."

"And what did it look like?" Asprey queried.

"I looked at it through my glass," James Geraldi answered. "Unfortunately, I couldn't make it out. You see it was turned toward the brightness in the east, so that I was a little dazzled. I should have said that it was covered with some sort of metal work . . . golden chasing, perhaps. But the box was the smallest part of the show. It had a setting . . . tall man against the sunrise sky. It had the man himself for the action. It had words, too. The oddest words that you ever heard in your life." He paused and nodded to himself in conviction. Then he said slowly: "What would you think, Edgar, if you heard a fellow like that suddenly say in a loud voice, as solemnly as any priest . . . 'Horus on the two horizons . . . golden Horus . . . Horus of the two eyes . . .'"

"The deuce," said the fat man. "I should say that he was a bit nutty. Or a poet, maybe."

"Would you?" Geraldi asked. "Well, that was all he said. I slipped on around the side of the hill and had a glimpse of the girl . . . apparently waiting there for her father to come down."

"How did she look?" Asprey wanted to know.

"She? Dashed unhappy she looked," replied Geraldi. "And looking up as if she half expected her poor father to go up in a cloud of fire. But I didn't glance at her too closely. She had a right to some privacy, I should say. I came home, with my mind made up to keep an eye on the pair later on."

"I don't make it out," Asprey commented, shaking his head. "What was it he said?"

" 'Horus on the two horizons, golden Horus, Horus of the two eyes,' " Geraldi quoted.

"Who the deuce was Horus, James?"

"You know something about Egypt?"

"I've skipped that. No. Hardly a thing."

"They worshipped the sun, Edgar. Do you want me to tell you about it?"

"I do . . . if this fellow Horus has a place in it."

"Of course, he had a place! They worshipped the sun, but they thought of it under a lot of different names. The sun god was the chief god, do you see? Now, you know, it went this way. Every town had its own chief god. But when the sun god began to be more important than their own village, the clever priests would add the solar disk to the outfit of their own deity. They would make him a god of the sun, too."

22

"A little confusing, Jimmy," said the fat man, "but I try to follow. A whole crowd began to claim the sun, then?"

"Exactly! But not alzl at the same moment. They split the old sun, not into parts, but they took him at different positions. For instance, there was Ra. He was the first of the sun gods, no doubt. And he remained at the top, in a way, because he was considered to be in the sun boat when it was floating across the blue waters at noon."

"You get poetical, Jimmy."

"I beg your pardon, I forgot. Then there was Osiris. He was the sun of night. That is to say, the sun as it disappears in the evening and as it comes up again in the morning. In other words, Osiris is killed by Set, the evil god of night, and, therefore, poor Osiris has to live underground and be king of the dead. But every morning he is restored to life, just as Isis restored him to life in the good old days. But you're tired of this history lesson?"

"Not a bit."

"Very well, then. The sun flushing up in the east is re-born Osiris. But then as he rises, the sun is Khepri, a scarab rolling the golden disk of the sun up the sky. You see, the heat of the sun hatches the eggs of the beetle. So they connect the beetle with the god. Khepri is the special god of creation. He himself rises out of the slime of the night every morning."

"I follow that. I can see how that myth came to be."

"But now, then, there was still an important position of the sun not accounted for. That was the most

23

beautiful of all. It is when the sun hangs in the east or in the west, not close enough in the horizon mist to have its cheeks pulled out, but looking bigger than in the middle sky, and all golden . . . all red gold. There you are, do you see, with your Horus. Horus of the two eyes . . . that is to say, of the sun and the moon."

"And you knew all this stuff?" said Asprey, smiling. "Or did you look it up?"

"Is there a public library in this town?" asked Geraldi. "No, I remembered that much. There's tons more, of course, that one could know."

"What was the headdress that you spoke of?"

"It looked to me like a wig such as the old Pharaohs used to wear."

"This is pretty rum," said Asprey. "The man's a nut. That's plain."

"If you look up his record, you won't think so. Six months ago, even, he did something frightfully brilliant in locating a tomb no one had ever dreamed of finding. Unluckily, the thieves had spotted the place a couple of millenniums earlier still. There was nothing but bare walls, I believe, for him to find, a broken mummy case, and a little scattered rubbish. But it was a great stroke. Results of years of study and guessing. No, Robert Christy Ingall is not a simple lunatic."

"He may be a complex one, though."

Geraldi shrugged his shoulders. "I've talked to you long enough," he announced. "Now talk to me."

"But what are you going to do about the crazy man, Jimmy? That interests me a lot."

24

"I'll have a look at him, I suppose," Geraldi said. "I'll investigate his possessions, some day or some night, and I'll particularly have a long look at that box and what's inside it, if anything."

"That should be easy," said Asprey. "A poor fellow with a broken-down brain . . ."

"Broken-down brain?" Geraldi echoed. "Who said so? But, as a matter of fact, let me tell you how this harmless fellow, as you call him, used to spend his vacations. Shooting big game in darkest Africa, my dear Edgar."

"And how did you learn that?"

"One has ears," Geraldi said shamelessly. "One walks about. If one hears a few words here and there . . . well, that can't be helped. This fellow is a famous hero in African hunting tales. He is also a great Egyptologist . . . which means a brain and a half, let me tell you. And, in addition to that, here he is in the Southwest standing on a hilltop and talking to a god of Egypt who died at least a couple of thousand years ago."

"Why here?" asked Asprey. "Why a hill in this state?"

"Yes," Geraldi said. "Boston is his hometown. Why does he have to leave all his relatives and friends and come down here to the edge of the world? Will he find something here?"

"That same Horus, perhaps," chuckled Asprey. "But now, Jimmy, I want your serious attention."

"You have it, unqualified."

"I asked you if you could work with me. You didn't answer. Now tell me?"

"It depends on the work," said Geraldi. "You and I, Edgar, are both crooks . . ."

"A rough, hard word," grinned the other.

"But we do different things, and we do them in different ways. Now, what I want to know is . . . is this work after my own taste?"

"I can promise you one thing," said Asprey. "This work is so dangerous that I couldn't imagine anything better suited to you."

"I'm not a salamander," answered Geraldi with a touch of irritation. "I can't live in fire, you know."

"You can," Asprey answered. "You can live in it and prosper. I've seen you. Well, I forgive you for the trouble you've made for me in the past. I put you a new proposition with enough danger in it to make you tremble, even if every hair on your head is a separate life. I want you, old son, to join me in the job of stealing that same box from the great Egyptologist and his pretty daughter."

Geraldi's brows flickered up. "What has Ingall done to me or to any man that he should deserve to have that box stolen from him?" he asked.

"In the first place," said the other, "how does he come by that box?"

"Go on," demanded Geraldi.

"I," Asprey began, "was nearer to that box than you were. And on the front of it, by means of my glass, I was able to make out a big lump of green . . ."

"Glass," Geraldi interjected.

"Emerald," said the fat man.

# CHAPTER
# FOUR

# "Dogs and Bones"

Two dogs may play cheerfully together for hours, but let a bone fall between them and instantly they are at war. So it was now with Geraldi and his companion, who sat glaring at one another with that quenchless hunger in their eyes. Then Geraldi made a cigarette and lighted it.

"Go on!" he prompted. He added, with that bright smile of his that showed a flash of the whitest of teeth: "You knew about the old Egyptologist all along. You dog!"

"He's not old," said the fat man. "He's not a year more'n forty-three."

"Did he marry when he was fourteen?" asked Geraldi.

"The girl's not so old, either. She's only twenty . . . even. She looks older. That's because Papa has given her a few things to think about."

"Go on, Edgar. Tell me the inside of the story, will you?"

"I can't," lamented the other. "I'll tell you how it is, though. I found that the slickest gang of crooks in the world was after this fellow. Five expensive birds,

Geraldi . . . five royal hawks all flying at one poor heron."

"That's strange," said Geraldi. "Who are they?"

"One is a pure-blooded Arab or something out of the way. His name is . . ."

"Seyf Kalam," Geraldi said.

"Great Scott! Do you know everybody in the world?"

"Once when I was taking a yacht down the Red Sea," began Geraldi, "on a hot evening, with the sails slatting on the masts, and the mosquitoes all around in black clouds . . ." His voice trailed away. "Well," he went on, "I know Seyf. And the other night, I thought I saw a familiar profile go past a door."

"Well," said the other, "Seyf is one of them. And I've spotted three of the rest. One is a talented Mexican crook of good family, with a Paris education that went deeper than books. I mean Pedro Oñate."

"I've missed that one," replied Geraldi.

"You probably know him, but not his name. Another is Lucien Rompier."

"I don't know him, either."

"Perhaps not. A great artist with a pen, that Rompier."

"Greater than you, Edgar?" Geraldi smiled.

The other extended his fat hands in a gesture of modesty. "Why compare?" he responded. "The fourth man of the crew wears an old Italian name to which he has no right at all. I mean to say Giovanni Strozzi."

"I know him like a brother," Geraldi remarked.

"You would," said Asprey. "Then there's a fifth man. I haven't been able to make him out. Perhaps you can.

Tallish fellow. Strong in the shoulders. A little pale. Handsome. Looks like an athlete. He runs the job, I gather."

"No, no," said Geraldi. "Strozzi never took orders in his life."

"He takes them now," persisted Asprey.

"Then," Geraldi announced with confidence, "the number five is what the newspapers are fond of calling a super-criminal."

"Friend," Asprey replied, "he is a little more than that. He's a man, Jimmy, worth a trip across the ocean merely to see. I've seen him only once in his real person. Then again, there was a certain something about a big Mexican muleteer that made me suspect it was the same chap in disguise. He seems able to step into any role and play it perfectly. Rather like the celebrated Geraldi."

"A very neat and kind compliment," Geraldi said, nodding his thanks. "And the five of them are after my Egyptologist?"

"They are."

"And they want what?"

"The box, of course."

"For the sake of the emerald that's on the front of it?"

"Undoubtedly."

"Is any emerald large enough to be the reward of five such fellows? I know the price of Strozzi and of Kalam, for instance."

"The others are just as high. But the emerald would be big enough to satisfy them all, I think. But, Jimmy, there's undoubtedly something inside the box. Otherwise, it wouldn't be wearing such a stone on its forehead."

"That's a reasonable suggestion."

"And, therefore, I say, this job is made to order for you."

"I have my little scruples," Geraldi said.

An expression of the keenest dislike glittered in the eyes of the fat man for a moment. But he mastered it quickly.

"Let me tell you," he said, "that I understand the little scruples, as you call them. But I want to point out to you that the Ingalls never owned an emerald like that one. Neither did Ingall ever find a box like that one . . . in Egypt. At least," said the fat man, leaning a little forward to make his point, "he never put it down on the records. If he had, at least a half interest would have gone to the Egyptian government. So you see, Jimmy, that your scruples about never taking from honest men don't need to bother you here."

"He found it in Egypt, beyond any doubt?"

"Right."

"And he held it out?"

"Make up your mind for yourself," Asprey replied.

"Well," said Geraldi, "I grow more and more interested. I'm very glad that you picked out this table for breakfast. In fact, I didn't quite suspect that you'd be willing to speak to me again."

"I'm a man of tolerance," said the other. "Besides, I believe in respecting the idiosyncrasies of humanity. Tell me flat . . . are you in for this?"

"To beat the five to the box?"

"Just that."

"It's odd," said Geraldi, "that they haven't succeeded in getting that box long ago . . . five masterminds, five master hands."

"You pointed out yourself that Ingall is not a fool . . . and that he's a hunter!"

"I pointed out a good many things that you knew already."

"I was glad to hear anything from such an esteemed collaborator. But to continue. Mister Ingall has been having a lot of bad luck lately. When he was in San Antonio, he went out for a ride in the early morning . . . his favorite time, as you've noticed . . . and a couple of burly brutes jumped him from the bushes. Bad fellows, gunmen, they were found to be. Well . . . he dropped them both. Oh, very neat work! He got a pair of bullets through his coat. That was all. Then again, one day as he and his daughter were driving along in a buckboard through the hills, three men blocked their road behind. Ingall gave his horses the whip. They galloped like wildfire straight into a pass where half a dozen fellows stood up and opened fire. The buckboard was jumping and bouncing like mad, and that probably disturbed the aim of the six in the mouth of the pass. But it didn't particularly disturb the aim of Ingall. His daughter grabbed the reins and the whip out of his hand. He stood up in that crazy, jumping buckboard like a sailor standing up in a fishing boat in a choppy sea. And he fought with a Colt in each hand, and with his long hair flying. He looked like a picture of Eighteen Forty! The wildest kind of Wild West."

"You were there," observed Geraldi.

The other colored a little. "I was showing you that the five have really been doing their best, but Ingall simply has been able to keep a step or two ahead of them."

"You were there," repeated Geraldi. He fixed his keen glance on Asprey and smiled in a peculiarly mirthless manner.

Something seemed to be swelling inside the fat man. It reached his throat, which worked violently. It reached his face, and he became a bright crimson. "I was there," he said rather hoarsely.

The delicate fingers of Geraldi tapped the table again. "Ah, well, you may be square with me, nevertheless. Did you intend all along to double-cross them, Edgar?"

"You'd be above that kind of thing, of course," said Asprey, half scoffing, half humiliated. "Well, two parts are bigger and fatter than five. Yes, I was with them, and I quit them . . . when I had a glimpse of you. I said to myself that so much talent would simply serve to clog the wheels of the machine. Now, Jimmy, you know everything. Are you with me, or are you not?"

"I'm with you," said Geraldi.

# CHAPTER
# FIVE

## "What's in the Box?"

Noon found the dining room at the hotel in San Felice more or less deserted, although Geraldi was faithfully there. The others scattered far and wide in the pursuit of all manner of occupations. But at night the same crowd was assembled, but even denser, so that some of the unlucky ones had to wait for a second table.

Miss Ingall, finishing well before her father, got up and left to give room to one of the hungry. Robert Ingall looked after her with a vague hesitancy, almost as though he thought it might be better if he should follow her at once. But he settled back in his chair.

"Hey, you!" said a voice beside Geraldi. "You're fiddlin'. You ain't eatin'. Lemme have your place pretty *pronto*, will you?"

This insulting request was met by Geraldi's accustomed courtesy. He finished his tea, stood up at once, and went from the room.

There was the rude beginning of a garden beside the hotel — a few plots of grass of the most ragged nature, and some groups of stubbed rose bushes. Through this Geraldi walked quietly to and fro. He strolled with his stick and his cigarette, wandering to the front of the garden and glancing idly up and down the street, or again to the rear of the hotel, where a Negro and a Mexican were loading a large wagon with the debris of a shed that had been knocked down by a windstorm not many days before. Geraldi paused and chatted with the two, or tried to chat, but they did not take kindly to his words and answered him with grunts. The Negro even went so far as to declare loudly: "They's some that is and they's some that isn't, but mostly it don't make no difference. You can't dress up pore white trash without the trash lookin' through!"

Geraldi, as though this had no meaning for him, wandered away and returned again as two men carried out from the house a long box, rudely made of unplaned pine boards.

"We got some more junk for you here," they said.

"Well, well," said Geraldi, as the two went past him. "What can all that rubbish be?"

"Rag and iron scraps, an' such," said the rearmost of the bearers.

Like a typical idler, attracted by all small things, Geraldi followed. The two men put down the box and puffed a moment.

"This'll about give you a load, Sam," said one of them. "Suppose we hoist this aboard and away with you?"

"Sure," said the Negro.

"But," Geraldi observed, "surely your wagon is only about half loaded?"

"And what business is it of yours?" asked one of the four. "You ain't gotta pull it, do you?"

Geraldi tapped the box with his stick. "Very big," he said, "big enough, I should even say, to hold a man . . . or a woman."

The Negro whirled on him, the whites of his eyes glinting dangerously. "What you talkin' about, white man?"

"I?" Geraldi stated. "Is there any harm, my dear fellow, in saying that this is a big box?"

"Harm?" echoed Sam. "I'm gonna knock the head right offen your shoulders, if you don't get out of here."

"Come, come. After all, what I said is true. It is big enough for a man. Suppose I peek in through the crack of that lot of scrap iron and rags, and such?"

The reply of Sam was delivered without words. He drew back his massive right hand, made it into a fist, and shot it straight at the head of Geraldi.

Geraldi cried out loudly with terror; his voice rang, piercing far and wide as he shouted for help, and shrank from the blow. The massive fist and arm shot over his shoulder, and, at the same time, the big Negro crashed against him, their legs entangled, and they pitched to the ground. But odd chance, as it were, put Geraldi uppermost, his elbow striking the back of Sam's neck. The black man lay without a quiver.

"Kill him, kill him!" snarled one of the three, and they came at Geraldi with a rush as he yelled again for help and scrambled to his feet.

They were too close for him to flee. And, at any rate, springing to his feet he suddenly appeared to lose his balance and toppled straight at the knees of the two foremost. They went over him with a lurch, while the fourth of the party stayed his rush and struck savagely at Geraldi's head with a billet of wood that he'd picked up.

Chance, as it seemed, saved Geraldi again, for he writhed to his knees in time to swerve from the descending blow. He had kept his hold on his walking stick all this time, and now, with a more frantic cry for help, he thrust the bone-shod point of the cane into the face of the other. He of the club went backwards, groaning, clutching at his eyes, and Geraldi sprang up in time to see a knot of men hurrying toward them from the hotel. But there was danger of a different sort now. One of the two who had tripped over him was up with a gun in his hand.

"You're gonna see death!" he hissed, and fired point-blank.

The yell of Geraldi was in itself enough to have spoiled the aim of that weapon, but in the confusion of his terror the cane had spun around in his hand, and, as the gunman spoke, Geraldi stuck out in instinctive self-defense. Just across the wrist of the other's gun hand that lucky blow descended. The bullet hummed harmlessly far away, and the other grasped a broken hand.

"We're done! Cut and run for it!" said the fourth of the crew, and instantly bolted, with his companions at his heels. The Negro alone lay prone and helpless as the crowd of rescuers arrived.

Half of them remained on the scene of action; the rest sprinted away after the fugitives.

"It was about the box," Geraldi explained, mopping his face with a snowy handkerchief. "I said it was big enough to hold a man. It made them very angry. They almost killed me. I don't know why I'm not dead. Thank heaven that so many brave men were near enough to hear me. I'm going to faint, I think. Has anyone a little brandy, please?"

"I seen it out the back window," said one man. "They jumped this bird." He added: "He was scared to death. They broke themselves up stumblin' over him. What's in the box, anyway?"

They tore away the upper boards. Then they lifted out the body of pretty Mary Ingall, tied hand and foot, and thoroughly gagged, but her eyes bright with life, and angry life at that.

# CHAPTER
# SIX

# "The Nerves of Mr. Wilbur"

Geraldi went to the bar of the hotel. He sat on a box in a corner and visibly trembled. His handkerchief was in one hand, continually dabbing at his forehead. In the other hand was a glass of whisky that he sipped. He was apparently totally unnerved.

"Why don't you swaller that off?" asked one of the curious crowd.

"This? But it's like fire, you know," Geraldi commented. "And, besides, strong liquor upsets me terribly . . . except just a thimbleful of cognac."

"Except a thimbleful of what?" roared one.

"Old cognac! Old grandmother!" they shouted at Geraldi, and burst into enormous, unquenchable laughter. He amused them hugely.

"You're ail so rough," Geraldi commented, admiring them with wonder. "So rough and strong! I've never seen such men! Thank heaven so many of you were near when I was in such deadly peril."

"Listen to him," snarled a disgusted voice. "All full of himself, ain't he? Never a word about what might've happened to the girl."

Someone tapped Geraldi on the shoulder.

"Mister Ingall wants to know, will you step up to his room for a minute?"

"Tonight? I'm so terribly shaken," Geraldi mumbled. "I really couldn't see anyone. I really couldn't."

"Aw, rats!" said the messenger. "Don't be such a baby. He ain't gonna eat you. The old boy simply wants to thank you. Come along and see him, will you?"

He dragged Geraldi to his feet, and led him faintly protesting through the door, while a fresh shout of laughter broke behind them.

To the second floor they mounted, and then the guide tapped at a door and pushed it open without waiting for an invitation.

"I got him here for you," he said, and thrust Geraldi into the room.

The door closed. Geraldi leaned against it, bowing and shuddering, like one trying to be polite and overcome with nerves. He was Archibald Wilbur, he said. Usually people called him Archie. And he laughed in a thin, foolish cackle.

The girl, in the farther corner of the room, bit her lip to keep back her contempt. But still her stern humor showed itself in her eyes.

Robert Christy Ingall led Geraldi to a chair and pressed him into it.

"Frightfully upset," Geraldi muttered. "Every nerve is broken and jangling. Hideous experience for me, Mister Ingall. Simply hideous. Bur thank heaven the hotel was so near. The men heard. The brave men. Rough people, but kind, Mister Ingall. They saved my life."

"I rather thought from what I heard," said Robert Ingall, "that the crowd simply had saved the lives of the four scoundrels. They've got three of them, now."

"Gracious!" Geraldi exclaimed. "How exciting! How terrible! The villains! I hope they'll be punished."

"I think they will be," said Ingall in his slow voice, for always he seemed to be thinking his way from word to word, speaking the simplest sentence as though he had to search for some means of expressing his thoughts more clearly.

"One got away," said Ingall. "The Negro is still rather helpless because of the force with which you struck him down. One fellow had a damaged eye and cut forehead. Another had a broken wrist where you tapped him . . . with your loaded walking stick. And, take it all together, I should say it was pretty lucky for the four that the crowd arrived before you'd beaten them to a pulp."

"Oh," said Mary Ingall, and drew a little closer. It seemed a new viewpoint to her.

"You're joking, of course," said Geraldi, with a high-pitched, nervous laugh. "I don't really remember anything. Except the first terrible moment when the Negro struck at me and we fell to the ground. I think my elbow must have come down on the back of his neck. He went limp . . . suddenly and horribly. Like death. Then as I tried to get to my feet, two of them fell over me, and a fourth man struck brutally at me . . . I hit out at him. Dear me. I don't want to think of it. And then the revolver. I knew that the bullet had gone through me. I . . . I . . ." He closed his eyes and lay back in his chair. "Have you . . . have you . . . ?"

"Brandy?" asked Mr. Ingall.

"Oh, no! I'd much prefer smelling salts."

"We haven't any," Mary Ingall stated. "But . . . could I offer you some sal volatile, if you wish?" Her voice was controlled. She kept the scorn from it. But she could not force any real warmth of kindness into her words.

"Perhaps I'll soon be better," Geraldi commented, "if I don't have to think of that dreadful affair. You . . . poor, dear Miss Ingall! How you must have suffered. How frightfully brave of you."

"Brave of me to be grabbed and gagged and slapped into a box?" she echoed rather angrily. "I was a blind ninny, that was all!" She even stamped a little, as though she promised herself that such a thing never would happen again. "But," she added, "I don't think that either of us have said a single word of thanks to you . . ."

"I'd rather that you didn't," Geraldi insisted. "Oh, I'd so much rather forget everything. I'd so much rather that it were all put away from our talk. You understand? Otherwise, I really couldn't bear up. I should faint, I think."

She had to turn her head away toward the window, all flushed with the rose of sunset now.

Robert Ingall said: "I'm sorry, Mister Wilbur. I don't want to wear out your nerves, but I must tell you how deeply I appreciate what you have done. I would like to speak a little, too, about the extraordinary coincidences which seem to have taken place during that battle royal."

"Dear Mister Ingall!" cried Geraldi. "You make me tremble! You're not going to talk about it any more, I beg."

"I was thinking, in the first place, what a rare set of circumstances took place in the very beginning. It was odd . . . but I won't remark on it . . . that you stayed there to meet that danger instead of running away from it as you could easily have done. Because, obviously, what they wanted was to get my daughter away, not to harm you."

"I was so stunned with horror and terror. If you had seen the dreadful face of that black . . . creature," Geraldi whimpered. He covered his face with his hands.

The deep, grave voice of the other went on. "I understand. It must have been a rough moment. But then the coincidences begin. He strikes at you and misses completely. Odd point number one. He rushes at you, and you become entangled with him so that you *both* fall. Odd point number two. In falling, you actually land on top of him, which is the oddest point of all. And, finally, for the fourth coincidence, you happen to so fall that your elbow lands on his spinal column and nearly kills him . . . a trick the Japanese understand perfectly. Have you ever been in Japan, Mister Wilbur?"

"Beautiful Japan," Geraldi said, clasping his hands together as though he were adoring a distant vision. "Let us talk about Japan. Will you talk with me about Japan, Mister Ingall?"

42

"I should be happy," said Ingall, "to talk to you about anything. But I have a rather analytical mind, and, if you don't object, I'd like to ramble on a bit about these coincidences. Will you keep track of them, Mary, my dear? I think I've added up four, at this point."

Mary, a frown of wonder on her brow, looked keenly at her father, keenly at Geraldi. The latter rose in haste.

"Really, dear Mister Ingall," he said, "if you're going to persist . . . I don't want to be rude . . . I should shudder at the thought of being rude to a gentleman . . . any gentleman . . . but one older than I . . . I should shudder at such a thought. But I must withdraw. I beg you to forgive me. I simply haven't the nerves. I . . . I . . ." He backed toward the door, making apologetic gestures.

"My dear fellow," Ingall stated, "if my nerves were half as good as yours, I'd be the happiest man in the world."

Geraldi seized the knob of the door. "You're pleased to scoff a little . . . you're pleased to make a little jest about me. You really are. But I don't mind. Good evening, Mister Ingall. Good evening, Miss Ingall. I hope that you'll recover perfectly from the frightful shock . . ."

"Good night, Mister Wilbur," said the girl.

"My dear Wilbur," Ingall remarked, "you act beautifully. You do, in fact, act the part so well that, if I didn't know, I'd be entirely deceived. Good night, if you wish."

Geraldi paused, his hand on the knob of the door that he had half opened.

At last, he closed it softly and came back into the center of the room. He had cast the odd mannerisms of Mr. Wilbur over his shoulder, as it were. "You're a keen fellow," he said to Ingall. "An old fox, I dare say, will usually catch a young one if he cares to."

Ingall put out his hand. "I don't think we really met before, did we?" he asked.

"I don't think we did," said Geraldi.

Strong as steel, their grips met. They stepped back a little from one another.

"And I," Mary added, with an embarrassed laugh, "was completely taken in. I've been an idiot, *I* want to begin over at the beginning and thank you in a new way, Mister Wilbur."

"Or does that name," Ingall said pleasantly, "go into the discard as well?"

Geraldi glanced at him again. His meaning was clear enough, and Geraldi shrugged his shoulders. "That name will do as well as another," he assured the two. "Shall we all sit down again?"

# CHAPTER
# SEVEN

## "Frankness on Both Sides"

They sat down, Ingall with a faint smile on account of
his triumph; Geraldi rather with a gesture of surrender;
and the girl gingerly, on the edge of a chair, as though
her mind were still full of thought.

"But," she said finally, "do you see what it means,
Father? He attacked . . . deliberately . . . four men . . .
four armed ruffians."

"With a walking stick," Ingall replied. "He used that
stick first as a sword to stab one of the brutes in the
face, then he used it as a club to break a hand."

"But," cried the girl, "but, Father, you . . ."

"We owe him everything," said Ingall. "Is that what
you mean?"

She stared at Geraldi as though still she were
computing and could not arrive at a satisfactory sum
total.

"Let's forget it all and drop it," he suggested.

"But I can't do that," said Ingall.

"I think you'd better," murmured the girl to her
father. "Talking doesn't do any good." She continued to
look at Geraldi in that half-frightened manner. He,
despite nerves of copper, began to grow a little

uncomfortable. Finally he said: "I want to be honest about this. I don't want you to think I was simply altruistic."

"Will you have a cigar?" asked Ingall. "Don't explain anything, my dear Wilbur. We'll chat of something else since you wish us to."

"But what *did* make you do such a . . . a brave thing?" asked the girl.

Geraldi said gently: "I have a pair of motives for most things . . . I like excitement, and I like money."

Now, although he said this in the quietest manner, her head jerked a little higher and rich color began to go up her cheeks.

"Look here, my friend," said Ingall, "I'm afraid you're going to make a confession to us. I don't want to drive you into a corner."

"Of course, you don't," smiled Geraldi.

"Perhaps I'd better go," suggested Mary Ingall, rising.

Geraldi stood up in turn. "You'd better stay here," he returned. "You'd better stay to hear the warning . . . or challenge, I may call it."

At this word, their attitude changed a trifle.

Geraldi, in the meantime, went on: "I am what you might call a gold-digger. Or perhaps you don't use such slang."

"I understand you," said the girl. "But what sort of a gold-digger? Some of them sell mines that are not, and some sell lots in cities in the sky."

"I have no talent in those directions," answered Geraldi modestly. "I am simply a professional gambler.

I may say with pride," he added, "that I've done a few efficient jobs cracking safes, and that I've held up a train or two for variety. Gambling, however, is my long suit, and in addition any sort of adventure that promises excitement and cash . . . or excitement, sometimes, even without the cash."

"We understand you," replied the man of science. "I've always rather envied that sort of a life."

"Have you?" asked Geraldi.

He looked with respect and also with amused curiosity at Ingall. The silver hair seemed absurdly out of place above such a tanned, healthy face. It was the face of a man who has just come into his intellectual prime, fit for a battle of wits — fit, also, for a battle of hands. It was a decided contrast to the beautiful face of Geraldi; it seemed that Ingall had been roughed out of strong stone. There was a granite hardness and immovability about him. His very smile was different from the smiles of other men. It was very like the archaic look of half-mocking and half-cruel mirth that the old sculptors of Egypt gave to their basalt gods and granite Pharaohs.

"I've always envied your calling," said Ingall. "The servant of society is, after all, a slave. All democrats love freedom, eh?"

"I don't think," Geraldi said, "that you would ever spend time to make dice or cards perform for you."

At this, Ingall did not change his expression, but the girl opened her eyes wide.

"I've had to give you a few keynotes with regard to myself," Geraldi responded, "because I don't like to pose as a modest hero. When I guessed what was in that box, I did the rest for selfish reasons."

"What on earth do you mean?" demanded Ingall.

"Very well. I'll be explicit. Suppose the four had taken your daughter away. Tomorrow, rather early, you would receive information that she is safely held . . . that no money is wanted for her ransom, but that she will be returned to you unharmed if you will give for her a little box, encrusted with gold and . . ." He paused.

Ingall and his daughter were on their feet, watching him.

"You understand?" said Geraldi. "I didn't want to risk the loss of that box. I have designs on it myself."

The answer astonished Ingall more than anything he ever had heard in his life, or anything he ever had seen. "I can follow that train of reasoning," he said deliberately. "But there's a flaw in it. And if you're in touch with those cowardly scoundrels who tried to take Mary away, you may let them know that if I had ten boys and girls and they abducted them all, I never would surrender the box . . . in exchange for them all!"

Geraldi could only look at the floor. He heard, but he could not believe.

"You've been wonderfully frank with me, Mister Wilbur. You see that I am frank, also. Partly because I want to protect Mary . . . I want to point out to you that no one can reach the box by striking at her!"

"I have to believe you," said Geraldi, but he could not keep a little stiffness out of his manner, a hard ring out of his voice.

"We'd better talk of something else," suggested Mary, her voice strained.

"I must give Mister Wilbur as complete a warning as he has given me," continued the father. "You aren't the first. As you know, others are after the box. Others have tried in the past. They have all failed. They always will fail. No man or men on earth possibly can take it."

"I know," said Geraldi, "you have a pair of detectives to help you. But *impossible* is a large word, sir."

"Of course it is," said Ingall. "But let me tell you that many have died in these attempts, Wilbur. More will die in the future, and I" — here he slowly stretched out one hand as though the truth were written on the palm of it in flaming letters — "and I have remained unscathed . . . and I shall remain unscathed in the future."

"This is absolute knowledge, of course?"

"Absolute, young man. Nothing could persuade me to deceive you."

"And nothing," said Geraldi, "could make me more set on obtaining that box." He went on to explain: "In all fairness I must give you one more opening. I've never troubled honest men, Mister Ingall. If you can explain that you have a right to this box . . ."

"Ah, but I have, I have!" cried Ingall.

"A legal right?" asked Geraldi. "An actual, legal right?"

Ingall raised a forefinger as though calling down a superior witness.

"My friend," he said, "there are higher rights than legal ones."

"Are there?" Geraldi answered carelessly. "At any rate, you don't really claim that the box is yours?"

"It is!" cried Mary Ingall.

"Mary, Mary," said her father. "Don't let him be deceived. No, in your sense, it doesn't belong to me. This odd scruple of yours," he added, "need trouble you no longer. The box is an open prize . . . and heaven have mercy on the souls of those who try to take it. Mister Wilbur, I've warned you frankly, sincerely."

He said this with an inexpressible gravity; and Mary Ingall slipped back into a chair, dropped her head on her folded arms, and began to weep softly.

Geraldi cast one glance at her, rose, and bowed to Ingall, and offered his hand. The latter took it without hesitation.

"What we've talked over is a secret to the rest of the world, so far as I am concerned," said Geraldi.

"Thank you. Of course, what you've explained to me is an absolute secret, likewise."

"In the meantime, look to everything with great caution, Mister Ingall. Examine your locks. I'm an expert in reading the mind of a lock. Look to your doors and windows. I don't make a great deal of sound when I come. I'm proud to say I have had a good deal of experience in all this sort of work. You need not be afraid of a shot in the back, however, or a knife in your throat at midnight. I don't use those methods."

"Thank you," said Ingall. "I appreciate your frankness. In exchange for your warning, listen to mine. If night or day I see a suspicious shadow near me, hear a suspicious sound, I'll send a bullet to probe the secret before I come myself. And I shoot straight, Mister Wilbur, though you may not have known it."

"I know it perfectly. We are all agreed. We are all in the open. I think this makes a fair fight of it, sir?"

"Entirely," Ingall agreed. He looked upon Wilbur with a sudden compassion in his eyes. "Ah, young man," he murmured, "think again before you undertake this work. Because, if you persist in it, as surely as there are powers in heaven, you are a dead man." He said this with a terrible ring of conviction; there was a hopeless belief in his face.

Geraldi bade them good night and went to his own room.

# CHAPTER
# EIGHT

## "Plans"

His room, by a really odd freak of chance, was just above that of Ingall, and, as Geraldi stepped inside the door, he was amazed to see fat Asprey on his knees, drawing up something through a crack of the floor on the farther side of the chamber. "You oily scoundrel," Geraldi commented casually.

Asprey, before answering, brought up a small, flat disk through the floor and then rose to his feet and began to coil some lengths of very thin, supple wire.

"You've been listening in," continued Geraldi, still very casually.

"Couldn't help doing that. You have advanced ways, Jimmy. You might be several strides ahead of me in almost no time. Look at yourself now. A hero in a minute." He chuckled, and, having finished rolling up the coil of wire, he began to rub his thick, soft hands together — a favorite gesture with him. "A hero," said Asprey, making his voice unctuous and musical. "One moment the shy and trembling youth . . . the next the tiger at work. How those four would have gone with wings, if they could have guessed that it was really

Geraldi who was up against them. You let one pull a gun. That was foolish."

"Not a bit," said Geraldi. "As long as I made a farce of it, only the hottest of the lot took to his Colt. If the four had seen me draw . . . well, I might have handled a pair of them, but the other two would have shot me to pieces. I took the safest way, by all odds."

"Safe?" said the fat man. "Safe as a lion in a tiger's den. But let it go. I've stopped wondering at you, Jimmy. Gradually I begin to understand. The flame eats the tree because it loves the wood, and the sap, also" After a short pause he continued: "I'm going downstairs and out for a little walk. If you happened to go down the same way . . . through the garden and into the vacant lots beyond it, you . . ."

Geraldi nodded, and his fat ally left the room at once with a quick, bold step that caused not the slightest sound, or so much as made the thin, pine flooring quiver. Then Geraldi put out the lamp and sat in blackness before his window and watched the treetops tipping back and forth across the stars. San Felice was still, or else there were those distant, single noises that make night more profoundly silent — the bark of a dog, a far-off, dying laughter. So Geraldi looked out upon the world and tasted his lie and found that it was good. And he promised himself that of all the antagonists he ever had encountered in the four quarters of the world, none would be more terrible in the proof than this same Ingall, with his strong, cold, cruel face.

Then he thought of the girl. She had looked at him with eyes as straight as the eyes of a man. But he could not fit her into the picture. She disturbed him in only one way. Why had she begun that stifled weeping? What had been said or done to break down her self-control? However, Geraldi remembered that women are fragile creatures, heroically strong for a single instant, then collapsing. And he put down her weakness to her nerve-wracking experience of that day. It might, indeed, have undone an older and a stronger woman than Mary Ingall.

After what seemed a sufficient interval, he determined to follow his fat companion, but he chose a unique mode of descent. Arm's length from his window a drainage pipe ran down the building from the eaves above. He gripped it, tried its strength, found it to be of iron and well-fastened. So he swung himself out from his window and went rapidly down, holding on by his arms only. A sailor would have been proud of such a feat. As he slid past the window of Ingall, he heard the steady voice of the scientist reading aloud. He even heard the clicking of knitting needles, and a domestic picture flashed oddly before the mind's eye of Geraldi.

Then he reached the ground, dusted his hands, and looked up the sheer wall with a nod of satisfaction. It was always well, in his experience, to have unexpected means of exit and entrance. Crossing the garden, he found Asprey beyond, pacing through a grove of pines.

"What do you make of them?" Asprey inquired in a professional tone.

"He's all man."

"I thought so," sighed Asprey. "I almost knew it. But I wanted you to pass on him. A brain, eh?"

"And a pair of hands. He's a lion, Edgar. There's no doubt of it. He's one in ten thousand."

"And the girl?"

"She'd make a secretary . . . or a wife."

"Wasn't that sobbing I heard?"

"She blubbered a little."

"What made her do that?"

"She'd been trapped, caught, and boxed, almost kidnapped," said Geraldi. "Enough to break down any girl, I should say."

"I tell you, Jimmy," said the fat man, "that Ingall is no ordinary fellow."

"I've said so."

"I mean he's extraordinary in an extraordinary way."

"Go on, Edgar."

"He's been touched in the brain. I'm almost sure of it. And what he depends upon to protect him and the box is a mystery of the first water."

"It will need to be," Geraldi asserted. "I intend to have that box in my hands before another twenty-four hours."

Asprey sighed. "I like to hear you talk that way. But I doubt it, rather. Unless Ingall is really cracked."

"He has the straightest, coldest eye in the world, man."

"But you see, Jimmy, just after he made you his profession of faith, the girl broke down and cried."

"I've explained that."

"A dashed silly explanation," said Asprey with conviction. "She went through that abduction like an actress on the stage. Steady as a rock. Still was steady when you came into their room. I heard her voice. Not a quiver in it. Perfectly natural. Perfectly at ease. I'll tell you what, Jimmy, it needed an extra special shock to down her, and that shock was furnished by her father."

"So?"

Geraldi lighted a cigarette, and Asprey said not another word until that cigarette was half finished. Then he continued: "The point is, that her father's belief in mysterious protection is his weak point, and the girl well knows it. That's why she began to cry."

"You're guessing."

"But I'm guessing a mile closer to the truth than you are."

"If you're right, I'm wrong."

"Jimmy," said the other, "I thank you for being humble. It may help us win the game. What have you in mind for our next move?"

"Get a pair of first-class horses."

"They're already got."

"I mean one of them will have to pack your tub of fat at a good gallop and keep it up."

"I have," said Asprey, "a half-breed, one quarter common range cayuse and one quarter distilled essence of deviltry. She'll carry even me."

"And for James Geraldi?"

"I have a long-drawn-out, lump-headed, slab-sided brute with the sweetest set of legs you ever saw in action."

56

"Do you know these horses, Edgar?"

"I know them, my dear fellow, like the inside of a book."

"Then there's half the job done."

"What's the other half?"

"The taking of the box."

"Tonight?"

"Of course."

"Very well, Jimmy. I'm under orders. How's it to be done?"

"*Amigo mio*, it's to be done very simply."

"I wait to learn."

"The room of the girl is beside her father's room?"

"Yes."

"In the middle of the night, you open her door with a key. I'll provide the key in the meantime."

"I have one, thank you," said Asprey.

"My dear fellow," said Geraldi, "how foresighted you are. It's a pleasure to work with you."

"But," said the fat man, "I don't like this business of going into a girl's room at night."

"Does it shock you, Edgar?"

"They lynch you on the double quick, in this part of the world, for even lifting an eyebrow at a girl."

"You can take my part of the job, then. Sit on the drain-pipe outside Ingall's window. When you make a noise and the girl yells for help . . ."

"Great Scott, Jimmy, do I have to wake her up?"

Geraldi laughed.

"Then, old boy, when you get a whoop out of her, you back out of that room on the double, and lock the door behind you. That yell of hers will bring her father like a tiger out of his room. As he passes through the door, I enter via the window, lock him into his daughter's room, and begin to search *his* room . . ."

"Ah, Jimmy," said the fat man, "what a child I am in these matters. I'll begin to learn at your knee."

# CHAPTER
# NINE

## "Success"

Man is not made to hang long from a branch, and Geraldi's wrists were aching before he had been many minutes clinging to the drainpipe that ran down the side of the hotel. It seemed to him that Asprey surely must have had ample time to work the key into the lock. Then it came into his mind that Asprey might have decided to betray him and take all the profits of the occasion with a lesser partner, who would be contented with a fixed sum of hard cash rather than a portion of the entire profit. There was another danger — if that grim fellow Ingall looked out from the window and saw a man wedged against the wall beside it, it would be very odd if he did not try a snap shot at the night intruder. So Geraldi's time spent clinging to the pipe was by no means pleasant. Then he heard the faintest of creaks, as though hinges were being turned cautiously. Immediately afterward there was a woman's scream.

In Ingall's room, springs squeaked, bare feet pounded upon the floor, and Geraldi heard Ingall's voice calling: "Steady, Mary! I'm coming!"

He did not wait for further indications but swung himself boldly through the window and landed cat-like on the floor of Ingall's room. Geraldi reached the interior door, closed it with a motion both swift and soft, and heard Mary beyond it, exclaiming: "I saw someone in the darkness. A hand touched my face. I wasn't dreaming. Try the hall door!"

Geraldi had heard enough. He went to his work, torch in one hand and the other rapidly reaching here and there. A gesture whipped the clothes from the bed and flung them in a corner. Another turned over the mattress — a mattress thick enough, perhaps, to contain the box. But a deft exploration showed that the mattress was undisturbed. Now he paused, flashing the light from point to point, trying to make his mind jump to some conclusions.

Above him, below him, feet were beginning to beat on the floors in answer to the shouts of Ingall. Ingall, apparently unaware that the door to his own room had been closed and locked, was giving his shoulder to the one leading from the girl's chamber to the hall, and every thrust of his weight sent a crash through the building.

There was a tall chest of drawers in the room. Geraldi wrenched the bottom drawer open, then the top. There was nothing in the lower drawer, and nothing other than a few clean shirts neatly folded in the top. Ignoring the drawers between, he tipped the entire chest to and fro, swaying its ponderous and clumsy weight with wonderful ease, but he heard no heavy object sliding back and forth.

He left the chest just as a heavy body lurched against the hall door of the room. Then another shock. More men than one had gathered there to break it down. But Geraldi knew that door. He had examined it with more than passing care that evening and had noted how the wood was seasoned and tough. Also, the thoughtful Ingall had reënforced it with a strong bolt of his own construction.

So Geraldi let the door be, for the moment, and flashed his light over the walls. One board projected a little beyond the others. Miraculously he gained a finger hold and ripped out that wood as though it were the thinnest of cardboard. A fine mortar dust swept into his face. That was all.

Then he turned back to the room itself and the two big suitcases in the corner. But they were a little too obvious. Grimly he returned to the chest of drawers, while someone gave a shoulder to the door leading to Mary Ingall's chamber and made it buckle and groan. Geraldi whipped out a bluenosed Colt and split the top panel of that door with a snap shot. He heard an exclamation of surprise and anger. But the whole place was a buzzing hornet's nest by this time. He knew that he had only seconds left as he jerked open the unsearched drawers one by one, letting them crash upon the floor as he swept a hand through the contents of each, until he came to the last.

The last one of all. If that failed, he knew that he dared not spend another moment in the search. The last one of all. And behold — under a loosely folded linen coat was a box of eight or nine inches square — heavy — flashing with gold, and the torch light was flared back at him from a great, blue-green emerald. He was at the window in an instant. A torrent of noise flowed up and down the hall, beat and roared through the girl's chamber. But had there been time for one of the keen-witted to get outside the house and watch the window from beneath?

All below him was dark and thick before his eyes, so recently dazzled by the light of his own torch. He climbed onto the windowsill and dropped down shoulder deep, the box between his legs. His right hand came in contact with the drainpipe, and, as he swung over to his narrow ladder of escape, he heard a door go down with a huge rending of wood, a mighty crash against the floor. They had rushed in from the hallway, he could tell, probably four or five men taking the door at one charge. He went down the drainpipe so fast that his hands burned, keeping his eye fixed upon the window above. A light darted from it, wavered, and fixed itself suddenly upon him. He thrust himself out from the wall with one hand, caught the box from between his knees with the other, and dropped.

A gun coughed. He felt the nip of a bullet before his eyes; never had good aim been baffled by so small a margin.

He landed lightly, whirled, and ran to the nearby pines at full speed straight down the side of the house as two men lumbered around the corner, guns in hands. The light licked down at him again like a long tongue. Two hasty reports over his head — but Ingall had perhaps found it difficult to get in a good position. He would have had to turn in the window and fire with his left hand, perhaps. At any rate, neither of those two bullets came close to him, and he swerved away to the left as the pair before him shouted and threw up their weapons.

He was in the brush before they fired, and, as he heard the slugs cutting with a rattle through the small branches above his head, he knew that he was safe. And the treasure in his hands. And all had been done on the very day when he had warned the enemy.

It was hardly remarkable if Geraldi laughed a little as he ran, swinging in and out among the crowding trees. He made straight for the far angle of the garden. There, dim among the shadows, he found two horses, with a bulky form in one saddle, the other empty. Cat-like, Geraldi sprang up.

There was a convenient sack attached to the saddlebow, and into this he dropped the box and got the horse under way with the pressure of his heels. They made straight at the fence, Asprey leading the way. No need for jumping. The fat man's foresight had cut away the dangerous barbed wire between two of the posts, and they whisked away into the muffling, thick sand of the street, twisting at once to the right down an alley. People were coming out from their houses; doors were slamming, windows crashing open.

Geraldi tipped to the side. "Carry straight ahead, man!" he called. "They'll spot two men riding together, otherwise, and follow us by that. Go on east of the town . . . to that hill where I saw Ingall. I'll follow around by a different route."

He half expected that Asprey, now that the prize was won, would be apt to do anything rather than leave the vicinity of the jewels, but, instead of protesting, the fat man waved his hand. Geraldi, therefore, doubled back, crossed the western side of the town, and circled around toward the eastern hill that had been appointed as a rendezvous.

San Felice was awakening with a roar. It was like the explosion of a great bomb, spreading by degrees from place to place, a noise composed of snorting horses, howling and barking of dogs, even the squeal of a pig, and, under all, the angry humming of far-off human voices. A dangerous sound, and yet the sweetest music to the ears of Geraldi. He smiled as he listened to it.

His horse had not been praised for nothing. Looked at from above, it seemed more like half a horse than a whole one — half a horse with a double head set on the end of the neck like an apple on the end of a rapier. But, nevertheless, it could gallop, and gallop it did, with a long and swinging stride, frictionless, effortless.

Geraldi looked back to the town and saw the spreading arms of it draw together, saw the lights draw back into a single, gleaming point. Then he knew that safety was theirs, for the time at least. The hill jumped up before him, girded beneath with trees, as with heavy mist, and out of those trees a single horseman rode and waited for him. He did not need a herald to tell him it was his companion in crime. The bulging, rounded lines of that rider proclaimed his identity. And, as Geraldi came up, they swung their horses on, side by side, silent, riding with care, but intent on putting a pleasant stretch of miles between them and the pursuit.

**64**

A pursuit it would be, too — as Geraldi well could guess from what he knew of Ingall. That astute old warrior, beaten by the simplest of devices, would not give up without a desperate struggle.

"Mountains?" asked Asprey at last, and waved his hand before him.

To the right went up the dark heads of the range. To the left those heights were broken into lower, tumbling hills.

"What good are long-legged horses in mountains?" asked Geraldi, and they aimed their course for the hills.

# CHAPTER
# TEN

# "The Wink of Steel"

It was four in the morning before they paused. Already the east was lightening, and they had blundered upon an excellent stopping place. A little creek slipped down the side of the hill with a whisper of speed, and the light of the day was freshening upon the willows and poplars that stood along the banks. It had been primeval forest, not many years before, but fire had leveled all this section. The huge trunks stood up like ill-made men, reaching distorted arms into the dimness of the morning, but everywhere the second-growth woods had sprung up to a considerable height.

It was the perfect time. In this light, fire could not be seen at any distance, and smoke would be a mere part of the morning mist, so they built their fire without too much precaution and prepared a breakfast. It had been no starvation trip planned for lightest marching order. Each of them had cunningly composed packs that would enable them to present an alteration in their appearance from point to point on their march. Asprey had seen to it that there was plenty of food and even a coffee pot.

They finished their breakfast. They finished their coffee. As Asprey lighted a cigarette, he looked up at the rose of the morning that was blossoming across the sky. "Well?" he said to Geraldi.

"Suppose we sleep on it?" came the response.

"We won't sleep much afterward, I'm thinking," said the fat man, and without another word laid himself down on the grass and was instantly snoring. Geraldi imitated that example. They slept for nearly two hours, calmly and well, and at last Geraldi wakened and found the other sitting up, looking with mild, beneficent eyes upon him.

He had taken from his pack a small guitar — smaller than any Geraldi had ever seen before — and now Asprey began to pluck the strings and sing in a large, rich voice that floated far away among the trees. The water ouzel, that had been darting fearlessly about above and through the spray of a small cataract in the brook, now perched upon a dripping stone on the bank and gave up his own music for a more skillful effort.

Geraldi, leaning on one elbow, listened drowsily, and watched a blue jay perched on the very tip of a small pine tree, looking restlessly about for mischief to perform. "I suppose it's time," he said.

"We might as well," answered Asprey.

Geraldi took the saddlebag, therefore, reached into it, and took out for their first examination a treasure so infinitely beyond their expectation that they looked it over in total silence. It was not merely inlaid with gold. It was heavily encrusted all over, and upon the encrustation a precious enamel had been laid to present certain strange figures. Inside, the box was sheeted with gold again, but this was merely a thin layer. There was nothing within; it was the sheer weight of the metal that had made the box appear to be loaded.

What Geraldi first saw was an enameled man in an enameled boat with high, curving prow and stern. Upon his head he wore what looked like branching horns, and between the horns reposed a large disk of green. It was upon that disk that they fastened the greater part of their attention. Asprey even asked to have the box tipped a little more into the light, and with a glass screwed into his eye he searched the green depths with hungry gaze.

At last he raised his head and removed the glass. Geraldi waited in the calm of a very great impatience.

"It's real," said Asprey, and sighed. "It's entirely a perfectly first-class emerald. Goodness knows how many carats in it. I'd be almost ashamed to guess."

"And here's another side," remarked Geraldi. He turned up the gorgeous form of a great scarab that rolled before it a huge, green ball that glittered and shimmered in the sunlight.

"My Lord! My Lord!" sighed the fat man. "Is there one on every side? No wonder Kalam and the rest were after it."

He applied the same scrutiny to this gem and finally announced: "There's a couple of flaws in it, but 'way down at the bottom of the heart of it . . . and that's a deep heart, son. Like the deep, green heart of the sea. Green fire. Green heaven. Ah, Jimmy, life is just beginning for us!"

They turned the third side up and saw what appeared to be a swathed mummy with a white crown, and above the crown arose another of those monstrous gems. They gave it hardly a glance. Upon the fourth side another figure walked, hunch-shouldered after the old Egyptian style, and he, in turn, had above his head another emerald no whit inferior to all the rest.

Speechless, they turned up the box, and upon its top they saw a larger figure than any upon the sides, enameled in the form of a man with a hawk's head above his shoulders — a marvel of cunning workmanship, so that every feather seemed indicated, and the steely sharpness of the formidable beak. Above his head, also, there was an indentation that extended quite to the bottom of the golden sheathing of the box, but that which filled the hollow no longer was present.

The fat man snatched the box and measured the empty hole, measured again the other jewels that remained. Then he laid the box upon the sand, where it glowed and flashed as though on fire. "Young man," he said angrily, "we've been done out of a stone worth all the others put together! Do you hear me, Jimmy? We've lost the head of the whole business. These other gems are simply pikers. That was the real prize. *That*, my boy, was an *emerald!*"

"It might have been a piece of green glass," said Geraldi.

"Don't say it, Jimmy," replied the other. "It does me harm to hear you say such a thing. It really does, Jimmy. Makes my heart ache to think you've no more sympathy and understanding for the rare old boy who planned this bit of jewelry. Green glass? Would he spoil his job by coming down to that note in the scale?"

"He wouldn't," Geraldi agreed. "Because I take it that this is the crowning point of the whole work. This fellow here with the hawk's head, Edgar, is our friend that I was telling you about . . . that Ingall talks to at sunrise."

"Hours?" asked Asprey.

"Horus," Geraldi corrected.

"Horus! That's it! Golden Horus . . . how did the rest of it go?"

"I'd as soon have him in enamel," said Geraldi, "if we could find the thing he used to wear upon his head."

"Good old fellows, they are," said Asprey with beaming sympathy. "Forced to carry around burdens like those, Jimmy. Sad, I call it, and never a word of complaint, I suppose, in the last couple of thousand years."

"Those are solar disks," Geraldi said. "Bum idea, that, Edgar . . . green suns, eh?"

"I never saw a better sun in the sky," said the fat man with energy. "Never saw a better one in my life . . . never one to equal the four beauties on the sides of this box. But if we had the top one of all . . ." He broke off with a sigh. Then he stood up and began to remake his pack. Geraldi followed suit.

They resaddled the refreshed horses, mounted, and rode down the dip of the hills.

"Which way now?" asked the fat man.

"There's only one way for us," said Geraldi.

"Explain yourself, old son."

"Where are we going to get rid of stones of this size?"

"I won't break 'em up," declared the other. "I'm dashed if I'll have them broken. I'd rather eat 'em first."

"Then" responded Geraldi, "we head for the East, take a ship in New York, and slide over to Paris. I know a little side street with a little black-faced shop in a tumble-down old building. There's a one-eyed rascal running it. He wears a dirty blue apron and keeps his spectacles high up on his fore-head except when he looks at a jewel. But he pays as much as a million and a quarter in hard cash for a single deal."

"I like him already," said Asprey.

"He keeps a son in a palace near Tours. Keeps that lad like a prince." There was reminiscent shade in his voice.

"I suspect that you played cards with that boy," suggested Asprey.

"He's an ambitious youngster," said Geraldi. "Lucky, too. He wanted to help his luck out, and, therefore, he learned a great deal about cards . . . you understand? He sat down to a little friendly game one day, and I happened to be at the table."

"I hope you taught him a little, Jimmy? You wouldn't let a promising young fellow like that waste his time, I hope?"

"He couldn't learn," said Geraldi, "except by himself. All went perfectly well until he made a slight mistake in his own deal . . . the cards seemed a bit wrong for him, I mean to say . . ."

"You switched decks on him?" grinned the fat man.

"What a suggestion," murmured Geraldi, but his eyes were too large and mild and innocent.

The blue jay, that had been perched on the top of the young pine, now came swooping with a harsh outcry just above their heads.

"Dash that bird!" exclaimed Asprey. "I hate those little bright beasts. They're spies, Jimmy!"

The latter made no reply, but after a moment he leaned pleasantly and said to his companion: "Keep your head straight forward, Edgar, and don't look behind you."

"Why not, man?"

"I saw the wink of steel a second ago."

"Ah?" murmured Asprey, growing a little pale, but setting his jaw firmly beneath its folds of fat.

"I saw it again, a second later. Unless I'm terribly in error, there are about six riders in that bit of woods, Edgar, and they want us."

# CHAPTER
# ELEVEN

## "Legal and Moral Rights"

When they had turned the next point of rocks, they sent their mounts down the slopes like a mountain river in June flood. They shot out from the woods. Pleasantly rolling country extended before them with good footing for the horses and the slopes never too steep for a fine gallop. The enemy came like volleyed arrows behind. There were not six, but seven of them, and they were mounted on excellent horses. There was hardly the slightest difference between their mounts and those of Geraldi and his companion, but what difference there was, was on the side of Asprey's purchases. If only the fat man's mount could bear up under the crushing impost of that tremendous weight.

Ten miles of honest galloping were put behind them, and now the best they could raise from their horses was a trot. But the enemy was dimly bobbing on the horizon.

"Jimmy," said the fat man, "I give you the credit for the whole idea, and the nerve to stay in the fire until you'd picked out what you wanted . . . but hand me a little credit for the getaway I provided, will you?"

At that moment, while his head was turned, his fine animal stopped short, and then jerked forward on its head. Asprey, heavily thrown, rolled head over heels and got up staggering in time to see Geraldi send a bullet through the brain of the horse. Staggering still, but not with the shock of the fall, Asprey came back to his companion. He looked at the country about him, but it was smooth-shaven. There was not a rock, there was not a bush, there was not even tall grass in which he could have attempted to hide. Then he stared at the smoking gun in the hand of Geraldi, and at the thin, hand-some face of that youth.

"Get on the horse!" commanded Geraldi. "I'll run along-side."

Asprey asked no questions. Fear was making his fat sides quake, and he scrambled into the saddle. His first gesture was to put out his hand to the saddlebag in which the box hung. "How could they have spotted us?" groaned Asprey.

"By thinking the way we thought. Nothing simpler. Ride, Edgar, old fellow, and we'll try to come to some place where we can fight them off."

Asprey groaned again, and started the horse at a trot. They slipped between two low hills.

"Shall I swing right up this draw?"

"Keep straight on! Keep straight on!" So commanded Geraldi, trotting lightly at the side of the fat man.

They went up a long, easy rise, and from the top they looked back at seven shadowy silhouettes streaking toward them from the distant rear.

"They've seen the kill . . . they've tasted horse blood, they want our blood now," said Geraldi. "Look at that!

Those horses, even, have new life. And this nag is a beaten dog." He pointed a little to the left. "You see that knot of rocks and trees? Make that, if you can, Edgar, and pray that there'll be water in it. We're going to have a siege even if we land that."

Asprey made no comment.

They turned straight toward the little oasis of rocks. It stood up for them like a ship at sea — and they, wrecked mariners on the shallowness of barges, with sharks about. Whip and spur went into the tormented flanks of the horse with the fat man working hard, and Geraldi running beside, holding to one stirrup. Although Asprey had chosen an excellent animal to carry the lighter weight of Geraldi, it never was meant to support his own poundage. The ten-mile run had taken the heart of the horse. Now it floundered drunkenly across the hills. Geraldi glanced back and took note.

"We can't make it," he panted. "Ride for the foot of the hill, Edgar, and we'll fight them off from behind the horse and try to get up to the rocks, one of us, by a rear movement. Ride, man . . . ride!"

Asprey rode, indeed. He was badly frightened, but fear did not make him incapable. His mouth set in a hard, straight line that made his cheeks bulge. He had the look of one grinning with pain, but he wasted no time in glancing over his shoulder at those grim riders behind him; he gave all his attention to wringing a little more strength out of that failing, shambling body of the horse, and steering it the straightest way for the hill of refuge.

They were near the foot of the hill now and had its long, easy slope before them. But in their ears were the yells of triumph and the beat of many hoofs, when a gun barked straight before them, and then in rapid succession a stream of shots was fired.

Utterly bewildered, Geraldi looked back and saw a horse down and a man rolling on the ground, while the rest of that pursuit split to either side and rode furiously for safety. At that same moment, totally spent, the horse under the fat man halted and dropped its head.

"We're lost and saved," said Asprey bitterly. "And dash the luck that's brought the entire world here to chase us this way and that. We never should have made that camp, Jimmy."

"We've done nothing wrong," said Geraldi. "You can't beat luck. It always has the top hold."

They left the horse and went slowly up the slope. No one appeared from behind the rocks that ridged its top, and they had gained the very crest and walked in through the first line of the defense before they could see what garrison was there. Then they found a big, blond cowpuncher, and with him the white head and the stern face of Robert Ingall.

The four looked at one another in half-amused, half-grim expectancy.

It seemed perfectly obvious what had happened. The gang of Seyf Kalam and the rest had guessed at the direction in which Geraldi would flee; so had Ingall, and he showed his self-confidence by taking only one man to join him in the pursuit. Geraldi began to chuckle.

"And why?" asked Ingall.

"Because," he said, "I can't help thinking about the view you had of us when we were scooting across the hills . . . with those seven fellows brushing us straight into your dust pan, so to speak."

Ingall did not smile. "I had no doubt whatever," he said. "I knew what would happen."

"You didn't strike out across the hills by guess?"

"My young friend," said Ingall, "I was led."

The blond cowpuncher put in: "By what, chief?"

"A thing which has no name . . . for any of you," said Ingall. "I think the box comes back to me, Mister Wilbur?"

Geraldi had tucked the saddlebag under his elbow. Now, for answer, he shrugged his shoulders.

"The box goes back to you?" echoed the fat man. "I don't see that. You've spent more years in the higher education, Mister Ingall. But I don't follow that idea."

"We can give you some reasons, maybe," the big cowpuncher suggested. He was a handsome fellow, with a face that looked younger than the pale, narrow sabers of his mustache, drooping on either side of his mouth. Now he moved his rifle a little. He carried it slung across the hollow of his left arm, ready at any instant to jerk the butt to his shoulder and cover a man.

But Ingall raised his hand. "Not a bit of that!" he declared. "We're dealing with a gentleman here who will see reason. But if you try force, my boy, he will kill us both out of hand. You don't know him."

The cowpuncher smiled, and his smile was as stern as Arctic cold.

"I dunno," he said. "I take my chances . . . but you're the doctor here, and I do what you say."

Asprey actually rubbed his fat palms together with satisfaction. "This is a lot better," he said. "We're going to talk this thing out . . . reasonable. All you have to do, Mister Ingall, is to prove that you have a legal right to this saddlebag and what's in it."

Robert Ingall sat down on a flat-topped rock and, taking off his hat, wiped his forehead with a handkerchief and then smoothed his silver hair.

"You might take a walk around the edge of the rocks," he said to the cowpuncher, "and try to make out what those fellows are doing. Then go down and bring up that horse of theirs as soon as it can walk. It will be dead in a few hours unless the stiffness is walked out of it. Here's my glass, so that you can watch the hills." He gave it in its case to the other, and still the cowpuncher lingered, frowning a little. Never had Geraldi seen a more perfect fighting type, keen as steel, and as cold.

"Let me hang around a little," begged the 'puncher. "You dunno. I might come in pretty handy up here, chief. You never can tell . . ."

He let his glance drift from Geraldi to the fat man, and back again, until his cold gray eyes steadied upon the smaller of the two and dwelt long upon him. And Geraldi looked back with an odd and baffled feeling that he was mated at last.

78

Ingall, however, seemed to prize the formidable presence of his hired man not a whit. He merely turned his head to him with a curt nod. "Take yourself off, my friend," he said. "Look over the hills. See if you can spot those rascals who were riding so hard a little while ago. Then come back with the horse."

The cowpuncher made a gesture of reluctant surrender. Still, after he had started off, he turned again and gave Geraldi a lingering glance. But finally he was gone from sight.

"Legal right?" Ingall pondered aloud. "It's true that I have no actual legal right. But I have a moral right."

"Moral right! That's good . . . that's rich!" said the fat man with a wink to Geraldi. "He has the moral right. You can keep the moral right, Mister Ingall, and we'll keep the box, thank you. Or," he added, "you can have the moral right *and* the box, but we'll hang onto the pretty green stones."

Ingall looked gravely, almost pityingly, at Asprey. "Do you mean that you would pry the emeralds out of their settings?" he asked.

"Funny, isn't it?" smiled the other. "It'd be sad to spoil that pretty little box. But you see how it is, Mister Ingall. I have no eye for art. I'd leave that to you. All the gold, even, and the fine enamel work. We'll simply take the stones and let it go at that."

Ingall raised a hand with a lessoning forefinger. "Let me tell you one thing from the bottom of my heart," he said. "Every man who tampers with the jewel work on that box is dead . . . dead from the day he touches it."

The contented grin of Asprey was somewhat dimmed by this. But he looked in bewilderment at Geraldi, as though wanting a little reënforcement in talking common sense to this strange fellow.

Geraldi seemed to be considering this appeal in some doubt. But at length he reasoned: "It's a very large haul, Mister Ingall. It's enough to make a man want to overstep the mark a little. But, as a matter of fact, I see that we would have been neatly scooped up by those seven riders if it hadn't been for the rifles on the hill . . ."

"Great Scott, man," breathed Asprey. "What are you about to say? Are you going to let them in on a split? If it's a fight, Jimmy, you know that you can count on me to handle this fellow . . . no matter how many lions he has killed. And as for the 'puncher . . . I think you can dispose of him fast enough."

"I know you have plenty of nerve," Geraldi said, at last coming to a conclusion, "but the fact is I recognize that moral right Mister Ingall was speaking of. We gave him a fair challenge . . . we got the box from him by fair craft and taking of chances . . . but now I think he's won it back. And here, as a matter of fact, it is." And he placed the saddlebag in the hands of Robert Ingall.

# CHAPTER
# TWELVE

## "Three Sad Men"

To the fat man it appeared a stunning thing, so that he gaped at Geraldi, and then at the saddlebag that Ingall had opened for a single glance, and then closed, and was tying its mouth once more.

"Jimmy," said Asprey at last, "is it the double-cross?"

"It's the square deal," Geraldi answered lightly.

The other started to speak, changed his mind, and went slowly away. His whole body seemed to sag. When he came to the first tree, he halted and leaned a hand against it until he had recovered from the shock. Then he went on with a fumbling step and vague eyes.

Ingall followed him with his glance.

"You've made a sad man, there, Mister Wilbur," he remarked. Geraldi did not answer, and the other went on: "I knew that it would come back to me. But I was curious to see how. And you observe, my young friend, the hand which took it was the hand which returned it." He laughed suddenly, and the laughter had an unpleasant ring; the light in the eyes of Ingall, also, was not a thing to be faced if it could be avoided, and Geraldi looked off across the hills.

"Our friends have ducked out of sight," he said, "but I think that they'll be back again. They have their eye on you."

"Ah, Wilbur," said Ingall, with a sudden change of voice and manner, "I am sorry for them. Just as I was sorry for you when you gave me your challenge yesterday. I admire courage. You all have shown it . . . wit, invention, grim determination, skill. It was a simple and neat little trick that took the box away last night. I thought for a moment that it would cost you a bullet through the head . . . but it is all futile. All these efforts to take what is mine are bound to fail. And if they seem to succeed for a moment, it is only that my own faith may be tested," went on Ingall, his voice rising higher and that fanatic ring coming into it once more. "As if I had doubt in my mind. But there is no doubt in me. I have faith. I have seen. I have seen the golden hand of the god."

Perhaps enough has been said to indicate that Geraldi had as few nerves as most young men, but now, as he heard the strange avowal that hinted at a creed outworn by two millenniums and more, he was slightly startled. It was not Ingall, oddly enough, that he thought of at that moment. It was Mary, the daughter of this man. Asprey had been right. It was a great deal more than the shock of her own narrow escape that had reduced her to tears the day before. And, worst of all, it was a thing of which he dared not speak. It was a subject that he shrank from. His own disbelief in everything seemed to weigh upon his mind like the mantle of lead with which Dante cloaked his sinners.

82

Ingall had risen to his feet, and now he walked back and forth with a long, slow stride. His eyes were still uncannily bright, and his glance roved. When it fell upon Geraldi, he had to steady himself to meet it.

"The time is now very near at hand," said the Egyptologist, "when such a revelation will be given to the world as will blast the minds of the weak and the foolish. Only to the chosen the truth will come home like a bird to its nest." He paused before Geraldi. "Young man," he continued, "there is metal in you that could see the truth . . . if it were as bright as the disk of the noonday sun, let me say."

Geraldi started.

"Oh," said the other, lifting his solemn hand, "as bright as the sun upon both horizons, the golden sun, like a hawk on both horizons . . ."

Geraldi stared at him with open dread. Ingall, seeing that look, mastered himself with an effort that turned him sallow of face.

"There must be time for everything," said Ingall. "We need to take great thoughts slowly, as a child learns to eat new food in small mouthfuls. But when the truth at last comes, there is with it an appetite . . ." He ceased speaking, and then added abruptly: "You have been sent to me for a purpose. Let me have a few days or weeks to see what that purpose may be. A purpose of good."

Geraldi could stand it no longer. He had to change this conversation, and he could think of only one topic that would serve his purpose. "Ingall," he began, "you have picked up a rare fellow in that cowpuncher."

"He?" said the other carelessly. "He was brought to me. There was a service to be done, and he was brought to me." He added in a calmer and more natural tone: "He shoots well, Wilbur."

"Did he drop that horse?"

"It was he. I told him only to fire over their heads, as I was doing, but the temptation was too great for him, it appeared."

"Did you think," asked Geraldi, "that you would stop that charge by firing in the air?"

"I hoped to," said Ingall in his darker manner. "For why should I wish to take their lives, seeing that their punishment will be greater than they can bear . . . through all eternity. Through all eternity."

Very glad was Geraldi to see the cowpuncher coming up the slope, and Asprey beside him, both pulling on the bridle. It was as though Asprey, after the shock that he had received, could not endure mere idleness. He worked with the 'puncher over the horse, driving it constantly up and down so that it would cool off gradually. But it was in very bad condition, and it persisted in stopping whenever it could and dropping its head down with a shudder.

"That horse will be no good for riding until tomorrow morning," said the big cowboy. "I'll rub him down, but he's fair shaken to bits. He never was cut out to carry a heavy-weight, it looks to me." He grinned toward Asprey.

"Take him down to the flat," Ingall said suddenly. "Face him toward the sun and keep him there for an hour. Then ride him back here."

"Ride him back?" asked the other, instinctively glancing down at his powerful body as though wondering how such a burden could be carried.

"Do as I tell you!" Ingall snapped shortly. "I don't expect you to understand."

Perhaps his long residence in Egypt had given him a rough carelessness in addressing his inferiors. Now the cowpuncher flushed a little and looked gloomily at his employer, but, as though he resigned himself at once, he shrugged his big shoulders and went off down the slope, dragging the dull-eyed horse behind him.

Ingall abruptly turned his back on Geraldi and retired to the shadows among the trees as though he wished to be alone.

"A nut," said Asprey lightly, hooking a thumb over his shoulder. He went on: "Jimmy, it's something deep . . . it's something grand that you have in mind. Let me in on it. I won't ask too many questions. You know that I'm with you up to the hilt in this little work."

"It's nothing up my sleeve," Geraldi assured him. "Not a thing."

"You've simply handed back the stuff to him?"

"I've simply handed it back to him."

"What right had you to do it?" asked Asprey, now growing suddenly purple, although he kept his voice down. "What extra claim had you to do it?"

"I don't know," answered Geraldi. "Except you'd be a dead man yonder in the hills, if I hadn't done what I thought was right when your horse dropped. And now I've done what I think is right again. I'll tell you this. I've nothing to gain."

"And I'm to believe that?" asked the other, his lips curling.

"I hope that you'll believe it."

"I'll be damned if I'll be such a fool," he said, and walked hastily away, pausing a little now and then as though the fresh ecstasy of his rage overwhelmed and numbed him.

Geraldi, in turn left alone, sat down on a rock and looked at the horse that the tall cowpuncher was keeping obediently turned toward the sun. The long minutes passed, gloomy minutes for Geraldi, as he contemplated the breakdown of what had once been a brilliant mind, until it had been lost in such superstitious folly as this. Then he rubbed his eyes and looked again with a new interest.

The broken-down gelding was beginning to crop the grass at his feet.

# CHAPTER
# THIRTEEN

## "Marvels"

It was no single marvel. A sick horse is like a sick dog. It will not eat. Only man seems to retain his appetite when he has no real need of nourishment. And although Geraldi looked on the quick recovery of the gelding as a most astonishing thing, that was not all. The full hour elapsed, and then the cowpuncher did exactly what he had been told to do. He jumped on the back of the horse and spurred it up the slope — and Geraldi stood up and opened his eyes, indeed, for the gelding came at a strong gallop.

He stopped the rider at the edge of the rocks. He wanted to know what had happened, what peculiarity of grass, perhaps, grew at the foot of the rocks, but the answer was decisive.

"The same as grows here," said the big man.

Geraldi shook his head in amazement. "I thought that was a foundered horse," he said.

"Look at him now," replied the cowpuncher.

The gelding held up his head. His eyes were bright. At that moment a buzzard stooped lower from the sky, although still at a great distance, and the horse lifted its head to follow the movement of the free-gliding shadow in the sky.

"What's your name?" asked Geraldi.

"What business is it of yours?" asked the big man with a ready ferocity.

"Come, come," answered Geraldi. "Don't be a bulldog. Is your name poison?"

"For some gents," said the other more fiercely than ever.

"Not for me, I hope," replied Geraldi. "Carry your name along with you, then, and good luck go with it and you." He even laughed a little as he spoke, but he felt far less content than he pretended, for there was something unspeakably ominous in the bearing of this man, and Geraldi, looking at him more closely, felt more and more convinced that he was something far beyond the ordinary. It was more than the magic of the dead god that had brought poor Ingall to this place, perhaps. It was the cleverness of this hired man of his. The very suggestion of that word made Geraldi shake his head. There was nothing servile about this handsome blond fellow. Not that Western range riders ordinarily are a servile lot, but those who have known the pain of labor for money carry the impression subtly inscribed upon their faces, and the writing was not to be seen in the brow of this fellow.

"I dunno," he murmured now, his quick, keen gray eyes constantly stabbing at Geraldi with a combination of watchfulness, suspicion, and savagery. "I suppose I could tell you that most people call me Mickey?"

"Mickey," said Geraldi, and knew instantly that there was a lie in the very suggestion. That Irish nickname has a cheerful sound to it. It is given to blue-eyed, red-headed Celts, to mischief-making, carefree lads, as a rule, and there was nothing careless or carefree about this son of battle. At least, every moment of his talk with Geraldi was like the clashing of swords. "You've taken an instinctive liking to me," Geraldi said, and smiled. "I can see that, Mickey. But tell me now . . . because I see you're a fellow with brains. What happened to this horse? Wasn't he dead beat an hour ago?"

"He was dead in his tracks," said the other, almost reluctantly turning his pale, fierce eyes from Geraldi to the horse. "I never seen a worse beat one."

"And you didn't see anything that could have brought him back to himself?"

"The sun," said the cowpuncher. "He stood down there and faced the sun."

He said it gravely, but Geraldi felt that in the words of Mickey there was the same suspicion and mockery and wonder that he himself felt on this subject. He almost wished that Ingall would hurry back from the trees so that he could ask him questions. Then he realized that it was a subject that nothing could have persuaded him to open again. He would have let ten mysteries of greater moment slide rather than see that wild look come back into the grim face of Ingall.

"Is that all, boss?" asked Mickey.

"That's all. Thanks."

Mickey touched his hat and went on. There was a useless mockery and contempt in this simulated salute, and Geraldi felt his blood boil as it had not boiled since he was a child. If Mickey for little or no reason hated him, it was apparent that he was beginning to hate Mickey. He wondered at himself, but the thing was there in his blood like a poison and would not away. He wondered at it. It troubled him, indeed, more than anything that had happened in a great time, for as a rule he had himself under the most perfect control. Whether in crime or in war, your great actor must be a man of a large and magnanimous temper, and that temper Geraldi usually possessed, but Mickey seemed to have snatched away his self-control. He had a wild impulse to shout after the man and hurl insults. Even after Mickey had disappeared among the trees, still Geraldi felt ill at ease. He had to walk up and down to curb himself.

He was glad when Ingall returned from the trees. These made a solid little group on the northeastern side of the hill, marching up to the tuft of rocks that was a natural fortress. The pines clustered together, and yet they seemed to have been planted in their close ranks by a human plan and fore-thought.

Ingall had decided, it appeared, that the day had gone so far that it would be better if they remained here until the morning came. There was a little spring among the rocks, a mere trickle of water and yet ample for cooking and for watering the horses, where it had collected in a pool. They could camp here in perfect comfort, and on the next day they could return to San

Felice with ease, where Mary must be waiting for them anxiously.

"But," said Geraldi, "there are seven men out there somewhere among the hills. They may have a chance, during the night, to rush us. Or else, they may be able to get together help and mob us during the return march."

Ingall smiled upon him with a superior knowledge. "Let me tell you," he said, "that no harm can come to me in this spot. And you, Wilbur, are my friend." He smiled as he spoke, and in a different manner. Then he enlarged his speech simply, seriously, thoughtfully. "Because, Wilbur, after a man has traveled for a while through this strange and foolish world, he begins to learn how other men are to be prized, and I never have met a fellow like you . . . with half of your hawk-like or panther-like nature, I mean to say, and with half of your nobility behind the veil."

He brushed his own thought aside. It was wearing toward the evening, and, calling Mickey with a sharp whistle, Ingall gave orders that camp would be pitched on that spot and preparations made for supper.

By the time supper was cooked, it was already close to thick dusk, and, as they sat about and finished their cigarettes and Ingall a long, thin, black cigar, the night settled over them. It seemed to change their position subtly. The last light banded the horizon with softest rose, and above the rose was a clear, transparent strip of green, and above the green the twilight blue began, thinly streaked with starlight, here and there. They appeared to be pressed upward from their hill, or as if the hill itself grew higher toward the heart of heaven. So they sat, surrounded with the soft evening.

Geraldi said, a little anxiously: "Suppose the seven slip up behind those trees, Mister Ingall? They could do that, easily enough, and blow us into the middle of kingdom come, eh?"

Ingall answered gently, as if to a child: "No harm will ever come to me or to friends of mine in this place, Wilbur."

The cowpuncher, at that, raised his blond head, glistening by the firelight, and looked across at Geraldi with the strangest of smiles. Geraldi frowned in return, and then the train of his thoughts was quite broken across.

Ingall with a choked cry had started to his feet, and Geraldi, turning his head toward the trees, saw on the black verge of them the strangest figure that ever met his eyes. It was a naked man with a loincloth wrapped about his middle, and on his head an odd dress from which branched something like horns. But the form of this man and his accouterment were the least of his strangeness. The horns on his head — the wig that he wore — the loincloth — all his naked body in addition, glowed and shimmered with a golden light.

Ingall staggered, and then, throwing out his arms, he went straight for that apparition. He began to run, reeling like a drunken man, while the golden form moved backward among the trees, glimmered, and was gone from view.

"Ingall!" shouted Geraldi. "Ingall! Come back!"

There was not an answer. Beside him, Geraldi heard the frightened, thick breathing of Asprey. He looked back across the fire, and there sat Mickey with a smile of devilish calm and content upon his face.

"Ingall!" Geraldi cried again, and started to run in pursuit. He thought that Mickey called something behind him, but he could not be sure. Only he knew that voice filled him to the very heart with suspicion and alarm. He ran warily, all eyes before and to either side, and a gun in his hand. So he entered the thick shadow of the trees, swinging from side to side to avoid their extending branches. His toes caught on a soft form, and he almost pitched to the ground. Then he whirled and knelt by the figure that he could dimly see stretched upon the ground.

"Ingall," he called softly, for he had no doubt of the identity of that moveless form.

# CHAPTER
# FOURTEEN

## "A Bolt is Turned"

He called again and received no reply. He lifted the head of the fallen man and leaned closer.

Then, in a dying voice, a pause between the words, Ingall answered: "The . . . hand . . . of . . . the god. Horus, golden Horus, on the two horizons you . . ." A shudder stiffened him, his head dropped back, and Geraldi knew that he was dead.

This, then, was ended. So Geraldi brushed Ingall and his fate from his mind. He lifted his head and looked around at the dull, shadowy forms of the trees, one blending vaguely with another. Out of them came a long, yellow blade of light, wavered, and then fixed on Geraldi. Although seconds are required to tell of the coming of that light, it was only a flash of fumbling before the radiance fell upon him. He leaped up and to one side, a gun in his hand as he sprang from the thrust of that bright sword. Behind him, before him, almost like an explosion and an echo, two guns spoke; two bullets kissed the air beside his head; and he fired in turn at the source of that light just as it winked out.

A stifled groan told him that he had struck the mark. Then, spinning about, the suddenness of that movement baffled the aim of a second gun, which now flashed through the brush just behind him. Straight at that flash Geraldi sprang and sent a bullet flying before him. The branches were cleared away before him. His shoulder struck a body that already was falling, and Geraldi himself tumbled headlong upon the ground.

His hand struck the metal coldness of a small, heavy box — the box of the golden Horus — the fatal box for which poor Ingall had been drawn to his death like an ox to the slaughter. He gathered it into the crook of his left hand and crouched, expectantly waiting. There was no movement in the form that he had shot down, and he felt a tigerish satisfaction in the thought that he had killed one of these murderers.

The whole grove was crashing with gunfire, now. Twice he heard curses loud and long, as bullets flew apparently close to some of these hunters after his head.

He heard a loud voice ringing through the trees: "Get him, or it's better to have lost the box! Get him, or we've worked for nothing!" The voice of Mickey. Was it not crystal clear? Poor Ingall's hired man was simply one of these scoundrels; he had hired murder, so to speak, and put it on a horse to ride with him like his shadow.

Another voice boomed from the opposite side of the trees, pitched deep, but carrying like thunder: "A couple of you take the outside of the trees. Hunt hard! He's poison for us all, if he gets away." That was his old, former enemy, his lately redeemed friend, fat, smiling, treacherous Edgar Asprey.

In a blinding stroke of red rage, Geraldi was on his feet to rush toward that voice, but better sense came to him. He turned back and made quickly for the edge of the woods. As he ran, he untangled the problem. It came apart like half-twisted woolen yarn. Of course, Asprey had meant well enough until he saw the box rendered back to Ingall. After that, he had sensed with the uncanny brain of a true criminal the identity of big Mickey. Quickly they had struck a compact between them — the golden god, or his lying semblance, had been enough to draw Ingall to his death. Now all their hands had no employment except to find Geraldi himself. A shudder of savage determination ran through him at the thought.

He reached the wood's edge. The steep slope opened before him through the rocks, and down it he raced. Soon he stopped racing, and began to jog softly forward. It was thickest night. In this hollow he could not be seen against any skyline, and his hope was high, indeed. Then hoof beats thudded softly, swiftly, toward him. He dropped to the ground, not flat on his face, but on hands and knees, his muscles gathered, and saw a rider sweep out of the darkness and into it again. He even saw the gleam of the gun in his hand and knew, somehow, that the man was the false Mickey. Then he stood up and began to run again, never sprinting, keeping well within his strength. He made for the nearest cleft between the hills, and through the cleft he passed and kept on with a swinging stride.

A light blinked, after an hour, to the left of his course. He turned toward it and saw the faint outline of a house draw up out of the night. It was a typical ranch house, he saw at once. The trees has been cleared away for firewood — the easiest the nearest. And the front yard was simply a bare stretch that made convenient places for the establishment of hitching racks.

Geraldi knocked at the front door, knocked again. He heard a long echo travel down the hall within, and then a window scraped up, overhead. A woman's weary voice called down: "Is that you, Bert?"

"No," said Geraldi. "It's an unlucky fellow who's had a horse break a leg. I want another. Can you sell me something?"

She hung in the window, hesitating. "I'll call Sam."

She called Sam. His steps trailed down the steps into the lower hall, while Geraldi turned his head and eagerly scanned the brows of the hills against the stars. If the hunt came this way, they surely would ride for the light, just as he had done.

Sam proved to be a fellow of fifty, with a red, bald head, and an undershirt and pair of overalls for clothes. He jerked his head at Geraldi. "Howd'ye. You wanna hoss, do you?"

"I want a horse."

"You got no saddle, neither."

"I have no saddle, either."

"You come along, and we'll fix you up," said the other.

One would have thought that it was the commonest sort of business for him to fit out customers with horses in the middle of the night.

"You're in a hurry?"

"A great hurry," said Geraldi in the most heartfelt voice.

"You know a hoss, son?" He led on around the side of the house, as he spoke.

"I know a horse, fairly well."

"You want something good?"

"The best, man. The best."

"Aw, now I like to hear a gent talk up like that. You come right along. I'll show you the best, right enough."

He took Geraldi to a corral. Then he turned up his lantern. It made a swinging light, a veritable signal torch that could have been seen from any point along the faces of those hills.

"Can't you drive those horses into the shed?" Geraldi asked anxiously. "Hold on."

A silver gray, stockinged in black, so that it seemed to be running without lower legs at all, swung past him with the excited swirl of the other horses in the enclosure.

"Hello! That one ought to do," Geraldi said.

Sam turned upon him with a jerk of the head. "Where you raised?" he asked.

"Texas."

"You were!" Sam exclaimed. "They can't read a book by lantern light in Texas, let alone a hoss. You want that gray?"

"Yes, and I want him quick."

"You can have him, son. But you gotta pay for him."

"Well, well, what's the price?"

"Eight hundred dollars will make that hoss yours."

"Eight hundred poor jokes," Geraldi stated impatiently. "I asked you the price of that horse, not what you'd pay for a racer."

"My son," said Sam, "they's a lot of other hosses in this here corral. You said you wanted the best one. You picked the best one. And I gave you a price on it. Now look 'em over again and try to pick one with a cheaper price."

Geraldi surrendered. "I'll take him then," he said. "But you're a confounded robber."

"Robber?" said Sam. "A gent paid six hundred dollars for that little old hoss a year ago, and, if he ain't growed two hundred dollars better inside of a year, I eat my hat."

He had brought a rope with him. Now he stepped through the crowd of horses, and with one jerk of his arm sent the noose flying. It settled on the neck of the gray, and he led him out of the corral.

"Now a saddle?"

"Now a saddle. Not an eight-hundred-dollar one."

"I got a good one I can give away for thirty dollars. You come and look at it."

So Geraldi followed to a shed that, apparently, had been built originally as a granary, for the floor and even the lower part of the walls had been polished by the pressure of countless rough-sided sacks. Bridles, saddles, and all manner of riding equipment down to leather chaps were scattered here upon the floor. A powerful room it was, with walls made of double layers of wood. The very door was a massive double slab. Rats would have a hard job breaking into this treasure-trove.

"I got the gray's bridle in the house," Sam explained. "You stir around and look these things over. I'll be back in a minute." He put down the lantern and left the room, grunting as he dropped down to the ground from the high step.

Geraldi had picked up a saddle when he heard a soft little click. Glancing over his shoulder, he saw that the door had been swung to, and at the same time he heard the loud grating of the key in the rusty lock as the bolt was turned.

# CHAPTER
# FIFTEEN

## "No Room"

Geraldi did not leap at the door. He simply called:
"And you're one of Mickey's arms, I suppose?"

"I suppose I am," Sam said cheerfully from the
farther side of the door. "Sorry I had to shut you up,
young feller. But you'll be pretty comfortable in there
till he comes and I can ask him does he want you."

"Look here . . . ," began Geraldi.

The voice of Sam answered from a distance. "You'd
better settle down. I'm gonna . . ."

What ended the sentence, Geraldi could not tell,
for Sam apparently was walking on toward the house
in perfect security that his door and his granary walls
would hold a stronger force than Geraldi. The latter
was inclined to agree. Geraldi did not even waste
time in sounding the walls or the floor. The very
look of them was enough for him. But he took from
beneath his coat the golden box that, it seemed,
must now go back to Mickey, Asprey, and their
company. The first glance at it by the lantern light
showed that the green orb above the head of Osiris
had been removed. He turned it hastily. Every one of
the emeralds had been torn from their settings, and

then, apparently, the box had been cast aside as a worthless thing.

He raised the lantern and glanced through the keyhole of the big lock. The light shone straight through — the key had been removed by the care of old Sam, and Geraldi started with pleasure. It left him a free hand for the work that he knew better, perhaps, than any other. In an instant he was on one knee and had unfolded upon the other a little roll of thin chamois that contained in flat pockets some narrow bits of steel of varying sizes. He tried one of these in the lock; he changed it for another and larger size at once; and then he began to work carefully, his ear close to the door, laboring by sense of touch, and by the ear, and by a peculiar extra sense that came, perhaps, from the examination of a thousand locks of all makes in the world.

The work had not gone on for a minute before he heard distinctly the beating of the hoofs of horses, the creaking of saddle leather. These sounds swept up close. Next voices began. Even the strong nerves of Geraldi gave way a little, and perspiration stood on his face. But he worked on carefully, feeling his way in the double darkness of the iron hood that lay between him and the workings of that old lock, and the rust that held it. Then there was the faintest of groans — something gave — the massive door sagged slightly open.

There was little religion in Geraldi, but now he flashed a single upward glance. Then he blew out the lantern, pushed the door just wide enough to allow his escape, and stepped out into the night, the box still under the flap of his coat and held in place by his left arm, as there was high probability that, otherwise, the glint of the metal might be observed even by starlight. He shut the door behind him, observing that eight or nine horses were now grouped around the hitching racks in front of the little house. There were many voices. The door opened, and there appeared the tall form of Mickey, accompanied by Sam and a lantern.

Geraldi stepped around the corner of the shed and heard the others come toward him. He heard Mickey turn and call to the rest. Asprey came, leading on the others, and exclaiming: "You never know. You have to make sure of a rat, once you get him cornered."

"Of course, you do," said Mickey, "and I dunno . . . it may be a better job to just burn the place down and let him toast inside of it. If we try to break in at one rack . . . a magnificent group of us."

"But it ain't Geraldi, really," protested Sam.

"It ain't nobody else," said Mickey. "And we had him. We had him in a net, and he slipped through. I don't know how, still."

"He's a snake," said Asprey with warmth. "You never have him, till you have him dead."

Geraldi, listening to those involuntary tributes, smiled to himself. He passed rapidly around the shed, slipped across to the front of the house, and worked in among the horses. They were tethered at one rack — a magnificent group of animals, and, standing out beyond the rest even in the dark of the night, a huge fellow with a noble, arched neck and a small, proud head. Geraldi quietly untied the reins and knotted them, pair to pair, in a long, loose chain. He took his post at the side of the big horse.

The whole force of Mickey was now grouped around the closed door of the granary.

"Geraldi!" called Mickey. "D'you hear me?"

Who was this Mickey, then? This illiterate cowpuncher, and yet able to command with absolute power such men as Asprey and Kalam, and the rest of those international criminals?

"He won't answer," said Asprey. "He's simply trying to make us curious. He'll never answer, until we've opened the door. And then he'll be out like a cat, a gun in each hand."

Mickey laughed a little. "To think of the great Geraldi bein' snagged like this!" he boasted. "To think of that! Hell, I gotta laugh." And laugh he did, more loudly.

Geraldi swung up to the saddle. He made himself comfortable. In the long holster beneath his right knee there now was a rifle — doubtless of the best make and fully loaded. His position could not be improved upon.

Mickey knocked at the door again. He called: "I'll tell you what, Geraldi. You come out here and give your oath not to make no trouble, and maybe we'll give you a fair trial and see if we can't reach an agreement. There's room in this world for you and me to be friends, maybe?"

"No room," Geraldi responded. "Not room enough for you and me on the earth or under it."

They had whirled about with a universal groan of astonishment. Sam even dropped the lantern. But from the ground it shone on them all and made their tall, awkward shadows stand high above them on the granary wall. They did not bolt to get out of the light. Neither did they shoot in the direction of Geraldi's voice. Bewilderment seemed to have gripped them. As for Sam, he actually had thrown an arm across his face, as though to shut out the terrible miracle from his mind.

"I've marked you all down," Geraldi announced. "Seyf Kalam, Lucien Rompier, Giovanni Strozzi, Pedro Oñate, my old friend Asprey, and you, Mickey. I'll learn more of you later. And I'll never leave your trail, my friends, until I've run you down. Do you hear? I want only one life to pay for the life of Robert Ingall. And I'll take a ransom from the others . . . each one an emerald to fit into the golden box, which goes into the safekeeping of the dead man's daughter, my friends, until every jewel is back in place."

He turned the head of the big horse, jerked on the lead reins, and so he moved off from the troop into darkness, and still that stunned group remained motionless before the granary door.

# The Bright Face of Danger

# CHAPTER
## ONE

# "Courage, Courage, Courage!"

If anyone had told me that I, Emily Lucile Ingall, would ever find myself planted in the center of a waste of sand, and rock, and cactus, I should certainly have refused to believe him. And yet here I am in this awful desert, where anything *may* happen, where everything *threatens* to happen, where I cannot even form the least idea of what *will* happen. I try to think patiently of Mary Ingall. I try to remember she *is* an Ingall, but one seems to lose all one's old anchorages out here on the rim of the world.

Even in the beginning I had a distinct feeling of uneasiness. I felt it the minute I stepped on the train. And every mile that the train whirled me west from Boston, the greater grew that sense of uneasiness. When we actually entered the Far West — the region beyond the Mississippi River, I mean to say — a sense of despair was clearly coming over me.

I fought against it, of course. I told myself that it was merely a nervous depression and that I would soon recover. I told myself that I was a victim of nostalgia; and I really think that people from Boston are drawn back to their birthplace by a great spiritual magnet. It is particularly so in my case. Nothing but my acute sense of duty and family affection could have reconciled me to the trip into this unhappy country called *the West*.

When I was a little girl, there was still a stretch of it marked white on honest maps. Unexplored. And I am sure that only a sense of shame keeps the geographers from putting white places on their maps still. *I*, at least, cannot imagine that men really know this region; I cannot imagine why they should *want* to know it.

But as the train plunged through enormous cañons and groaned up endless grades, I wondered what induced men to leave civilized places for such naked grimness. As for the women — of course, we have followed men as slaves follow their masters. Other women, I should rather say, for it has ever been a source of pride to me that I have scornfully refused to wear chains.

As the train wandered across this gloomy continent, I could not help referring to the strange letter from Mary Ingall that had brought me so hastily from my home. I already knew it word for word — it was graven on my memory — but I found myself returning to it again and again with the morbid fascination that the psychologists tell us draws the criminal back to the scene of his crime. I particularly remember a singularly scholarly lecture on this absorbing subject by dear Professor Hamperwitz, at the ever-delightful Minerva Club, one of Boston's — but I must not weaken myself by thoughts of that lost paradise — rather let me steel my spirit by comparing the text of poor Mary's letter with the actualities as I have found them. It began:

Dear Aunt Emmy:

My poor, dear daddy has died. You have had the news before this, and I haven't had a chance to write sooner. Not a chance in three long weeks . . . because I'm involved here in . . . I don't know what . . . I can't say what.

At the beginning, I thought that I could tell you in a letter. Now I see that I only can explain to you when I see you.

But will you come? I have no right to ask you. But to whom else can I turn? I need a strong, brave woman to help me. I need someone with a strong, quick brain, and with courage, courage, courage!

Oh, dear Aunt Emmy! I remember that you went with poor Daddy on two of his hunting trips. He used to say, "As brave as Emmy," just as other people will say, "As brave as a lion." So you see that I turn to you, helplessly. If you will not help me, no one will.

But how shall I say why I need you? I can't! I can't write it in a letter. I must simply make a blind appeal.

I have taken a charming little villa among the hills. Or should I say a villina? It isn't really very large. The hills rise into mountains north of me. The plains begin to the south. A river winds through the valley, and the valley itself is filled with all sorts of growth — trees and flowers you never have seen before, perhaps.

You could be happy here, I hope. It wouldn't be for very long. There are horses, too. Splendid horses! You know that the Spanish horses were rich in Barb and Arab blood, and, when they ran wild, they became the ancestors of the stock on these plains. There would be riding for you, and hunting, too. From wolves to grizzlies, dear Aunt Emmy.

But could you come? Will you come?

What more should I say? I can't explain. I only can say that I need you desperately, quickly! Don't wire or write to ask questions. I couldn't answer.

The rest of this strangest of strange letters was concerned with directions for reaching the "town" where she would meet me. I use the quotation marks advisedly.

As I sit here and reread the words of that letter, my indignation rises. Especially when I come to the paragraph **I have taken a charming little villa,** *et cetera*. But let me learn to be patient — I have little doubt that I shall need patience and fortitude — above all, fortitude — in this strange, barbarous region.

The train at last was only ten miles from the station. I looked anxiously from the window, waiting to see green hills begin to appear. Alas, no green hills were in view, but baldscalped mountains, naked and done for. Like that poem of Browning's. From the other side of the train, I could see a smaller country. I won't say of

112

hills. A wretched jumble and junk shop of broken land — that was what it was.

Then the train slid to a stop. I was hurried off. It seemed as though the train was unwilling to delay to let me off at such a place, and the wheels barely stopped turning before they began again. My baggage literally was flung down upon the platform while the engine began to get up speed again. It was outrageous, and I have written to the president of that company a letter that should bring some results.

Then I turned and looked about me for the town. But there was no town. There was a wretched little station made of timber with a coating of sand. It looked like a reddish sandpaper, really. There was one little street stretching away from it, but the half dozen buildings were almost lost, just then, in a great whirlpool of dust that was sweeping across the place.

Of course, I was a little bewildered, and then I saw a small wagon with two horses galloping before it. They came on at full speed. The brakes screamed. The driver leaped over the wheel while it was still turning and came up the bank toward me. The driver was not a man. It was a girl, wearing divided skirts that actually were much more like trousers. As she came closer, she waved a gloved hand at me, and then I saw — saw that she was Mary, poor Robert Ingall's child. My own niece. She was as brown as an Indian; the edges of her hair were sun-faded. In short, I only recognized her because I expected to see her.

I was much too bewildered to ask questions, or to protest. I merely said that we must have a man to handle my luggage, and I wondered where the porter was.

"We get on without porters in this neck of the woods," Mary said.

"Neck of the woods?" I echoed her. I looked at her again. Of course, I couldn't believe my ears — was this the modest, gentle, well-trained girl whom I had last seen? She actually caught hold of the largest of my cases and dragged it across the platform, upended it, and tumbled it with a crash into the back of the carriage — buckboard, as they call it here. I took one of the others, silently, and saw Mary take two more, one in either hand. Over the pile of baggage she spread a black canvas.

"Dusty a bit," Mary said to me in explanation.

As if there were some peculiar end to be attained by an economy of words. I could not answer. It is always best, I feel, to allow a new situation to develop; first judgments are apt to be wrong. I got into the wagon, and we drove up the street.

"I gotta stop at the post office and get some bacon," Mary remarked.

But my powers of spelling break down. I only faintly imitate the language that I heard that well-bred and well-raised child using. It stunned me. I merely observed — as she swung the wagon around with a dizzy lurch — "Are these samples of your horses, Mary?" They were heavy-headed, roach-backed caricatures of horseflesh. It was almost libelous to call them horses at all.

114

And what answer did she make? "Two of the best," said Mary. "Run till they'll drop. Gamest little beggars in the world. That's Jinks on the left. That's Shanghai on the right. They call him Shanghai, because he takes charge of you when you least expect it."

The conversation of a girl finished in the best schools. I looked straight ahead and made myself smile. But I could see at once that I had been deceived.

We dashed down the street. Everything was done at a gallop. We came to a halt with brakes that screamed again, and a dust cloud overtook us and poured a liberal handful of unpleasant particles down the back of my neck.

It was a little one-storied shack in front of which we had halted. Over the door appeared a battered bit of lettering. I seemed to make out **Post Office**. Another offered **Meat and General Merchandise**.

On a cracker box sat a long, gaunt idler. He got up, and for a salutation he touched the brim of his shapeless hat with a forefinger. It was a simpler thing than a salute, and much easier than raising his hat. For, incredible as it sounds, this fellow appeared to know Mary. Yes, he addressed her by her own name and said — "How's things?" — or some such mumbled formula. And *my* Mary answered cheerfully: "Fine and dandy, Jake. Go in and ask for my mail, will you? And get me a side of bacon. I'm all out."

# CHAPTER
# TWO

## "A Patient Sufferer"

I shrink from relating what follows, but in order to prepare myself for the ordeals that doubtless lie before me I have determined never to spare my own feelings, even to shirking the recital of the most sordid details.

In response to Mary's request the tall fellow named Jake nodded, spat at a nearby post, and hunched up his shoulders — in appreciation, I suppose, of his own aim. Then he went into the shop.

"They're awfully obliging," said Mary. "You never saw such people as we have around here, Aunt Emmy. They'll do anything in the world for you, day or night, bless their hearts."

I pretended that I did not hear, and I had a good excuse, for at that moment a great gust jumped down the street and almost tore the hat from my head. I never have seen such a wind as blows here. It leaps on one like an invisible tiger, strikes, and is gone.

Jake returned. He gave Mary some letters and put a large parcel wrapped in greasy brown paper into the rear of the buckboard. Then he deliberately rested his foot on the hub of the nearest wheel and opened a conversation, wishing that Mary would go to the next dance. She admitted that she might be a little busy but that she'd come if she possibly could.

At last we drove on.

"Mary," I could not help inquiring, "do I infer that you have been at dances with that man . . . and actually danced with him?"

"I've danced with him," said Mary. "Jake is a grand dancer. You wouldn't think so, would you? But you never can tell about people around here. He does all the latest steps, and everything. He studies them out of a newspaper that has a column called 'Terpsichore.' Jake is a good fellow," she concluded, and I felt that there was no fit answer to make to such a remark. Possibly — possibly, I say — there may be women and aunts who would have found the words for the moment.

I will not dwell upon the ups and downs of the cattle trail that Mary called a road, and that we followed with the most frightful juts and jars for ten miles. And during most of that time, Mary kept the horses in a canter — a sort of hand gallop that, in the dialect of these singular people, is called a lope. Once, when the breath was jolted from my body in an audible gasp, Mary slackened the pace for a moment. She said to me simply: "That jarred you a little, didn't it? But you'll turn into India rubber before you've been out here long. You'll lose weight for a couple of weeks," went on this girl for whom trips had been engineered through Europe, through Asia, on whom too much money could not be spent. "You'll lose weight for a couple of weeks, and then you'll change. I'll put ten pounds on you in a couple of months, and every pound of it muscle."

Again it was impossible to answer. Two emotions were swelling in me: indignation, of course, and pity for poor, dear Robert Ingall whose work had come to this.

At the end of ten miles of such labor, we drew up in front of a house. It should not be called a house. My sense of exactitude rebels at the misuse of the word. It was a wretched little place of two rooms — a kitchen and one other. The floors were bare earth. In the kitchen a stove staggered, leaning at a great angle. The beds — that I should live to call such structures beds! — they were shelves built insecurely against the wall. "Bunks," Mary called them. I thought of books about the sea. It was like a wretched forecastle. **A charming little villa!** That phrase rang in my mind like a bell.

Mary, as I explored, had dragged in my luggage and left it lying on the earth. Then she unharnessed the pair of horses, hobbled them, and turned them loose to graze.

I came to the door of the shack — I cannot call it a house — and looked about me. The valley is filled with strange trees and flowers. It is a dreary waste of sand and rocks, with tallstanding cactus, grotesquely made, and shrubs and dwarfed trees that throw only a ghostly pretense of a shadow on the sand, their leaves are so small and, as I have discovered, often hanging with their edges turned up — so as to escape the force of the sun.

And the sun! Even in Boston an August day will be warm. Although I pity the weak creatures who find it necessary to leave our city at *any* time of the year. But until I came here, I never have known what the sun could be. It falls in rain. No, in solid sheets that rebound and cover the earth with blinding, liquid waves. It falls upon one with a weight. I know it sounds trite. But when I try to explain how the sun falls over these hills, I can only say that it is like the flashing and fall of ten million swords of white fire.

So I looked over the landscape. Do I remember something in the letter about **pleasant hills rising to mountains in the north and . . .** I shall not look at that wretched letter again to quote exactly. I cannot trust my temper.

Mary came in, dragging a set of double harness.

I made my voice carefully polite. "And there is a river, Mary, is there not?"

"Oh, yes," said the shameless child. "You see?" She swept her hand toward the center of the valley. There I saw what looked like low-lying smoke stealing here and there, a faint cloud of desert vegetation.

"The water comes down in June, when the snows melt," said Mary. "They tell me that there is running water sometimes for a whole month."

I looked her in the face. With wonderful hardiness, she met my eyes, and went past me into the kitchen.

The kitchen. I have mentioned the stove. Have I spoken of the "cooler" in one corner? A wooden frame covered with sacking. On the top, a pan of water that, by means of rags, drains down the sides of the cooler. And the evaporation of the moisture keeps everything inside as cool, say, as melted butter. There is a table of rough pine. The upper surface has not been smoothed with a plane, but use has given it a sort of grubby, even surface. There is a chair made out of a box. There is a stool. Otherwise one may stand in this house, or, in the bedroom, sit down on one of the bunks.

The bedding consists of straw mattresses — very little straw, and that in lumps. And over the mattresses are spread a pair of dingy, gray blankets. From the walls hang saddles, slickers — tarpaulins to shed the rain, it must be understood, or oilcloths — harness, Spanish atrocities — and, finally, there is a rack of guns. I counted three shotguns, one sawed-off a short distance from the stock, and four rifles, three of them repeating Winchesters. There were no fewer than seven revolvers. Enormous things that fire bullets almost half an inch in diameter.

I asked her who used those weapons.

"I do," she said.

"These?" I insisted, and took one of the ponderous revolvers from its place.

"Be careful, they're loaded," said Mary. "Of course, I use them." She took the gun from my hand and showed me where the sights were filed off and the trigger also done away with. "It makes a lot slicker draw," Mary explained, while I wondered at her.

She stood in the doorway. "You see that rock with the black face? I'll put a white spot on it." She fired, and without raising the gun shoulder high. I saw a little white spot appear near one edge of the rock. "Thumbs!" said Mary. "You see how it is, if you want to shoot fast? And if you have to shoot at all, you want to pour in the lead. You don't aim. You just get the hang of the gun and sort of feel your way to the target."

"I think I'll lie down," I said. I went and stretched myself on the bunk that was assigned to me. The air was close, hot, and still. I was very tired, but still I could not sleep. Too many images were jumping across my mind in a swift succession. I was seeing the wild mountains, like ridges of ocean in an incredible storm, frozen in place. No, not frozen in place, because all is motion, motion. There is nothing fixed in this fierce, bright land. Men and mountains are as flexible as water.

At last, I could endure it no longer. I sat up and opened my bags. The leather was burning hot to the touch from its journey out in the buckboard. I took out some few of my dearest possessions — those little trifles a woman will bring with her even to a desert — hoping that the sight of the familiar things would restore my balance and normal tranquility. Alas, I overestimated even my powers of endurance. One glance at the photograph of Boston Common, with its well-cared-for, luxuriant verdure, and the bitter contrast with the dreary waste in which I found myself unnerved me. I was fain to return the picture to its cover. The heart is, after all, but human.

I try to be reasonable. I try to tell myself that, after all, Mary is not mad. Is it I who have departed from my senses? I almost feel that must be the answer. I am sick with disdain and shame. I have been tricked and cozened into coming to a dread "end of the world." And why? I hope that I shall not have to ask direct questions. I hope that there will be grace enough in her to make her come to me and beg my forgiveness for her shameless falsehoods. I hope that she will prove that there is one drop of the honorable Ingall blood in her veins. And this girl is the daughter of that dauntless hero and spotless knight — Robert Ingall.

Thank heaven that has spared him the suffering of having his heart wrung on her account as mine is, at the moment. I shall do nothing in haste. When one has journeyed for five days on a train, one has learned patience. And, after all, I think that I have not shrunk from my share of burdens, my share of mysteries, in this world. Truly did the poet say: "The end is not yet."

# CHAPTER
# THREE

# "A Beautiful, Black Panther"

Exhausted by my emotions and the trials of this terrible day, I must have closed my eyes for a brief moment, blotting out for the instant the dreary picture of this wretched landscape, this wretched house. As I recovered myself, Mary came into the doorway, swinging a riding quirt in her hand.

"Enjoyed your nap, Aunt Emmy?" she asked rather ridiculously, for, of course, I had not slept.

I smiled at her, as politely as possible, and gave her no other answer.

"I thought," she continued, "now that it's cooler, we might go down to the tank and fetch up some water."

Water! It seemed almost impossible that there should be such a commodity in this hot wilderness. I put on my hat, or rather I started to, when she stopped me.

"You'll just blister the back of your neck," she said. "Take this." And she plucked down from the wall a battered straw hat with a tall crown that came to a peak.

I put it on. The sun was close to the horizon, but still it was fiercely hot. Mary had caught a new horse

— there seemed to be a dozen scattered over the bleak hills near the house — and she had put a large leather sack on either side of the saddle. Leading that pony — all the horses are hardly larger than polo mounts — we went on over the first low hill, and I came in sight of the water. I had been prepared for a good many shocks since my arrival, but this was too dreadful. A "tank" makes one think of a large, wooden reservoir, naturally. As a matter of fact, it is simply a mud hole, partly filled with stained water. When rain falls — if ever there is rain in this unfortunate land — it must deposit a considerable sheet of water here, but now all the outer margin was dry, baked, and deeply cracked. As we walked on, a great spider ran out of one of those cracks and scurried away. A hideous thing. Inside the cracked pattern around the edge of the pool there is a broad margin of mud, liberally colored with green slime, and inside the mud banks lies the water.

I had to stay on the verge of the mud, while Mary waded in. With a bucket, she dipped up thick water — *thick* is a word I am using purposely. Finally she filled the leather sacks, and we went back toward the house. I could not speak.

In the red of the sunset, I helped Mary to strain that unspeakable water through several folds of cloth. Of course, it is boiled before using, and although flavored with vinegar . . . ?

Our supper came next. Bacon — fried crisp, I'm thankful to say — was the meat. We had potatoes boiled in their jackets. There was a sort of cornbread, baked in

**124**

flat, rough loaves. There was plum and apple jam, to my surprise. And there was black coffee, incredibly strong. Yet one can drink a great cup of it and feel no ill effects — life here is so strenuous, makes so many more demands upon one's physical powers.

Mary was constantly gay. From the moment of my coming she had not mentioned her deceptive letter to me — I use as mild a word as possible — and neither had she referred to the mystery that had made her send for me. And her silence made a more and more favorable impression upon me. At first, I expected abject apologies. But, after all, she was showing a good deal of courage and firmness in facing my disapproval, which she must have felt.

She apologized for having only bacon. But, as she said, the usual fresh meat was rabbit, and I would be tired of that before long. Perhaps I could hit the rabbits, she said, but they were beyond her skill. I was absurdly pleased by this little compliment, and after coffee I really felt rather comfortable. We washed and dried the dishes — the tins, I should say — and then we sat on a blanket in front of the house. The fierceness of the day was gone entirely. There was no moon, but the stars were wonderfully bright, and each lay, as it seemed, in a pocket of black velvet. A wind was stirring, and it brought us far-off sounds that seemed to be drifting in from the horizon. The lowing of cattle, perhaps, the howl of a wolf, the yelp of a coyote, and the hoot of an owl — but all those sounds reduced and made small as all living things are made small here.

"The voice of the desert," Mary calls it. I think it's a good title.

I discovered that I had brought no cigarettes, but Mary offered to make one for me, and she did it very neatly with brown wheat-straw paper and tobacco.

"You're not smoking yourself, Mary?" I asked her.

"No," she said.

"Then how have you happened to learn how to roll them so well?" I asked her.

"I roll them for Jimmy."

I wondered, with a little shock, who Jimmy might be. At least I could be glad that it was not Jake.

"You roll them for him, but you never try them yourself?" I asked her.

"Jimmy doesn't think women should smoke," she responded.

This really worried me. "And who was it that taught you to shoot . . . with your thumb working the hammer, I mean?" I asked her.

"Oh, Jimmy taught me," she said in the most matter-of-fact way. "He knows all about such things."

I was just able to shut off a stream of questions that came tripping up to my very teeth. Questions are very little use, as a rule. Because they usually can be answered by yes or no — elaborated a trifle for the sake of politeness.

We sat for an hour in front of the house. I think we hardly spoke fifty words. There was no need of talk. The desert night was like a play; we were the audience. And when we did speak, our voices were hushed, as though we were afraid of interrupting the action.

"I'll have to turn in," said Mary at last. She stood up. Then she said suddenly: "You can wait until tomorrow to let me explain, or try to explain, Aunt Emmy?"

She spoke so gently and simply that I was half ashamed of the bitter things I had thought during the day. And she put that thought into words at once, for she said: "I'll try to explain tomorrow evening. It's no good talking about hard things during the day. The sun won't let you." She added: "Hush! Did you hear something?"

I did, immediately afterward. It was the snort of a horse, in the distance, coming up from the valley.

"Who could it be? Who could it be?" Mary said, with a hint of fear in her voice. She went into the house and came out again — carrying a rifle.

It was only a few days before that I had been in the middle of Boston's law and order. I can't tell you what it meant to me to see Robert Ingall's daughter coming to the door of a house with a rifle in her hands, like an Indian squaw in the wilderness.

Out of the blackness I saw a faint silhouette. Then, against the stars, I clearly saw a rider, and his horse. A whistle floated up to us.

"It's only Jimmy," Mary sighed with much relief.

I stood up in my turn. I wanted most desperately to see the face of Jimmy, as may be imagined. And my own relief was tremendous when I heard the clear, quiet voice of a man who has rubbed out all local accents by much travel.

"Are you there, Mary? Are you there?"

English, I thought. You know how much they use that phrase?

"Here I am!" called Mary in the happiest voice. It over-flowed with brightness, like a fountain playing in the sun. "I'm not alone."

"I'll turn my horse loose to graze," said Jimmy. He dismounted a few steps from us, unsaddled and unbridled his pony, and turned it loose.

All this before he greeted me. But I was not offended. In this country, the necessities of life take the oddest precedence over all formalities. One feels it instantly and grows accustomed to blunt manners.

"You'd better hobble him," Mary suggested. She had gone into the darkness a few steps toward Jimmy, but there she stopped as though she didn't want to desert me.

I could feel her excitement over his arrival — excitement, happiness, relief. I wouldn't vow that it is love. But a wonderfully near neighbor of that moon-shiny state, I must admit.

"He won't run away," Jimmy responded. A very pleasant voice, I still thought it. "He's used to me, and he'll tag around within call."

I liked that, too. A man who has a horse that will answer when called is apt to be a man worth knowing. I was intrigued by other bits of information — that he fired revolvers by sense of touch, so to speak; that he disapproved of smoking for women. Above all, that he was, to Mary, an all-important Jimmy.

She introduced us in the darkness.

"Aunt Emmy, this is Jimmy Walker."

"I think you'd better use the right name," he said.

"Do you think so?" she said thoughtfully. "Well, then, he is James Geraldi."

He shook hands with me.

"We'd better go inside and have a light," Mary recommended, "because Aunt Emmy will want to see you, Jimmy, of course."

Curiously, he wasn't the least embarrassed. Nor was she. But I knew that I was rather crimson when, at last, the lantern was lighted and the flame turned up. They were as calm as could be, smiling at one another and at me with the most perfect good nature. I looked straight at him. It was possible to be frankly curious, for he was actually holding the lantern close to his face so that I could view him.

And the first thing I thought of was a beautiful black panther.

# CHAPTER
# FOUR

## "An Incredible Story"

By this, it may be thought that I refer to a blackamoor, another *Othello*. But he looked sleek, handsome, Oriental — not dangerous. If I had suspected that poor Mary was fond of the fellow before, of course, I was in a panic now. I looked from James Geraldi to Mary. She seemed so clean-souled, so thoroughbred, so like an Ingall, that my heart bled for her. Now, I don't mean you to infer that Geraldi looked the part of a sneak or an abandoned villain, but he was of a different order from Mary, and people like Mary. You could have dropped him from almost any distance, and he would have landed on his feet. Does that give an idea of what I mean?

Mary was saying: "She doesn't know even *that* name, Jimmy."

"Suppose I explain," he said.

"No, you don't need to," said Mary. "We have to do a tremendous lot of talking . . . it will all come out. Take the chair, Aunt Emmy, and I'll open the meeting."

I sat down. I really needed to sit down.

"Excuse me," said the voice of Geraldi.

He was gone without a sound, and I looked blankly at Mary.

130

"It's better that way," she said. "We never know. One has to keep watch."

"For what?" I asked her. "Are the coyotes likely to come here and drink the tank dry or eat your horses?"

She smiled at me, without answering, as if I were a small child and she mysteriously grown up and wise. In fact, I felt increasingly absurd and subdued.

"I'm going to begin at the beginning," said Mary.

"You'd better, I suppose," I stated.

She went to a corner of the kitchen and opened a tin cracker box and took out of it something wrapped in a dishtowel. When she opened the dishtowel, she placed in my lap one of the marvels of this world. A golden box large enough to fill both the hands of a man, and worked over with Egyptian enameling of a kind I never had seen, despite the innumerable specimens Robert had brought home. On each side there was a figure — Ra, Atum, Osiris, Kheperi, or is it properly Khepera? — and on the lid of the box, and therefore larger than the other figures, a hawk-headed Horus. All the work was perfect, except — strange to say — that the solar disks, which apparently had been above the head of each figure, had been torn away. Perhaps they were particularly jewel-like bits of enamel, I thought.

"You remember that last tomb Father opened?" Mary asked.

Of course, I remembered — the one in which he was supposed to have found nothing but rubbish.

"But in the rubbish," Mary went on, "was this box."

I looked at her. She was so matter of fact and steady that one would have thought she was saying the most trivial thing. But gradually the significance dawned on me. The discovery of such a box would have meant newspaper headlines over all the world. In addition, it inferred other things.

Mary did not wait for me to draw my own deductions. She said: "You know that Walpoie said every man has his price." I grew hot with anger, but she went on: "On every head except the Horus, there was a solar disk, and every disk was a great emerald. It was a treasure, of course, but it wasn't the cash value that excited Father. You know how he was interested in Egyptian mythology?"

"Sometimes he talked almost like a believer," I remembered.

"It was a very hot summer," Mary declared. "He worked frightfully hard, and, when he found this box in the rubbish of the old tomb, it had a tremendous effect on him. He stopped the excavations, and he left Egypt at once . . . and he had this box with him. You remember that his manner was rather odd when he came to Boston? Then he received news of some sort that made him very excited again. You see, Aunt Emmy, in this box he somehow felt that he had the key to . . . heaven, suppose we say."

"Mary!" I could not help breaking out at her.

She nodded. She was as sure as could be of everything she said. She was speaking of her own father. Then she went on: "He decided to come to the Southwest. He wanted to come alone, but I wouldn't let him. I was terribly afraid all the time. I thought then, and I think now, that what led him on was an offer from some criminal to restore to him the fifth emerald, the one from the head of Horus. That was the lure that brought him here."

"But why should they want to bring him here?" I asked. "Why couldn't they work on him in Boston?"

"Because in Boston he lived in a big house, surrounded by servants. Because Boston is filled with police. Because, perhaps, some of this band of criminals are too well-known to metropolitan police. At any rate, they drew him down here. He was wildly happy. I was terribly afraid. I suspected what would happen. I protested with all my might. He simply threatened to put me on a train bound for Boston. So I was still.

"Poor child," I could not help saying, and she gave me a faint, sad, little smile. That instant I knew that, no matter how she had allowed herself to change in this wild country, at heart she was still the same — she was still our Mary.

"One day in San Felice," Mary continued, "I was seized, bound, gagged, and put in a large wooden box . . ." I cried out in horror. But she went straight on, as smoothly as you please: "They were about to put me on a wagon at the rear of the hotel when a young man who had been watching them asked what was in the box. They tried to drive him away. There were four of them. He routed them all." She paused and looked at me with fire in her eyes. "With a walking stick, he did it," she declared. Then added: "That was Geraldi."

I hadn't the slightest doubt now that I had seen him. Four men are much bigger than one. But four men are much bigger than a black panther, too.

"After I was set free, Father sent for Geraldi to thank him. He was pretending to play an effeminate role under an assumed name, but Father saw through that. Then Geraldi told us frankly that he believed we had stolen goods from Egypt, that he intended to get those goods from us, and that he gave us fair warning."

"Mary!" I exclaimed. "This same Geraldi?"

"This same Geraldi," she said with an odd smile. Then she said: "Father was perfectly secure . . . in the protection of the god."

I shuddered.

"But that same night, with unbelievable courage and cunning, Geraldi and another man drew Father out of his room . . . by appearing to threaten me . . . found the box, and escaped with it . . . and rode off from San Felice. Father and another man followed the trail. But the band of thieves was following as well. They jumped Geraldi. He and his companion fled until the other man's horse broke a leg. Geraldi refused to leave him. They went together . . . the other riding and Jimmy running . . ."

"But, Mary," I began, for, of course, I wanted to stop her at such a point of heroism, but she went on. "They would have taken Jimmy and the box and all, if it hadn't been that they came accidentally to Father and his companion, who drove off the crooks . . . and then Jimmy, in reward, simply handed back the stolen box."

"My brain swims, Mary," I said honestly.

"It will swim still more," said Mary, "in a few moments. Jimmy's fellow robber was a scoundrel. He was furious with Jimmy for giving back the box, and he

134

opened negotiations, quietly, with Father's man, Mickey. Now Mickey, it appears, was really a member of the band of criminals . . . the organized thieves. And while Father and Jimmy sat by the supper fire on a hill, Mickey invited up his band."

I stood up. She was white, but she talked on rapidly and steadily: "They lured Father into the woods by a horrible trick. Geraldi followed him and stumbled on his body. He lived long enough to say that he had died by the hand of a god."

"And that was the hunting accident?" I asked her, sick at heart.

She paid no attention to me. "Jimmy found the box . . . he had shot down one of the murderers. With the box he fought his way out of the woods. He was almost caught at a neighboring farmhouse, where he found that all the emeralds had been torn away from the heads of the gods. But he slipped through the second trap, too . . . he's a hard man to catch . . . and he warned Mickey and the rest that he would never leave their trail until he recovered the four emeralds . . . or had taken four lives."

"Wait a moment, Mary," I begged nervously.

"I'm almost done. He came to me and wanted to send me back to Boston. I refused to go. I told him I intended to stay in this country until I had done something about finding the murderers. He spent a day or two trying to persuade me, after he had given the golden box back to me, and then . . ." She stopped, with a little shudder. "They made another attempt. They came back and tried to kill *me*."

I turned to ice.

"Jimmy stopped them," she said in a trembling voice — it was unsteady for the first time in telling this wild tale of horror and surprises. "He saved me, and he begged me to leave after that. I refused. I had an idea, which was that they wanted the golden box for some mysterious reason, and that they never would scatter until they had obtained it. This was our chance, you see. I kept the golden box. It was the bait. I went with it to an exposed and lonely place where they could try to get it if they would. And when they made their attempts, Jimmy would be somewhere near . . . do you see the idea, Aunt Emmy?

"But how could I live here, seeing Jimmy every day, without some woman to live with me? And what woman is there in the world good enough and brave enough to do such work except you, dear Aunt Emmy? So I wrote you a series of prodigious lies. You never would have come if I had told the truth. You simply would have had me examined to test my sanity. I sent the lies because I knew that once you were here you never would desert me . . . you'd help me through the trouble."

There was a world of almost timid appeal in her voice. I simply took her in my arms and kissed her. I had no other way to answer.

# CHAPTER
# FIVE

## "Which Color Angel?"

Of course, after that, I had to sit down and think. One needs to make pauses in order to add up results and draw deductions. I drew enough to take my breath. That Robert Ingall had done a dishonest thing. That he had done it in the imagined service of a Egyptian god. That Mary was a pure-blooded little heroine. That she was being served with a quixotic devotion by Geraldi, apparently a man who lived by his wits — I put it mildly. That she was probably in love with this handsome fellow. That she now was acting as a bait to entice the most murderous danger. That I, Emily Ingall, now sat in the trap to keep her company.

When I had made up that list and unknotted my tight fingers, I found Mary watching me. She smiled into my eyes. How old she seemed, and wise — the baby.

"I knew that you wouldn't fail me, dear Aunt Emmy," she said. "So did Jimmy."

"What does he know about me?" I asked her.

"I told him about you and the big gray horse," she said.

"Bother Jimmy," I said. But I was pleased.

James Geraldi came back into the house. He put a saddle blanket on the floor and sat down on it, cross-legged. Mary, with the most astonishing shamelessness, pulled the stool over beside him and rolled a cigarette. He took it from her. I saw their eyes meet as she lighted a match and held it for him. They smiled on one another. Breathless and very tense, I watched them.

How far had this affair gone? I was still a little dizzy, but this thought cleared my mind astonishingly, for the matter of the golden box, the emeralds and all, and the revenge for Robert's murder — all of these things seemed little or nothing compared with the welfare of my dear Mary.

"And now that you are in the trap, Miss Ingall?" queried James Geraldi.

I did not answer him directly. Mary had dropped a hand on his shoulder and patted him.

"Mary," I said to her bluntly, "aren't there some other things that you'd better explain to me?"

She took her hand from Jimmy's shoulder and smoothed his sleek black hair. She looked at him and not at me as she answered: "You've not been West long enough really to understand," she said. "But Jimmy and me are partners."

I was too worried to pay any attention to the bad grammar. But I wonder what Miss Borden-Jeffreys would think if she could know that one of her pupils used such language.

"I haven't been here long," I agreed. "But I'll try to understand, if you'll use words of one syllable."

138

"Well," said Mary — and she made a pause and looked at the sagging rafters overhead. "A partner," she began again, "is a friend. With nothing to gain by the friendship," she concluded.

"A partner," she tried again, "is like yourself."

She made a third attempt: "A partnership is a common stock. Everybody owns everything."

"A sort of socialism?" I suggested a little dryly.

"A partner," said Mary, "is never looking for the main chance. He's just looking for partnership."

"That," I said, "sounds a good deal like a riddle. What's the answer, Mary?"

She replied: "It's something you feel, but you can hardly put it into words."

"Suppose," I said, "that you each tell me what you expect to get out of the other?"

"Of course," said Mary. "I hope to bring the murderers of Father to some sort of justice . . . under the guns of Jimmy. Besides, I expect to have this box made perfectly as it was in the first place and take it back to Egypt. So that there won't be a shadow of a ghost of a suspicion to fall upon the name of Father."

"You expect to get back the four emeralds . . . and then take it to the Egyptian government?"

"Yes."

"And would you consent to this?" I asked Jimmy.

He looked gloomily at me. "I don't see any good reason why we shouldn't split the profits," he declared. "But Mary doesn't see it that way . . . and we're partners." He laughed a little.

"What *do you* get out of this dreadful affair?" I asked him.

"Robert Ingall was my friend," Jimmy answered, and his words were close-clipped, and there was a little ring in them.

"You wait here in the middle of the desert," I rehearsed. "You have a treasure in your hands. A band of proven thieves and murderers is going to try to take that treasure away from you. You are miles and miles away from the protection of the law. You are only one man. And here is a young girl. I hope that I don't have to argue to prove what a mad thing this is."

"You don't," said James Geraldi. "I realize it. So does Mary. But we know that you would understand why it has to be done."

Then I tried another tack. "Those emeralds are, of course, very valuable?"

"They're worth hundreds and hundreds of thousands of dollars," Jimmy replied, "perhaps millions. I didn't see them out of their settings, and I can't tell how many carats. They were almost flawless and perfect in color."

"Very well, then," I went on logically. "This is a pretty piece of enamel work . . . this box. There are several pounds of gold in it. But, after all, it's a trifle compared with the price of the emeralds."

"So it seems," affirmed Geraldi.

"Then why should those determined scoundrels wish so much to get the golden box when they have the lion's share of the value of the thing already?"

"That," said Geraldi, "is the present mystery. To solve it we want to wait."

"You know that you both, probably, will be butchered?"

They sat quietly watching me, not as though my warnings were of interest, but as though they were curious to see my reactions.

"What can one woman and a man do against the rush of a dozen desperadoes?" I asked Geraldi, point-blank.

He picked up his rifle. "There are fifteen shots in this," he said. "Under my armpits I have two revolvers, with six shots in each. That makes twenty-seven bullets. More than two apiece for twelve men."

I refused to be put off by such mathematics. "And suppose that they slip up to this house in the darkness?" I asked him.

"They don't like the night," he answered. "I believe they feel that I can see in the dark." He laughed again softly. I was glad to see that Mary drew just a trifle away from him and looked down at his sleek, black head with a little shudder.

However, I no longer felt that the odds were so terribly long.

"And every day," went on Geraldi, "I can jump on my horse and go for a gallop over the hills to see if the birds are drawing near our net. Or sometimes I can slip out and go softly on foot, from place to place. One never can tell when there will be an opportunity, and once we catch one of the birds . . . its song may draw in the others."

He laughed again very softly, very musically. Again Mary's eyes narrowed a little. So did mine, I fear. And I could see that this beautiful youth was just as dangerous as poison.

"We'd better go to bed," said Mary.

"There are only two bunks in the house," I pointed out.

"Jimmy always sleeps outdoors."

"Good heavens!" I exclaimed.

But he reassured me: "My horse is as good as a watchdog, and he always stays close by me."

I gasped, for just at that moment the beautiful head of a black horse was thrust into the doorway, and great bright eyes looked at me with an almost human intelligence.

"There's Peter now," Mary announced. "Come in, dear."

Actually, the horse walked into the room and stood there switching his tail, and watching his master. He was a perfect creature. A sixteen-hand glory, I should say. There was not a speck of white on him except between his eyes a snowy diamond mark. It seemed, in that dim light, to shine like a star. When I saw this fine stallion coming in like a dog I felt — I don't know how. Like an Arab in a sheik's tent, I suppose. But it made that wild, free place still wilder and freer.

Jimmy Geraldi stood up and said good night. He waved his hand, and Peter backed out before him. They disappeared — there was a sudden beat of hoofs. When we went to the door, we saw a shadow flying over the top of a hill against the stars.

142

"You see?" Mary said. She seemed to have lost her strength. She was clinging to me. "Isn't he terrible, and beautiful, and wonderful?" she asked.

"He is," I said frankly, for I felt that he was all those things. "What is he doing?"

"Oh, he's just having a spin with Peter ... nighthawking, you know."

Yes, like a nighthawk, I thought, flying over those hills more swiftly than any poor quarry could travel.

"Mary," I said suddenly, "what do you think of him?"

"I think he's an angel," she said as quick as a wink.

That took my breath. I had hoped that she saw both sides of him. Then she added: "But I don't know, Aunt Emmy, whether he's an angel of light or of darkness."

# CHAPTER
# SIX

# "Facts, But No Theory"

I wakened this morning with a fragrance of cooking meat, and never did I dream anything more delicious. I had slept like the dead, it seemed. In the middle of the floor there was a wash boiler half filled with water that was steaming, and I guessed that I'd been wakened by someone bringing that water in for my bath. It seemed a great deal of service, just then, and I jumped up like a guilty person, took a quick bath, and hurried into the kitchen.

There was Mary, singing, and rosy, and wonderfully pretty. She smiled at me. "*You* slept!" she said.

"And you, my dear?" I asked.

"I always sleep, when Jimmy is watching the place," Mary responded.

It made me rather grave and serious, at once. It took the bloom from the morning to be called back suddenly to the mystery of Mary's relations with that strange young man. When I say there is a bloom in the desert morning, I mean exactly that, and such a bloom as I never have known in New England. The sun is fierce with heat before it is six diameters above the horizon, but the face of the desert clings to the night as if it is afraid of the day. By that I mean that in every hollow the shadows are stretched out flat, and a thin mist makes a veil of purple over the sands, and all the rocks stand up and turn gold and blue with the slanting light, and one feels an upward spring of the heart.

Mary took a great roast from the oven. "Is that too strong a diet for your breakfast?" she asked me.

I told her that I never would be contented with mere rolls and coffee again so long as I lived. I never knew what hunger was before. But I asked how the butcher had managed to bring this meat during the night.

"Jimmy is our butcher," she told me. "He took a dip into the hills during the night, and there he found this and brought it in. The rest of it is hanging in the shed."

Jimmy again. Jimmy Geraldi at every turn of her talk.

We had breakfast like barbarians. Who were the 16th-Century earl and countess in England who breakfasted on a quart of ale, a quart of wine, and a chine of beef? I understood for the first time how they could do it. Actually, we reduced that fine saddle almost by half.

"And where is Mister Geraldi for breakfast?" I asked her.

"Mister Geraldi," she said with a touch of mockery at my formality, "has gone out to hunt bigger game than deer. He'll eat cold meat when he comes back. He doesn't care . . . hard tack or roast chicken . . . so long as he's happy."

"And he's happy? He enjoys this sort of experience?"

"You saw him last night," said Mary. "What did you think?"

It gave me an excellent opening. I couldn't help leaping at it. "I don't know what to think of this situation . . . I don't know what to think of him. I don't know what to think of you, Mary."

She waited behind her cup of coffee, her hand perfectly steady. It irritated me to see that, after all, she didn't much care what my opinion might be. She didn't want me there to fill a useful rôle — chaperone. Good heavens, I would as soon try to chaperone an eagle and a thunderbolt.

"Of course, you're bewildered by this strange place," said Mary, apparently willing to help me out.

"By you, my dear," I told her. "But how can I help it? Poor Robert Ingall is dead. As for the golden box and the emeralds, they are nothing to me. But you, Mary? What does this mean to you? What is he to you?"

"Jimmy?"

"Yes, yes."

"I told you . . . my partner."

I threw up my hands. Then I hastily took another sip of coffee. "You may say that, but you can't mean it," I told her. "I'm not very familiar with men, but I do know a little bit about women. You can't live as you do, practically alone with such a man, without feeling something more . . . or less . . . than partnership."

"You want to know if I'm in love with him?" She put it frankly into small words; it made the problem and the difficulty both seem smaller, to listen to her.

"I would like to know that," I said.

She studied, crumbling a piece of cornbread in her strong little brown fingers. "So would I," said Mary.

**146**

"Ah," I replied. "Then you don't know? You haven't actually lost your heart to him?"

"I don't know."

My jubilation ended. "It's rather sad," I could not help saying. "You must know something about it?"

"I know a great deal about it. I'm full of facts. I'm ready to take an examination on the facts. I'm crowded and jammed with 'em."

"What sort of facts?"

"Facts about Jimmy."

"So I judged."

I was rather dry, but Mary merely laughed.

"I know this," she told me with the same studious searching for the truth. "If he were to say . . . 'I want you,' . . . then I'd go to him over deserts and . . . over mountains."

I sighed. I had feared that.

"But," Mary continued, "if I go away from him, finally, and he has said nothing at all, then I'll know. I can't tell. But I'm fairly sure that I could get along without him."

"Ah, Mary dear," I said. "I'm so glad to have you say that. I'm so glad."

"Oh, yes," she answered, "my heart is not made of such friable stuff as the heart of a heroine in a mid-Victorian novel. And if I go away from him, I'll soon find some young man who wants to marry me. Because I'm not ugly," she said with that paralyzing 20th-Century frankness, "and I'm . . . open to reason. I don't want the world with a fence around it. I want a husband and babies, someday."

147

I blushed a little and filled my cup again, not that I wanted more coffee but that I hoped that Mary wouldn't see I was ashamed of her language.

"Of course," I said, "you'll settle down to a normal, natural life."

"But," she went on, "I could see rocks ahead, even in that smooth sea."

"What sort of rocks do you mean," I asked her.

"Suppose," dreamed Mary, her chin propped on the palm of her hand, "suppose that in the midst of things . . . say in Boston, even a harbor of safety like Boston . . . suppose . . ."

"Well?" I urged.

"That one day, while leading little John by the hand, and wheeling Mary Anne before me, I should see Jimmy Geraldi go galloping by . . ."

I sat stiff and erect.

"If he went straight ahead, it would be all right. But if he were to turn and say . . . 'There's room behind me.' I'm afraid that I would leave John and poor little Mary Anne to stand and cry on the sidewalk, while I ran to him, and jumped up behind his saddle, and galloped off to . . ." She stopped.

My heart was ice, as may be imagined.

"Come, come," Mary soothed, as brisk as can be, "it's not as bad as all that, you know. Nothing will come of it all."

"And he," I asked. "Does he dream? Does he . . . ? But, Mary," I went on, growing a little confused, I'm afraid, in my talk, "is it quite necessary to roll Jimmy's

148

cigarettes, and sit beside him, and pat his head as if he were . . . a big Newfoundland dog?"

She nodded, as much as to say that she had thought about all that, but then she answered me: "You mean I could hide my heart behind a veil . . . put on a front?"

"I don't know what you mean by that," I said. "But I believe that there are ways in which women can make themselves difficult."

I blushed to say it, really, but Mary said very quickly: "That would be no good. If I made a mystery of myself, he'd be after me at once. Like a tiger, really. If I tried to be difficult and make trail problems, the way most girls do, he'd solve them and me. In an instant he would be making tremendous love, and I would be completely . . . dizzy. No, that would be a disaster."

"Mary," I reminded her, "you're an Ingall. You have a backbone of pride and . . ."

"Stuff," said Mary. "I'm only a girl . . . and he's a demon. The only way is to do exactly what I've done. He can see, if he cares to open his eyes, that I'm in his hands. And, for that very reason, he never would think of me except . . . as a partner." She raised a sad little laugh, and shook her head. "Besides," she added, "I'm not quite the stuff that interests him. He likes a girl, Aunt Emmy, with a dash of spice about her. You see how it is?"

"Spice?" I repeated.

She smiled at me. "He has known," she explained, "adventuresses, princesses with damaged titles and pretty ways, clever women smugglers, girls, Aunt Emmy, who have a sort of extra-legal profession."

149

"A neat phrase," I commented.

"Don't be scornful," Mary said. "Those are the girls who attract him, and I hope that I won't finally be inspired to follow their example."

I, who had started with such high hopes of getting to the bottom of this affair, now wished that I hadn't asked a question. Mary herself said it for me.

"You see, Aunt Emmy, I'm full of the facts, but I can't put them together into a theory."

# CHAPTER
# SEVEN

# "A Picture Too Vivid"

The conversation upset me. I wanted employment, so I made Mary go about other affairs, while I cleaned the dishes and put the house in order. But as fast as I worked with my hands, my brain insisted on working, also. It was like taking a walk, and not being able to walk away from one's thoughts.

When the housework was finished, I picked up one of the Winchesters and went over its mechanism. I never had used one of those guns before, but they're perfectly simple and beautifully made. I took it with a loaded magazine and went out into the open in Mary's big straw hat. I tried that gun standing, and I tried it kneeling. I even tried it lying down. I tried it at a hundred yards, and from that up to four hundred, picking out all sorts of targets. I spent a crowded morning struggling over sand and rocks to look at my handiwork and then take aim at something else.

I was very stale. One loses the knack of drawing a tight bead. Finally my shoulder was very sore from the kick of the rifle, and I had used up pounds of ammunition. I went back to the house and found myself alone. Mary was out somewhere. The golden box stood in the middle of the kitchen table, glistening with a sinister beauty, and I stared at it with an odd feeling that one of those figures with their archaic smiles would begin to speak. If they could have told me all the crimes and the misery that they'd brought into the world because they once were crowned with emeralds, that would have been a romance to hear, wouldn't it?

Just after noon, when the shadows were beginning to lengthen a trifle, I heard hoofs scuffing through sand outside, and Mary rode in, red with the heat. She pulled the saddle and bridle from her horse, came in and hung the saddle by its stirrups from a peg, and the bridle was thrown into a corner. I picked it up and found a place on the wall for it. I was cleaning the rifle I had been using, and Mary, after she had helped herself to three glasses of water and vinegar, nodded to me.

"You're making yourself at home, Aunt Emmy," she said.

I smiled back at her.

"And are you going to be able to stand it?" she asked.

"As long as you need me and I can draw breath," I told her — and it did me good to say it, and say it with such vehemence.

She answered in the one way I didn't want to hear her speak. "Ah, Jimmy knew you would feel this way."

I was beginning to hate Jimmy. And the more I saw of Mary, and the more clearly I saw that she was a treasure in spite of her little outlandish roughness of manner, the more I hated Jimmy Geraldi — to think that she was, as she said, in his hands. But there are ways in which one can plant discord. I determined to be wily and dark. I wished, in fact, for a touch of witchcraft to help me out.

We had lunch, a nap afterward, and we woke up at the same time, in the late afternoon. My head was burning with the heat and with the dreams that had been running through my mind. Mary was standing at the door.

"I see Peter coming up the hill across the valley," she said, lowering the field glass that she held, "and Jimmy's not on him."

I was at her side instantly. That might mean anything. She gave me the glass, and I could see the glistening form of black Peter and a man in the saddle with folded arms.

"But there's another man walking a little behind the horse," I said at last.

She caught the glass from me and looked again. "Ah," she said, and dropped the field glass at arm's length. "That's Jimmy." She went to the bank and sat down, slumping back against the wall. She had been dreadfully shocked, although she wouldn't show it until her fear had been proved wrong.

The two men and the horse came straight up to the house, and an unconscionable time they were in coming.

"Is it one of them?" asked Mary under her breath, a dozen times at least, "or has he simply picked up somebody?"

Of course, I could not guess.

But finally they arrived.

On Peter, that looked as if he had been going hard, was an Oriental-looking fellow — swarthy skinned, with smoky eyes, and a long, narrow, rather handsome face.

Geraldi, who walked beside him, helped him down from the saddle carefully, and then we could see that the stranger had been wounded in the right thigh. There was a red-stained bandage around it. Once off the horse, Geraldi picked him up and carried him lightly into the house.

He is not a large man, this Jimmy Geraldi, and yet I was not surprised to see his strength. He put the wounded man on my bunk and then we cut away the trousers and exposed a clean hole through the flesh, larger on the inner side, where the bullet had come out.

Geraldi and Mary did most of the work. I scraped lint busily. After a while we had the man comfortable, bandaged, his wound filled with iodine — poor fellow — and then a drink of water — a long one — followed by a still longer drink of coffee. After that, he leaned back with a blanket rolled under his head and smoked and actually smiled at us — the same odd, archaic smile that the Egyptians carved for their kings and their gods.

"We've had a long trek," Geraldi said, looking at the man, "and here we are home at last. Mary, I want you to meet Seyf Kalam. You'll excuse Miss Ingall if she doesn't shake hands with you, Seyf? Also, this is another Miss Ingall, come out here to visit us." He added: "She will not want to shake hands with you, either. However, we are going to be understanding, not foolishly hostile."

I looked at Mary, and by her quivering lips and pale face I understood. This was one of the gang of the jewel thieves. This was one of the murderers of her father.

Seyf Kalam looked from one to the other of us. He said in perfectly good English, but with a queer accent: "I am not guilty of the worst thing."

Mary cried at him suddenly: "*You* come from Egypt! Yes, yes, and I've seen your face there."

"No," said Kalam, and shook his head.

Geraldi rolled another cigarette and handed it to the wounded man.

"Don't trouble Seyf with questions, please," he advised. "He's tired. But you might show him the golden box, Mary. He's interested in that."

She went obediently into the kitchen, and, as she did so, Geraldi said: "You were the golden man among the trees, Seyf. You were the fellow who lured Ingall into the trees. Is that correct?"

"I? No, no," said Kalam.

"I didn't hear your answer," said Jimmy Geraldi. "I asked you if you were the man who did the mummery of the golden god, and drew Ingall in to his death in the dark of the trees?"

Kalam's face suddenly looked like highly polished copper, it was so covered with perspiration. "Yes," he said at last.

"That's good," Geraldi said. "Because once we begin to tell the truth, we can get on. We can reach an agreement."

Mary came back with the golden box and gave it to Geraldi. He, in turn, gave it to Kalam. I've never seen such hungry greed as he showed when he clutched it and turned it this way and that. Reverently, you understand, and yet hungrily. Actually, the tip of his tongue ran over his dry lips, and he suddenly asked for water again. The excitement had thrown him into a fever. After he had drunk, he examined the box again in the greatest detail, staring at each side, opening it and staring again inside as though he were reading print.

"It's a pretty thing, Seyf," Geraldi agreed in a gentle voice. "Lovely, isn't it, Mary?"

He turned to her. She was looking fixedly at him, with dark hatred in her eyes. Not hatred of him, of course, although I thought so for a startled instant. It was simply that she could not face the murderer; therefore, she looked to Geraldi to know what would happen. He understood and answered her at once, but by speaking with Kalam.

"Seyf," he said.

"Aye, Geraldi," said the other. "I beg your pardon," he added in a quick, guilty voice.

"It's quite all right," said Jimmy. "They know my name. Now, Seyf, you understand the agreement?"

Kalam blinked and drew in his head a little in a shrinking movement that sent a tremor through me. "If they bring in the emerald for me," he said, "you will perhaps let me go, Geraldi?"

"Perhaps? No doubt at all. I'll let you go scot-free."

"And how can they do that?" Kalam asked, swaying his head a little from side to side in his sorrow. "Who can persuade them that you will not shoot them down as they come in to bring it?"

"They have my old friend . . . Edgar Asprey. He's with them," said Geraldi, and he smiled. A white flash of a smile that turned me to ice. Whoever his friend Asprey was, *I* was glad that I was not to stand in Asprey's boots on some day to come. "Edgar will tell them that I can be trusted," Geraldi continued. "My word is as sacred, Seyf, as the sun of Horus."

Kalam lowered his eyes, and muttered something that sounded like Allah. "But if they should not bring it?" he asked.

"Then we take you out and brace you against a rock and put a loaded gun in your holster," Geraldi stated. "And I take my distance from you, and, at a given signal, we finish the fight that we began yonder."

Kalam stared at him like a bird at a snake. It was plain that he had no mental question as to how that fight would terminate.

"The will of Allah," Kalam said faintly, and closed his eyes.

So did 1. 1 was seeing the picture too vividly.

# CHAPTER
# EIGHT

## "A Lordly Lion"

Almost immediately afterward, Mary went into the kitchen to cook supper, because it now was dusk. I went with her, and we worked silently together.

Finally I said: "Would he do it? Would he really do it, Mary?"

She whirled on me. "Fair fight!" she said. "Why not? Why not?"

But I knew that her anger covered the same thought that was in my own mind. It was *not* fair fight, and no matter how wolfish a fellow this Kalam looked, a wolf cannot be penned with a tiger.

Almost as though he knew, and did not want us to talk alone, Geraldi came in at that moment. He was very cheerful and said something about having started the ball rolling. He even sang a few words of a song, and, taking half a dozen tin plates from the shelf, he began to do a soft-footed dance around the kitchen, singing his own song, always looking upward, and yet instinctively weaving back and forth among chair and stove and table while from his hands the plates went whispering upward, glittered in the air, and floated down into his fingers in a steady stream. It did appear to me a particularly skillful performance. It was as though trained birds were flying through the air, enchanted by this magician's song. Vaudeville, you will say, and, of course, it was. Yet there was something more about it — something delightful, and uncanny, and terrible, too. I mean, that he should have been so light-footed and light-hearted at the very time when danger was becoming momentarily a more terrible threat to all of us in that house.

We had one of the crew of murderers, and the rest were reasonably sure to descend on us by day or night to rescue their man and revenge his capture. But Geraldi sang and danced and juggled tin plates in the kitchen.

"Is Kalam safe?" asked Mary.

"He should be left alone," Geraldi answered. "It gives a man a better chance to think."

"Especially," I said, "when he hears a song and dance in the kitchen."

At this, he flashed one of his keen glances at me, but he made no remark.

We had supper in the kitchen, Mary and I. Geraldi took his own food and a plate for Kalam into the bedroom, or bunkroom, perhaps I should say. We could hear his cheerful voice chattering to Kalam, and the deep, soft answers of that captured man. Mary looked exceedingly dark and prepossessed with thought that, I knew, was partly assumed to keep me from asking questions about a disagreeable subject. Of course, I said nothing more about Geraldi, or Kalam, or the terrible tomorrow that I saw before us. I simply talked

**159**

as lightly as possible about Boston, and our family and friends there. I judged that this would not make her any happier, and I was right.

I wanted to make her see, in every way I could, how impossible it would be for her to fit into the life of Geraldi, or for Geraldi to fit into her background. She had, as she had said to me, all the facts about him, crowds of facts about him. I wanted to help her put those thoughts in order and come to a logical conclusion.

Geraldi came into the doorway, saying: "There's a light coming across the valley. I think one of them is coming up to bargain about Kalam's release. I'm going to leave you two alone to talk to the stranger about Kalam. I don't know what will be said. There may be a good many threats, of course. But you'll take nothing but the emerald in exchange for Seyf. You understand?"

"Yes," said Mary.

Geraldi disappeared His rifle flashed as he stepped past the open door.

Naturally I stared at Mary for an explanation. "You don't mean that he's actually left us alone, here?" I asked her.

"Of course," said Mary, almost in a tone of irritation. "Because while one of them comes up to bargain, the others may try a rear attack, or some such thing."

"But when the bearer of the light comes, Mary, and finds us alone . . . ?"

"He'll guess that Geraldi is lying somewhere in the dark. He's sure to guess that."

**160**

I saw the point. It was simply a matter of who would have the quickest brain in this game of chance. If he who came to make the bargain out-guessed Geraldi, then, perhaps, Mary and I would receive bullets through the brain and Kalam would be spirited away — and the golden box with him.

I got down the rifle that I had used that day. My right shoulder ached a little at the mere thought of pressing that iron-bound stock in place again, but I feel much more secure with a weapon in my hand. When I looked around from making sure that it was loaded and in readiness, I saw that Mary actually had placed the golden box in full view upon the kitchen table.

But I said nothing. I cleared away the tins and started to wash them, with the rifle leaning against the sink. What would my well-trained Boston household say if they could see their mistress in such an environment?

Mary set about dusting things, sweeping, making a great fuss, as though she were putting the place in order for a guest's arrival.

Then a voice called loudly, not far from the shack: "Geraldi!"

The call was repeated, and Mary said: "I think that's Mickey's voice. He's the leader of the whole crew."

"Hey, Geraldi! Will you come out and talk?"

Mary went into the open doorway. "Geraldi's not home," she called. "Come in and have a cup of coffee, will you?"

This was followed by a little silence, after which I heard the snort of a horse, close at hand, and then, suddenly, I knew that a big man was standing with Mary against the black of the night.

"Mickey," I heard Mary say, "this is my aunt, Miss Ingall."

I turned and nodded, with a tin plate in one hand and the wet dishrag in the other. I almost dropped both the rag and the plate. I could not believe my eyes. This leader of the ruffians, this chief of scoundrels — was — I can hardly bring myself to utter the name. I recalled that summer I spent with a party of friends in Skye, and the little hotel in Portree, and the kindly fat host who always brought out half a dozen different sweets at dinner time, and the trips we took fishing. How well I recalled it. It was not so many years ago. And the bright spot of that summer was the handsome, big, young Englishman who went fishing with us outside the harbor, when we caught the mackerel. It was he. It actually was Lord Winchelmere, done up now like a typical cowpuncher of the rougher type, with battered leather chaps on his legs and some tarnished-silver conchos strung Mexican fashion down the side of them. He had on a sombrero of the Mexican type, too, with a high-pointed crown, and a band of silver-and-gold work. It looked a frightfully hot thing to wear in this boiling weather, but Lord Winchelmere looked just as cool as ever he did on those fishing trips through the fogs of the Hebrides. His face was browner and just a little older. Not much. I was struck with a sudden point of similarity between him and Geraldi. That is to say, one could hardly guess within ten years of the probable age of either of them.

**162**

It was a dreadful shock. Suddenly I knew that, if such a man were interested in this affair, then it was certain to be of the utmost importance. And if ever his hands were given to murder, then life and death after that would be nothing to him. In that first glance I thought him fully as formidable a man as Geraldi himself. Yet in a different way. He was much larger, of course. And with his tawny hair and the two deep creases in his brow, he had the same leonine look that we had noticed those years before.

He nodded to me pleasantly enough and said that he was glad to know me, but he did not come forward to shake hands. I was glad of that, because in the position where I stood I was well within the shadow, and he could hardly recognize me except by some great effort of memory that would recall my name.

I went on washing dishes, half turned toward the two of them, and always ready on an instant to snatch at the rifle. It was wonderful to see the coolness and the ease of Mary as she faced that giant of a man — knowing him to be the chief cause of the murder of her father, even if his hand had not actually struck the knife home — and yet keeping all malice out of her voice, out of her eyes.

I was proud of her. I felt, once more, as though I were the junior, watching a much older person do a difficult thing. How difficult it was to do. It was to be a duel, of course, between them, he striving to find out if Geraldi was near, and she striving to give the impression that he was just around the corner. But if ever he broke down her guard — if ever he had a flash

**163**

of understanding of the truth — then heaven defend us all. Mary's revolver, my rifle, would be very useless, indeed. It reminded me of my first lion hunt, when we heard the great beast in the brush, and before he came out into the open. Even my hands shook with the beating of my heart.

He began at once by saying: "I've come about the Egyptian."

"He *is* from Egypt, then?" Mary said cheerfully.

Had he given away a point already? I looked at him askance and saw that he was looking down at her with the faintest of smiles.

"I guess you knew that, ma'am," he said.

"Sit down," urged Mary.

"I don't mind if I do."

# CHAPTER
# NINE

# "The Upper Hand"

This Western dialect that he spoke he handled very well, so extremely well that I had to look at him again to make sure that I was not wrong. I *couldn't* be entirely sure, after all. I had to wait and watch again. Still my heart beat so fast and hard that my eyes were dim with the excitement of it all.

He sat beside the table and fingered the golden box. "Pretty thing, ain't it?" he commented.

"It is," Mary replied. "I like it a lot."

"Of course, you do," said his lordship. "Look at the way that enamel is laid on. I never seen anything to beat that. Looks like paint, only it ain't."

"It *does* look like paint," said Mary, as cheerful as ever. "And heavy, isn't it?"

He was weighing it in his hand. There came into his face a tense, wan look, as though he were starved. Starved he was, and for the possession of the very thing that he now held in his hand.

"Have some coffee," Mary suggested. "It's still pretty hot."

She poured it out for him with an inviting smile. I really thought that she was overdoing the thing a little

— considering what this dreadful creature had done — but then the truth flashed into my mind.

It would never occur to anyone, of course, who had not been here in the West. Out here, where perhaps there is only one house within a hundred miles — a hundred miles of desert — hospitality is a sacred thing. Sacred because it's so necessary. If you turned a man hungry from your door in such a place, he might starve in consequence.

The result is that all that has to do with hospitality is an extremely rigid, unwritten law. For instance, I've heard of a hunted man walking into the house of his greatest enemy, hanging his saddle on a peg, and eating a piece of bread off the table. By that simple ceremony he became immune from danger so long as he remained under that roof — and under that roof he could remain until a sense of pride drove him away. He never would be invited to leave!

And this, I realized, was in the mind of cunning Mary. Because hospitality lays a strong claim upon the receiver as well as upon the giver of benefits like these, and if young Lord Winchelmere actually drank that cup of coffee — or so much as tasted it — then his hands would be tied if he were at all ruled by the law of the land. And even if that law meant nothing to him, it would ruin his reputation through all the cattle country, and even the worst criminals would shrink from associating with a man who accepted food and shelter from two women, and then acted as an enemy to them. However, he probably was desperately thirsty for that coffee, and Mary had managed it all so well and

166

smoothly that he actually had the cup at his lips when something stopped him.

I do hope it was not my caught breath.

At any rate, he suddenly lowered the cup.

Mary flashed one side glance at me, and it cut me like a sword. "You forgot to put in sugar, didn't you?" Mary said sweetly, and offered to put in a spoonful.

He pushed the cup a little away from him and shook his head, looking up at her all the time with that faint, wise smile of his.

"It's a little too hot," he said. "I'd better let it cool off a bit."

He had remembered. I felt something between pleasure and pain. Pain that Mary had failed to trap him, pleasure that he had not fallen too low to respond to such a custom of the Wild West.

"And how is Seyf?" he asked.

"He's very comfortable, I think," Mary replied. "Do you want to go in and see him?"

He half rose, and then slumped down again. "I'll take your word for it, ma'am," he said.

"He's well enough to travel . . . in a litter," Mary said pointedly.

"I've brought a litter," said Lord Winchelmere. "Poor Seyf. Suffered a great deal of pain, maybe?"

"He didn't show it," Mary said. "He had plenty of nerve."

"Of course," said his lordship. "Plenty of nerve, but rather a slow hand, I should say. Rather a slow hand." He repeated this with a definite hardening of his face.

"I'm sorry that Jimmy isn't home," Mary said next. "He would have been glad to see you."

He looked across at her steadily, reading, reading in her face — but I could vow that he could not make out the truth. "I'm sorry, too," he said finally. "I would've been right glad to see him. Ain't been home for supper?"

"Just in to snatch a bite, and off again," said Mary.

"He keeps pretty busy," said his lordship.

"You know how men are," was Mary's response. "Always gotta be doin' something."

I marveled at her, her language, her easy way. Oh, Robert, that girl of yours could do well on the stage — and in great roles.

"He rides a lot," went on his lordship, still obviously fencing for an opening that would tell him the truth.

"Never can tell when he'll go sweeping off. And never can tell when he'll come dashin' in," Mary stated.

"Kind of a nervous way, ain't it?"

"His? Oh, I don't know. Besides, he enjoys riding a lot. Especially since he got that fine horse from you."

I looked at his lordship and saw that he had grown decidedly red with anger.

As a matter of fact, Mary had previously told me that the beautiful black horse, Peter, actually was taken from Mickey by Geraldi and made his own mount. It was a wicked thing for Mary to say, but it was a stroke that told. Would she be tantalizing him unless Geraldi were near to back her up?

Suddenly he said: "Suppose we get down to business, Miss Ingall?"

He threw a glance at me, but I pretended not to understand. I was dawdling through the dishes, taking my time, and taking it in the slowest possible fashion, for I wanted to keep in the shadow. If he really were his lordship, then one glance at my face in the light would be enough to remember me by. I don't know why I wanted to keep unknown. I felt as though it were a card in my hand — this bit of knowledge — if knowledge it were. Thank heaven that I played my part in that way, as will be seen presently.

"Aunt Emmy knows everything," said Mary. "We can talk before her."

"Very well," said Mickey. "We might as well talk, then. I gotta be gettin' back. Now, you got Seyf, and you got him good."

"Jimmy did," Mary said with the brightest of smiles.

"Him or you, it makes no difference. Your side has a trick," said Mickey. "Now I'm gonna tell you what I'll do. Just turn him over to me, and I'll see that you get a chance to slide out of this shack, all three of you. You can take everything with you. All the hosses . . . except my black, of course, that Geraldi stole from me. I'll give you my word that you can clear out from the shack, and no bones broken, and get away to the railroad."

I wondered what Mary would say. My own heart leaped at the thought that I could have a safe-conduct from this dangerous little shack.

"And we take the golden box?" Mary asked.

His face wrinkled with emotion — actually wrinkled and grew old. "I suppose so," he responded.

"But then," went on Mary, "you understand that Jimmy would hate to part with Peter."

"Is that what he calls the black hoss?" snapped Mickey.

"Yes."

"He don't answer to that name, though."

"Oh, yes. He follows Jimmy around like a pet dog."

The dull red went up the face of Mickey again. "A hoss like that . . . ," he began, and then realized that he was about to say a foolishly malicious thing about a mere dumb beast.

"In fact," Mary continued, speaking suddenly in a dry, crisp tone, "we couldn't make any bargain such as this. Jimmy already has told you the price of any one of your men. He told you the night he took Peter away from you . . . together with the rest of your horses."

Mickey pushed back his chair from the table. She had tormented him even to the limit of *his* endurance.

"You mean, one of the emeralds is the price for Seyf Kalam? A mere Egyptian, a sort of a . . ."

"That's my final word," snapped Mary. And she stood up from the stool.

Mickey glowered at her. Then, with a sudden movement, he snatched a bit of paper from his pocket and flung it on the table in front of her. "There you are," he said. He rose and turned toward the door, and Mary hastily unwrapped a great, green, flaming beauty of a stone.

I was staggered by the size of it. But Mary calmly tried it against one of the empty spaces above the enameled idols on the golden box. It fitted. "Very well," she said.

**170**

"You're contented?"

"It's what Jimmy told me to ask for."

"Afraid to stay and ask for himself?" Mickey hissed bitterly.

Just then, far off on the desert, we heard a sharp rattling — a rattle with a ring to it that one cannot forget. Gunfire! It was the sound of rifles.

One burst of that, and it was ended.

Mickey turned back from the door, and his eyes were positively yellow with savage joy and triumph.

I understood, of course. There was hardly a doubt that he *had* ordered some sort of a rear movement against the shack that night, and Geraldi, ranging far afield, had come up with those riders in the night and checked them. But at a distance. At a great distance. You see? Such a man as Mickey would not need a great head start. Doubtless down in the valley he had several fighting men waiting to receive him, ready to check any pursuit if he came with a rush away from the little house taking Kalam with him. And Geraldi was hopelessly distant — even the full speed of Peter would make him a whole minute too far away, perhaps. In that minute, everything could happen.

So Mickey turned on Mary with that dreadful gleam in his eyes. I cannot tell what happened. It seemed to me that she maintained a perfect calm as she remarked: "Some of your boys out shooting rabbits, Mickey?"

"Shooting at a coyote, more likely," Mickey sneered. He strode to the table and picked up the golden box and placed it under his arm.

I saw Mary's small hand grip the butt of the revolver that she wore like a man at her hip in a heavy holster.

"Don't be a little fool!" he cautioned her. "And you," he flung at me, as my hand stole out to the rifle, "keep your hands sensibly employed, will you?"

I answered: "You seem to have the upper hand, Lord Winchelmere."

It struck him like-the blow of a club. The golden box seemed to become too heavy for his arm to hold, and it slipped down onto the table again, and he went a pace back against the wall.

# CHAPTER
# TEN

# "His Lordship's Grace"

I don't mean to say that he was completely unnerved. But he was more than half stunned. He watched us both, but the yellow triumph was gone from his eyes, and his lips had parted, and his cheeks were drawn. Ah, heaven be praised that I had kept that small secret in the shadow of the room.

I saw that Mary was watching him like a hawk, and I had a terrible knowledge that, once she thought him off his guard, she would snatch at her revolver and try to fight him like a man, bullet for bullet. I could only pray that she would not do that.

We were saving time. Every second that passed was bringing her that much closer to the return of Geraldi. Unless, indeed, that rattle of guns had meant his downfall and black Peter was now racing riderless across the sands — or standing, perhaps, to mourn for his dead master. But, otherwise, after that exchange of shots, surely Geraldi was flying back to undo the mischief which that alarm might have done in the shack. Surely he was coming at the full speed of that glorious black horse.

If I could entangle his lordship in talk for another few instants . . .

I heard him mutter something beneath his breath. "I a lord?" he forced himself to say, and laughed, and made his voice stronger in that way. "Me a lord! I gotta laugh at that. Lady, I sure gotta laugh at that. Now you two back off into that corner, and do it *pronto*."

I did not stir. "I remember you very well, Lord Winchelmere," I insisted. I stepped out a little, so that the light came against my face more fully. "You remember that summer in Skye, of course?"

He rubbed his knuckles swiftly across his forehead. "Never heard of such a place," he stated. "Skye? What Skye? The blue sky, of course?" He laughed.

Although he was making a desperate effort, he was not succeeding in the least in covering up his first admission. I saw, too, that he was terribly eager to make me change my mind about his identity. Perhaps he was still in good standing on the other side of the water, I thought. And perhaps he was now making his great effort to undermine my mind.

"But you'll remember in another moment," I said to him. "You'll recall how you and my cousin and I went out before the harbor and caught mackerel. How the fog came down. And how we had to toot our horn on the little launch all the way back to the town. Of course, you remember that! And the sailing ship we almost ran into at its moorings. Oh, yes, Lord Winchelmere, I remember it all perfectly. So will you, in a moment. You preferred the Hebrides to the Alps, I remember you used to say, because of the wilder atmosphere."

I didn't pour out these words in one burst. I took my time. As though I were thinking my way from phrase to phrase. All the while I knew that Geraldi was sweeping back to us — or else lying dead on the sands.

Ah, that was a great moment. And since I had recognized him, I wondered with a most practical mind whether he would still try to argue, or else would — well, simply blot us both out and try to escape with the Egyptian before Geraldi came racing home.

That same thought went like a shadow over his face. If ever I read murder, it was in those keen, bold eyes. But, in an instant, he had changed his expression. He caught up the golden box and leaped to the doorway, keeping his head half turned toward us. There in the doorway he paused for a single instant. His lips curled. Then I heard distinctly the swift pounding of hoofs.

He strode back to the table and put down the box. Stiff desperate danger was in that man, I knew. He was struggling terribly with himself. Should he wipe us out and then take his chance of meeting Geraldi, hand to hand? He was capable of that, I felt. Still he hesitated, and raised his head, listening.

We listened, all of us, tense and eager. Soon we knew it was not one horse. No, no, it was more than one. Two — three, even. Therefore, it must be Lord Winchelmere's men. He, making sure of that, looked straight at me with a dreadful smile, and I told myself that my time on earth was short, indeed. For he never would forgive me or forget that I had recognized him. Perhaps it was the total undoing of his life.

The horses came nearer, so that I could hear the swishing of the sand as they stiffened their legs and slid to a halt. Then into the doorway leaped Geraldi! What a glorious picture he seemed to me. And prepared for battle with the light dripping down the barrel of a revolver held in either hand, and his nostrils flaring a little, and his eyes narrowed against the brilliance of the light, after his ride through the darkness.

Lord Winchelmere said quietly: "We've been just striking a bargain, Geraldi, and I've given Mary Ingall the emerald . . . as duly agreed." Deliberately he reached down for the cup of coffee and drained it at a draft.

Ah, well, I may be growing old and foolish, but I could not help admiring that villain's self-control, and the quickness of his wit at that moment. I admired, too, the calm way in which he turned to Geraldi — whose two guns had winked out of sight that instant.

"Now, for Kalam," said Winchelmere.

Geraldi paid not a flash of attention to the big man after the first look. He walked across to Mary.

"I'm sorry," he said. "I played the fool. I played the perfect fool. But I saw them coming, Mary. Half a dozen slipping over the sand . . . the snakes. With the night glass I couldn't make out the horses being brought on behind at a good distance. Well, it was idiocy, but I couldn't resist the temptation to slip around, tumble one sleepy fellow out of the saddle, and then bring on a pair of the horses and scatter the rest. I forgot their guns. Confound them, I forgot that. But they had a glimpse of me, and they opened up with every rifle in the pack. I beg your pardon, Mary, for such a childish thing as I've done tonight, and I thank my stars that I got back here in time."

She gave him a very wan smile. She had borne up with the most magnificent courage all through the test. There had only been an instant of weakness at a time when the strain was superhumanly great. But now she slipped down on the stool and rested her face in her hands.

Geraldi touched her shoulder. "Good girl. Brave girl," he said, as though she were little more than a baby. Then he directly turned on the big man. "It might have been unlucky for them," Geraldi began, "but I promise you, Mickey, that it would have been worse for you . . . in the long run, my fine friend."

Not very savage words, but savagely spoken — softly, with almost a purr that will wake me up at night for years to come.

I could not help putting in: "Mickey isn't the name, Jimmy. Let me introduce you . . ."

"Ma'am," his lordship interrupted me, "you ain't gonna tell that fool yarn to Geraldi, are you?" Even he, I learned, could be clumsy, when he was too desperately cornered. I said as quietly as I could: "I'm introducing Harold Allen Brompton, Lord Winchelmere. I think that's the whole name and title, isn't it, my lord?"

His face was bright with perspiration and yellow with agony. I've never seen a man so tortured. But suddenly he bowed to me and then to Geraldi. "It appears that you are right," he conceded.

# CHAPTER
# ELEVEN

## "Lords and Ladies"

That lucky remembrance of his identity had, I think, been tremendously useful to us. It had stopped his headlong impulse to take advantage of the distance of Geraldi from the house when we two women were alone with him. Now it had an effect that surprised me a great deal more.

Geraldi took the announcement of the name with an actual outcry of astonishment, and one who knows him understands how little apt he is to show great surprise at anything.

"You're Winchelmere?" he cried to the big man. "You're actually Winchelmere?"

His lordship threw a glance at me that should have blasted me. "That is my name," he admitted. But even then, having admitted so much, he was still slow to speak the words.

I noticed that Geraldi would not take his hand or make any movement to do so, and he stated: "This will be surprising news to your friends in England, my lord. All the Duttons will be surprised, I'm sure. And the Hendons will not be happy, will they? And particularly the beautiful Miss Hendon?"

That same dangerous red began to rise again in the face of Winchelmere. I saw his left hand gather into a fist twice and twice relax slowly while he was speaking.

"You're acquainted with all those people?" he asked dryly.

"By name . . . or one way or another," Geraldi said. "I prospected for diamonds with Joe Hendon in South Africa, you know."

"I didn't know it," said his lordship.

"I heard a great deal about you from him."

"No doubt," said his lordship, biting his lips.

"About your political ability, for one thing," said Geraldi, with the most charming smile and a nod of his head. One would have thought that he was showering roses of compliments upon his unlikely lordship. "And about your well-known eloquence on the platform, you know."

"Suppose we have an end of that," suggested Winchelmere, with an upward jerk of his head. He was very angry.

"End of what? Of your eloquence on the platform?" asked Geraldi. "That would be a pity, my lord. Hendon used to say that you were bound to be prime minister one day. Unless, Hendon was apt to add, you let your hatred of corruption and vice and graft of all kinds become too blind a passion. You know, your lordship, that one mustn't go too far along it, or you wind up where you began, don't you? Because every road, after all, is apt to go in a circle if you travel it far enough."

He chattered on like this in the most cheerful manner, and he was torturing Winchelmere with every word he uttered. I saw the big man suffering more and more. But I couldn't pity him.

"You have something on your mind," he said at last to Geraldi. "Now, what do you propose?"

"It's the most simple thing in the world," Geraldi stated. "Blackmail, in short."

"I guessed that."

"You would," Geraldi replied with terrible point. "But now, old fellow, to begin with, I'll tell you. You bring in not one emerald, but four of them. And after you've done that, I'll give you my guarantee that not a word of what's happened out here shall go back to England, and Mickey shall finish as Mickey began."

"Otherwise, you spread the whole news broadcast over the old country?"

"Not broadcast," Geraldi corrected. "I don't believe in newspapers. But just a friendly note to Joe Hendon, and a picture or two of you. That would be enough."

His lordship had the steadiest of nerves, and he showed it now. "It means the wreck of my life," he said.

"It does," Geraldi agreed. "I'm sorry for that. Reform needs her advocates, every one."

Lord Winchelmere made a gesture as though abandoning the thing of which he had been speaking. "Let it go, then," he said. "Let the whole thing go."

"Is your reputation on a foundation as insecure as that?" asked Geraldi. "Are you going to chuck it away like this?"

"You can't use it against me," Winchelmere said. "As a matter of fact, I suppose that I couldn't have carried on the double rôle very much longer. I'm going to give up the chance of a political career, a few cheers here and there, a few editorials of praise, in exchange for the emeralds . . . and the golden box."

"I don't want to be rude," said Geraldi, "but I do ask you to think that over again. It means chucking everything. You're done with decent people. No more lords and ladies. No more hats touched to you in the street. No more whispers as you pass. You've thought of that, Winchelmere?"

He had not thought of it in such detail, of course, and he felt the spur and showed that he felt it, but he merely shrugged his great shoulders. For he is a magnificent man. He stood there like a tower, with Geraldi — looking hardly more than a boy in comparison — stinging and lashing him.

At last his lordship said simply: "That's done, Geraldi. We'll go on to something else."

"The emerald, then," Geraldi said, and he didn't appear in the least downhearted by this change. "Let me see the emerald, Mary."

She pushed the paper toward him.

"Besides," said the big man, "I have to get on. My men can't wait the entire night. So I'll go get Seyf Kalam, if you don't mind. Is he in the next room?"

"He is," said Geraldi, "and probably close enough to the wall to hear everything that we've been saying in here. He'll be another to spread the story about his lordship. But wait until I've looked at the emerald."

"The girl already has seen that it fits," said the big man, moving toward the door.

Geraldi gave the jewel one glance. Then he took a revolver from his pocket and dropped the barrel upon the green brilliant. It crunched to a thousand bits. Geraldi let the gun lie.

I couldn't help noticing that it pointed straight at Winchelmere.

"Did you bring a real emerald with you?" he asked.

There was no argument. The big man simply hesitated for an instant. Then, as though he saw that there was no appeal, he slipped his hand into a pocket and finally brought out a little chamois roll. This he undid, and in the center of it lay one of the real stones. I had thought that the other was too beautiful to be improved upon. But I saw the difference here — the deeper blue-green, and the light that lived inside the stone, instead of on the facets.

Geraldi gave it hardly a glance. "That will do, then," he said, "and you're free to take Kalam with you, whenever you please."

Lord Winchelmere still hesitated. "Look here, Geraldi," he began, "after all, there's no reason why I shouldn't be frank with you. I want that golden box."

"I'm certain you do. That's why you and yours are staying so close to me. Isn't that perfectly obvious?"

"Perhaps it is," said his lordship. "I know I'm a fool, but the sight of the thing has fascinated me. I want it more than I want my own heart's blood. It's a treasure of art, Geraldi, and I have a proposal to make to you. It may sound the idea of a madman, but . . ."

"By all means," Geraldi coaxed. "I can't think that I'd ever accuse your lordship of madness. But step on with your idea, old fellow, and let's see what it's worth."

Always the same light and cheerful tone. His lordship seemed to grow enthusiastic. He leaned his big hands on the edge of the table, and one felt that, if ever he reached Geraldi with the sheer grip of his fingers, he would break him.

"Geraldi," he said, "you now have one of the four emeralds. There are still three more, and every one of them, as you know perfectly well, is worth ten times the weight of that golden box or the enamel on it."

"Perhaps."

"Now, then," continued his lordship, "you know that I've always been a fellow who gratified his impulses. I'll tell you what, man . . . I'll bring you the other three stones in exchange for the box. Is that agreed?"

I really thought that Lord Winchelmere's mind was gone. I looked from him to Geraldi, and found that Jimmy had a grim little smile as he listened.

"You've brought one stone. You get one man tonight," he said. "Afterward, we'll try to deal for the other three on the same terms. After that is done, and the box is complete, you and I will make up the final account and try to come to some agreement."

One could tell what sort of an agreement it would be. Lord Winchelmere answered: "I know you very well, Geraldi. I respect your cleverness and your talents. But before we're through with one another, I shall convince you that you're a mere mechanical worker in these fields. I suppose I must say good night?"

He bowed to us, one by one, and went through the door, with Geraldi behind him.

We heard them carry poor Kalam out to the stretcher. There were a few quiet murmurs of voices, and then Geraldi came back to us.

"I can't believe, really," he announced, "that Winchelmere is such a fool."

"As to offer the stones for the box?"

"What? No, no, but to let me know that there is more in the box than meets the eye. I'm going to sleep for an hour or two in the next room. You two have a look at that box and see if you can find something . . . a secret compartment, say, in the bottom of it."

# CHAPTER
# TWELVE

## "For the Sake of Golden Horus"

It will be plain that Geraldi had taken a very strong hold on my imagination when I confess that it seemed very strange to me that he should need sleep. There appeared to be enough energy in him to continue working through all sorts of perils. He had hardly left, when I said to Mary: "This is a dangerous business . . . I mean, staying here in the night with a lamp lighted while Geraldi is sleeping."

She answered: "What would they do? Suppose they slipped up and peered through the door and found us sitting here over the golden box? They'd suspect that Jimmy was somewhere in the darkness, with his rifle."

"Do you think they'd hesitate to shoot us down," I asked, "for the sake of making a dash at the box?"

She smiled a little. "Do you think they're as terrible as that? They wouldn't murder women, you know."

I didn't share her surety. At the same time, I felt rather ashamed of my suspicions. I suppose that one could put them down as childish.

"I've looked at the box a thousand times," Mary sighed. "I don't see what good it will do to examine it again."

I was astonished. I mean I was astonished that she should hesitate to do exactly what Geraldi had told us to do. For my part, I had been dominated completely.

"Very well," I told her. "Your mind is full of this thing and tired of it. You tell me what you know about it, and then perhaps I can find a new starting point."

She was perfectly willing and sat down beside me. We turned up the side with the figure of Osiris, newly recrowned with the emerald. About the figure were incised the most delicately made hieroglyphics.

"What do these things mean?" I asked her. "You know something about hieroglyphics."

"Father went over these with me a good many times," she said. "I've even copied them all out for him. This beside Osiris reads . . . 'Sun of the night, father of justice, and king of the dead, glorious Osiris, dying and reborn, as Nephthys and Isis remembered you, as Anubis and Horus and Thoth remembered you, remember me, also, because I am your servant.'"

"The me," I said unnecessarily, "is, of course, the king in whose tomb this was placed?"

"Of course," Mary replied.

We turned to each of the other inscriptions. Mary translated, and I wrote the translation down.

That to the great Ra ran:

**Boatman over the celestial waters, strong Ra, you have conducted me through the twelve perils of my life as you yourself every night pass through the twelve serpent-guarded gates of Tuat. Conduct me still after death, through the**

blue waters of the sky, and through the darkness.

The inscription for Atum was:

**You make the two lands green. The Nile is great but you are greater; and you are more cooling to the spirit than is the evening wind cool to the temples of a weary man. After my death, if you remember that I have repaired your temples and made your priests happy, repair my strength and make me happy, also.**

The writing for Khepri was a little longer. It seemed as though the sacred scarab was particularly a favorite god for the dead king, and he broke out:

**You created all things, holy beetle, but first you created yourself. You rose out of the slime of the world, and every morning you rise again out of the wet east. To you, the sun is not hot. You warm your hands by holding it. You lift it up like an egg and show it above your head to the world. So after my death take me in your hands and for the sake of the jewel I give you, show me to the kingdom of the dead as a king.**

"There was a little bribery in this, you see," Mary explained, as I finished writing down that translation, and we turned to the top of the golden box where the great figure of Horus stood with the empty indentation above his hawk's head.

There was more writing here than in any other place. Undoubtedly, after worshipping the sun in his other important forms, the dead king reserved a special degree of adoration for Horus. He had caused to be written:

> **Your beginning is beautiful on the edge of the horizon. But you are the horizon and the center of the heavens. And you shower down your beauty on everyone and on every land, great hawk of the sky!**
>
> **Your light is as strong as the talons of an eagle. You pick up the souls of men and carry them away to the tower of the sky. When you sleep in your horizon, the men of the world sleep and the lions come out to kill. When you rise, the lions flee to the hills and to the desert.**
>
> **Great hawk of heaven, golden Horus, maker and unmaker, wise and rich, as you place the yellow sun on the edge of the sky, giving it to men, so now I place on your head another yellow sun, although it is hidden from the eyes of men. But from your eyes nothing is hidden. Take this gift; take the gift of my soul, also, and give me a kingdom among the happy.**

Mary, having finished this rather long bit of translation, waited for my pen to stop its scratching,

188

and then she asked me a little wearily: "What do you make of all this, Aunt Emmy?"

Now, as I wrote down some of these words, a thought came to me. But I didn't reveal it at once. I asked if she had a ruler. She had none, but she had a fragment of steel tape, and I measured the box with this. It was nine inches high, and about ten inches long. I measured the cover and found it just two fifths of an inch thick. Then I measured the inside of the box. Allowing even three fifths of an inch for the thickness of the base, that box should have been at least eight inches deep. On the contrary, I found it only seven.

Mary had guessed what I was after long before I finished, but she waited with a rather wicked little smile for me to reach a conclusion. Only when I was about to announce my answer, she looked at me and said: "Of course, the bottom is more than an inch and a half thick. Father measured it, even with a micrometer. I have his exact figures, somewhere."

It made my inspiration seem a very thin section of cloud drift. But I tapped the table and shook my head. "Jimmy," I said, "says that there is something in this box. And so there must be."

"Then he'd better find it," Mary said.

"Perhaps I had," said the voice of Geraldi from the doorway, and he came in to us.

We hadn't been working there an hour — and in that time a tired man had slept, rested, and come back to us refreshed. He's not like others. He stands by himself.

Jimmy sat down at the table, and, taking the box in his hands, turned the box upside down.

"How would Lord Winchelmere know about a hidden something in this box?" I asked Mary.

"Kalam came from Egypt," she said.

"Lord Winchelmere," Geraldi murmured with that dangerous white flash of a smile that he occasionally showed. "I thought for a moment that the price of that name would be all that we wanted. Even as it was, I think that we owe a good deal to you, Miss Ingall."

He said it in such a way that I grew foolishly red, foolishly happy. However, my only excuse is that the words were spoken by a beautiful monster, for that's what he is, this James Geraldi.

He looked at the bottom of the box for a long time. It was a flat slab of solid gold, unmarked, except for a few scratches in the soft metal. At last he took out a large handkerchief and asked Mary to tie it around his eyes. She did as he requested, and then he began to tap across the face of the box, tapping in each spot first with the tip of his finger and then with a fingernail. He worked so for a half hour, I should say, and gradually played across the golden plate from one end to the other.

"You'd better go outside, both of you," he said finally.

We went without a word.

"What sort of mummery is this?" I asked Mary indignantly.

"Don't talk," she answered impolitely.

We stood at a little distance from the door, but where we could look back through it and see him bent at his work in the lantern light over the red-gold flash of the box. He had given up tapping with his fingers, and now he used as a hammer a small pocketknife, with which he was going over the surface as carefully as ever, his head straining first to one side and then to the other in a sort of agony of attention. Suddenly he called out.

We went running in and found him with his forefinger pressed against the exact center of the bottom of the golden box.

He tore the bandage from his eyes. "Here," he said. "Dig here. Where's that hammer and the chisel, Mary?"

She ran to get them, and, when she came back, he had scratched a thin circle around the point at which his fingertip rested, and then identified that particular spot with a prick of his knifepoint.

"Now," Geraldi murmured, picking up the small chisel and the hammer, "for the sake of golden Horus . . ." And he struck the chisel into the gold. It curled back in a shining furrow before the advancing edge. Around he went, and then made a second, deeper circle. It was wonderful to see the neatness with which he worked, and to listen to the quick clinking of the hammer blows.

"Watch the door . . . I'll watch the window," Mary said in a sudden, hoarse whisper.

I *did* as I was told. I had the same shuddering fear that eyes would peer in upon us.

Then Geraldi said: "So the sealed door is opened."

We turned with a start. He had lifted out a thick plate of shining gold. Then he dipped into the cavity that was exposed and produced between thumb and forefinger a great yellow stone that shimmered with

191

secret fires. "The golden sun from the head of Horns," he said. "A yellow diamond, my dear friends."

# CHAPTER
# THIRTEEN

# "A Precious Stone"

I wish, now, that I never had seen that wretched stone. But at that moment it looked to me like a miracle of beauty. I took it in the hollow of my hand. It was not a sparkling, flashing thing. It had been trimmed into a circular form, that was all. There were no facets cut to give it brilliance. Only, in the heart of it there was a wavering flame. Mary was at my shoulder, watching, too. I looked up and saw nothing but mirth in the eyes of Geraldi as he studied our intent faces, and once more I shuddered at him. Why? Well, I can explain that.

What made me look up was the length of the silence and the great beating of my heart, as I confessed the thing that makes men and women commit crimes. I don't really mean to say that I would have stolen even a jewel like that yellow beauty, but for the moment I could understand why men committed murder for such stones. Women, as well. And there was a tight, tense look about Mary's mouth that made me understand that she was thinking the same thing, feeling the same fierce greed.

But Geraldi laughed. Money, then, was no lure to him. Not even beauty was the attraction that dragged him into the ways of darkness. I fear that I grow a little poetical. But he committed his sins for the sake of the bright face of danger alone. Why, one may say, that's a higher impulse, a greater and a finer thing. Granted. But not a human motive. Anger, hate, jealousy, greed, love, ambition are the mainsprings. But this man was different, and, because of the difference, I almost hated him, then. There might be a new world in which a race of creatures like him would prosper and make their new laws and live by their new creed. How long would they last? They would burn themselves up in a year, so far as I could guess. He was like the yellow diamond for the head of the Horus. Brilliant and beautiful to see and with a secret flame in him, but totally inhuman. It struck all the pleasure of that rich find out of my thoughts. And then it seemed to me that I saw the way before me as clearly as a straight road is leveled by engineers.

I said to Geraldi: "I want to talk to you. Will you come outside with me?"

"Don't let her tempt you," Mary said to Jimmy. "She may try to get you to run away with the diamond."

Geraldi went with me out into the night.

"Now," I said, striking at once into the theme I had prepared on the spur of the moment, "what's to be done?"

"Whatever seems the best next step," he answered.

"You intend to stay here?"

"Of course."

"Why do you say of course?"

"What could be better than the way things are going now?" he asked me. "When we came here, we had the golden box. Now we have one of the emeralds, and the diamond as well ... which is worth more than all the other stones and the gold together. Besides, we've warmed up his lordship, and he'll reach into that uncommonly deep mind of his and try to pull out a masterstroke of some sort. It was an exceedingly rash move on his part ... to suggest that the box was worth all the emeralds. By this time he's cursing himself for having made it, and he knows perfectly well that we have in our hands the yellow diamond. Now he has to come to us and come to us quickly, and when he comes ... why, we'll finish collecting that harvest of emeralds, Miss Ingall. And there you are."

He finished speaking and laughed a little. When he had finished laughing, I heard a little contented purring sound in his throat, like that which a cat makes when it is by a warm fire — digging its nails into the rug from pure animal pleasure. Geraldi thought that this was the only way. Half a dozen dangerous brigands to stand against; half a dozen sets of brains to defeat. It was ideal for him.

I said: "I understand this. From your viewpoint it's simple. But not from mine or Mary's."

"And why should Mary object?" he asked me, rather coldly skipping any volition of mine.

"She wouldn't object, of course," I said. "Not so long as she thought that you wanted a thing done in one particular way."

**195**

He looked steadily, and I was rather glad that there was nothing but starlight for him to see me by.

"That's a little broad, I think," Geraldi said.

"I have to be broad," I replied. "There isn't time for diplomatic approaches. But you know perfectly that you'll make use of her to please yourself."

He waited a moment — to control an angry answer, I suspected. Then he said: "Perhaps you look at this thing in the wrong way. She and I spoke about a partnership. Did you know the terms of it? Did you think that I was in this thing for ... for money, perhaps?"

"Money would never tempt you," I answered readily enough.

"Ah, but it would," he answered me frankly.

"Money to live on, yes," I replied. "Money to please your fancy in clothes and fine living, now and then. But not money for its own sake. Money is trash to you."

"That has the sound," he told me more cheerfully, "of a fine compliment, but ..."

"But it isn't," I said cruelly. "You have devised this exquisite trap of yours and baited it with human beings. Whatever the trap catches, you turn over to Mary. Very well. That's a magnificent gesture. On the other hand ... she continues to the last moment to be the bait."

"She isn't afraid," he said. "You underrate her courage."

"I don't a whit," I snapped. "Of course, she isn't afraid. She's too dizzy with love and excitement to be afraid of wild lions." It shocks me when I think of the boldness of that sentence. But I was desperate.

"I don't understand that," Geraldi said as cold as ice. "I think that, perhaps, we can't arrive at a quiet conclusion. We'll have to manage to get on without it, Miss Ingall."

He would have drifted back toward the house, but I stopped him short by saying: "Let's be perfectly honest. Admit that you want to keep this up not simply to restore to her what she should have inherited from her father."

"I thought it was all to go back to Egypt," he said.

"And it may. But half the price of it would go to the restorer. On what do you think that Mary is to live, Mister Geraldi?"

"Is she poor?" he asked me.

"As a dormouse," I told him. "Her father left very little."

"That's a consideration," he said.

"It is." I went on: "You see for yourself that she needs the money. Her half of the emerald, the diamond, the golden box would be an ample competence to her, wouldn't it?"

"Rather," Geraldi agreed. "You think I should chuck this business? And let that pack of cutthroats go free?"

"We can't take the law into our own hands," I replied.

"You have to admit," he argued, "that things have been going on pretty well for us . . . in the service of the golden god." He laughed. He was trying to put the talk on a better plane for him, but I kept him down to brass tacks.

"What odds are against you, Mister Geraldi?" I asked.

"Why . . . I don't know," he said. "Nothing is won in life unless a little chance is taken."

I counted out my points. "They have free hands. They can act as they please, and they have a dozen pairs of hands to use in their work. You have yourself . . . and two women. Enough to make bait, you say. But, after all, I think the visit of his lordship has altered matters a little."

"His lordship made some very bad blunders," he pointed out to me. "I don't see, otherwise, how his visit has changed things a great deal."

"Even Napoleon made blunders from time to time," I reminded Geraldi. "But it's clear now that you have against you a man almost, if not quite, as strong as you are yourself."

He sighed.

"And he has others with him who are not fools," I continued. "You've shown splendid dash and brilliant courage and prodigious cleverness. But you know that battles can't be won by brains alone. You have to have force."

"You want to place what we have in Mary Ingall's hands and send her back to Boston," he said bluntly.

"I want exactly that," I said.

"She never would do it," he said. "She wants to see the murderers of her father brought to justice."

"Do you think," I asked him, "that it is actually best for her to stay here or to go home?"

"She is a proud girl," Geraldi stated flatly. "She would think the boldest course the best course."

"I don't ask what she thinks. But you, in all honesty. Which is the wise and safe way for a young girl? To stay here in this death trap, or to go back with what she has?"

He avoided me, strangely, by saying: "Besides, you know that, if we give up this work, we've left the service of the golden Horus. And we'll none of us have any luck, Miss Ingall, if we become traitors to his service. You can see that, of course?" He laughed gently, inviting me to take another viewpoint, quietly suggesting just that stroke of superstition that throws women off balance in their judgments. But I hewed to the line.

"I'm not talking superstition. I'm asking you point-blank a serious question. What is best for her to do?"

"As for that," he answered sourly, "as for that . . . from the viewpoint of sheer common sense . . . perhaps it would be better for her to go back. But she never would do it."

"Ah, but she will," I assured him.

"Try to persuade her, Miss Ingall," he challenged.

"Not I. I never could move her," I admitted. "But suppose you go in and persuade her with your own words."

199

# CHAPTER
# FOURTEEN

## "Geraldi Tries"

He seemed to see the point of what I had said in all its implications. He resolutely turned his back upon the door of the shack. "You can't expect me to do that," he replied very stiffly.

"But I do," I answered. "You agree that it is best and safest for Mary to withdraw at once. *I* can't help her with persuasion as long as she feels that you're bent on carrying this terrible business through. But you can do it with a word."

"I never could manage it," he said.

"Try, then," I urged him. "I'll wait out here in the darkness and watch. I haven't any doubt about what you can do with her."

He hesitated. He shifted from one foot to the other like a small boy. "I'll tell you what," he said, "it's a bit too much. You're asking me to send her out of my life. That isn't fair."

He admitted, by that, that he had ample influence to persuade her. He had shifted the argument straight over to the most personal basis, and I suppose he felt that I would have too much personal delicacy to talk any more. But there was no delicacy about me that night. I thought that I saw the whole future of Mary Ingall resting in my hands. I did what I thought was best. Heaven forgive me for it.

I said to him: "If she stayed in your life, Jimmy, what would the end of it be for her?"

He had no ready answer for that, and I went on cruelly. "Would you marry her, Jimmy? Is that what you have in mind?" I heard him exclaim impatiently. Then I said: "Your brain is too clear not to see all the possibilities at once. If you married her, you would have to settle down to a steady regular life. No more excursions around the world. Hard work. I don't know what. Insurance, perhaps real estate. Because you could be very persuasive, I'm sure."

I waited for him to answer. I saw that my words were battering him terribly. So I went on: "The Ingalls have influence in Boston. It might be that they would be able to place you in some office. I don't exactly know what sort of work. But if you were very industrious and obeyed orders, at the end of fifteen or twenty years there might be a junior partnership, and, in the meantime, Mary would be bringing up a pleasant family . . ."

"That's enough," Geraldi said.

There actually was a shudder in his voice. I had no doubt that he was filling out the details of the picture of the life ahead of him, in case he did what would be best for Mary, as I had sketched it. Nevertheless, I stuck to my guns, no matter what pain I gave him. We can be cruel, we women. But I kept in mind always Mary.

"You know, Jimmy," I said to him, "that although you're fond of Mary because of her courage, her simplicity, her pretty face, her big heart, you're not in love with her. You don't want to give her up. You don't want to have her at the right price. On the other hand, you know that in this human world one can't have something for nothing."

"You're frank," he said with bitterness.

"You're living from day to day, reveling in the danger of this place. I'm trying to look into the future and see the life of Mary as it will have to be," I told him.

"Very well," he said at last. "I'll do my share. I'll go to her and try. Stand out here, if you wish, and see me play the cards for you."

I felt a sudden and hot shame, then. It was perfectly plain that he wasn't a villain, not in the bookish sense. I suddenly remembered that he was only a boy; nature simply had made him not as other men are made.

He went in to Mary, who was still turning the great yellow diamond in her hand. She lifted her head with a start and smiled as he came beside her.

I, like a guilty thing, slipped closer to the door. I could hear all they said in their quiet voices.

He spoke at once: "I think that we've gained enough out of this, Mary. You'd better start back East tomorrow."

What joy sprang up in her eyes. "Are you going, Jimmy?" she asked him. "Are we all going?"

"I?" he said.

At that, she jumped to her feet. "Aunt Emmy has been talking to you?" she asked.

202

"She has," he said.

"Don't put a bit of stock in what she says!" cried Mary. "I've never heard of such a thing. Leave this place . . . when everything is going on so well?"

Almost his words, you see.

"They are not going on so well," Geraldi responded.

"In what way?"

"Ever since his lordship stepped into the picture, I knew that we were in for very hard work. Ever since he appeared, I saw that this was too dangerous a business for you. You must go."

"And you? And you?" she asked rapidly.

"I? Well . . . I'll drift off somewhere . . . out of the path of the anger of Winchelmere."

He said it like a man bitterly confessing the truth. But I knew that he lied. Once we were gone, he never would leave the trail of Winchelmere. He would have an extra spur to urge him on, after Mary's departure. She strained her eyes at him, as though he were standing at a great distance, so hard was she trying to read his mind.

"Do you mean that, Jimmy?" she asked him.

"I mean it."

"Cross your heart?"

"I cross my heart," Geraldi assured her. "It's the only thing to do, Mary. We're in the middle of a fire. You can see for yourself. Winchelmere is a dangerous fellow. I never saw a more dangerous one. And he has a set of clever and hard fellows behind him. Even if I wanted to carry on a fight with him . . . seeing how things now are, and that we have a big part of what we've started after ... I wouldn't want to have my hands encumbered by a pair of women. You can appreciate that?"

I winced as I watched the changing face of Mary.

"Of course, I can see that," she said slowly. She was as white as blanched linen. But she kept her eyes straight on his and made herself smile. "You must know what's best," Mary murmured.

"I do. I'm sure that I do," Geraldi said. "We'll start in the morning," he added.

"We'll start in the morning," admitted Mary.

"The first pink of the day," Geraldi stated.

"The first pink of the day," Mary repeated like a parrot.

"Well, good night," he said.

"Good night," said the lips of Mary, but they made no sound.

Geraldi turned on his heel and came out into the night. When he saw me, he paused for an instant.

I said wretchedly: "I'm sorry, Jimmy. Heaven forgive me, if I am wrong. I only mean to do what's right."

He said in the lightest and most cheerful voice imaginable: "Of course, you're right. I see that you're a surgeon of the soul, so to speak, and surgeons can't always have anesthetics at hand. There must be a little pain. Good night, Miss Ingall."

Ah, heartless, one would think. But it wasn't that. For at that moment, as I saw him step away and instantly vanish in the darkness, I realized that he was in hot torture, pain such as he never had felt before, perhaps.

I did not dare go back into the house until the light was out. I paced restlessly up and down through the darkness. I made myself look up at the stars. I repeated silly little bits of information about them — that Arcturus was fifty times as large as our sun — that he was running away across the face of the heavens. But always my mind kept leaping back to Geraldi. Not to Mary, strangely enough. She occupied a secondary place in my thoughts. But I kept asking myself if it were true that Mary could have been an anchor and a cable strong enough to hold Geraldi in place. For, if she were, then I was stealing a vast treasure from the world in preventing that man from becoming a part of civilized humanity, law-keeping humanity.

At last, when the shack was dark, I went in and undressed and lay down on my bunk. It was a windless night. The air was close and thick in the room; the blackness was appalling and stifling. I had a strange feeling that Mary was getting up from her bed and coming to lean above me in the darkness.

However, I used all my will power and closed my eyes and began to put myself to sleep. If a ship two hundred and twelve feet long weighs a thousand and ninety-eight tons, what will a ship of the same lines and two hundred and fifty-one feet long weigh? I've tried to work that problem out for years — lying in the dark. And sleep always jumps over me before I get the answer. It began to gain on me now, as I worked out the foolish fractions with an absorbed attention. Then, all at once, I was wide awake, listening with a racing heart and a tingle in all my nerves. For I could hear a soft, regular pulse of sound, never loud and never ended. It seemed to come from a great distance across the desert. I never had heard anything like it — and yet in a way it was wonderfully familiar. It frightened me and laid a load of grief on my heart. I couldn't tell why.

There was a faint stir in the darkness. Then, suddenly, I knew. It was poor Mary Ingall, sobbing in her bunk, and stifling those sobs. And I, miserable, lay still, with both my hands clenched, knowing that whatever she needed, I could not do anything for her, I could not attempt to console her or to soothe her. For I was the one who had dealt the blow. It was an ugly thought.

Mary went to sleep, at last, but sleep was gone for me. A dozen times before the morning I heard her moan in her dreams. Only at the very end I must have drowsed, for suddenly I heard a quiet, cheerful voice.

"Time to start, Aunt Emmy." And there was she, as bright and gay and pretty as ever, ready for the day.

# CHAPTER
# FIFTEEN

## "A Wild Ride"

We had an uncooked breakfast of raisins and hard crackers and vinegar-flavored water. Then he went out to the horses. The dawn had turned from the first gray to the faintest pink, and the vast desert looked soft, and cool, and habitable, and the mountains were like cheerful, friendly faces.

"But you've made a mistake," Mary said. "You've put my saddle on Peter."

"No," Geraldi said with an almost rude shortness. "I've made no mistake." He explained immediately: "You'll be carrying the box, I suppose."

She didn't argue. He gave her a leg up into the saddle, and there she settled herself. She looked very blank and white for a moment, but a few seconds after we started she was cheerful once more, and the color was back in her face. Only, she could not meet my eyes. And when I spoke to her, she only pretended to look at me, sweeping her glance toward me, but never letting it rest upon my face.

Geraldi stayed with us for a time. He said to us: "We have the three best horses that we possess. Oddly enough," he added, with a little sparkle in his eye, "they all belong to Lord Winchelmere and his men. However, we'll use them without any conscience this morning. We've about ten miles to go, and I'm going to ask you to keep to the trail. It's the fast way to reach the town, and the obvious way for Winchelmere to watch. But I don't think he'll suspect us of trying to do the obvious thing. He'll block the other suspicious ways for our escape. Perhaps he'll leave this way open. I want you to ride on together. You're a pretty fair judge of pace, Mary. You'll know how to rate Peter along so that you'll make fast time all the way to town, and yet have a sprinting reserve in hand in case of a pinch at the last."

"Yes," said Mary.

"Let Miss Ingall ride ahead," he said.

"Yes," Mary answered.

"I think that's all," Geraldi said. "I'll drop back and look after the rear of the procession, you see."

"Yes," was Mary's reply.

"That's all," Geraldi added.

"I think you've forgotten one thing," she said.

He rode up beside her, an anxious look on his face. "The box is tied into that saddlebag, and arranged so that it won't jounce around," he explained.

She held up her arms to him and drew his head down and kissed him.

"Good bye," she whispered. Then she put Peter into a gallop, and I went blindly after her.

I had been prepared for everything, I thought, but I hadn't been prepared for this. And, after all, she was a prophet. An extra sense must have told her what was going to happen. I can't explain it, otherwise.

I saw Geraldi, with a cold, stern face, drawing back to the rear, and I noticed that he was mounted on a beautifully made gray horse, rather small, but full of life and looking a racer in every point. Mary, of course, was invincibly mounted on Peter. The big stallion knew her well enough, and, although he turned his head and whinnied back once or twice to his master, still he was willing to go on kindly under the hand of the girl. I had a big, ugly-headed roan gelding. Although it looked like a cartoon, it went like an Irish hunter, and, with all its force, it had a mouth of silk. I was prepared to meet a very severe challenge before I would be overhauled on such a horse as that.

I lost Geraldi over a hilltop, then I saw Mary drawing up a little and waving her hand to make me go ahead.

I drove the roan past Peter, who lurched and tossed his head, angry at being put in the rear. I even managed a smile and a nod to Mary as I went by, but there was, however, no smile in my heart. The premonition of disaster was beginning to possess me. I tried to reason that it was because of the odds against us, and the cleverness of Lord Winchelmere. But I knew, deep down, that it had been that one word of farewell between Mary and the man she loved.

I rated the roan as well as I could for the ten-mile journey, taking into consideration the state of the sand, so we went on at a good clip and put the miles rapidly behind us. After a time, I felt much better. The roan went like a fine machine, tireless and long-striding. With the pink of the morning turning to rose, my confidence grew stronger. We were more than halfway to the town.

We were passing, I remember, a big tank with the flush of the sky spread over its still surface like rich lacquer, when something made me turn my head, and I saw three horsemen fly over the top of a hill off to our right. They appeared for only an instant, and then dipped out of sight behind a big wave of sand. But I knew that it was the beginning of the hunt. Lord Winchelmere had found us out, and he and his men were driving at us. If they could gain ever so little, they would shut us out from our return. Certainly they would at least come within gun range of us. And I hadn't the slightest doubt, in spite of what Mary had said, that they would open on us as readily as they would on armed men.

I looked back. Mary already was swinging up beside me. "Bear a bit left," she shouted, "and give the roan the whip!"

I was already doing it. That fine fellow, with never a falter over rough or smooth, flew away at full speed and gave a trifle to the left. Mary had rated Peter just beside me, and, fast as the roan was racing, the big black stallion simply floated beside us, head high and ears pricked, while my horse was laid out as level as a taut string, from nose to tail tip. I could not help thinking of Geraldi. He was that way. There was between him and other men the same difference that lay between Peter and most other horses.

Mary was glancing continuously to the right. Toward the enemy, I thought at first. Then I saw a silver streak break out between two little swelling hills of sand. It was Geraldi, jockeying his horse to incredible speed and bearing out to cut off the other riders from our line of march.

We poured out of the hills into the flat. There was the town, its windows winking with golden fire in the morning light, not more than three miles away — a matter of minutes at our speed. At the same time I saw the rest of the danger on our right.

In the lead were three fellows racing, bent low over the necks of their horses, and keeping a true line to cut off the way to our goal. Aye, and I saw in an instant that all the good fortune in the world never could make us beat them out. Behind them came four more, riding with equal eagerness, but distanced either because their horses were not quite so good, or because they weighed more in the saddle. One of them was unmistakably his lordship, riding beautifully, keeping well up in spite of his crushing bulk on the back of a horse. But, at the worst, why could we not admit that we were blocked from our goal, and bear to the left, sharply, and ride away? I turned my head in that direction and saw the answer. Four more riders were foaming down at us from the northwest. They were spread out in a line. Obviously they were the net into which his lordship hoped to turn us. And then despair jumped into my brain and turned me sick.

The hard, clear voice of Mary rang at my ear: "Keep riding! Keep working!"

That cleared my eyes again. She herself was a little white, I thought, but she was riding like a jockey and keeping Peter, with his immense stride, well in hand.

"Go on!" I cried to her. "Go on, Mary! You can get past them!"

I could see that the black horse had an almost infinite reserve of strength and speed left in him. But Mary made no answer. She only glanced again to the right.

Then I saw the little gray horse flash out again into plain view, with Geraldi sweeping him forward. I thought that Geraldi, at that moment, looked no larger than a stripling boy. And going out with such wild courage to face such odds. He could not win. I felt that. I dared not look again, but kept my eyes straightforward.

We were coming rapidly toward a focal point. Guns began to rattle. I saw the thin streaks of smoke snatched away from the guns of the three, while Geraldi went straight on, never answering. Closer and closer.

"He's mad!" I shouted.

Then his hand went up with a gleam of steel in it. We were so close that I could see the Colt jerk up at the muzzle as he fired, and instantly the leading rider of the trio threw his hands above his head and leaned slowly to the side, farther and farther. At last he toppled, rolled over and over on the sand, and came to rest in an oddly twisted position. I didn't need a doctor's certificate to tell me that he most certainly would never rise again.

There was a veritable roar of guns now. They paid no heed to us. But the remaining two in front were driving

212

straight at Geraldi with smoking six-shooters, and in the rear the galloping four were turning loose their rifles. Not aimed at us, but at least half a dozen random bullets hissed close to my head. Terrible sounds that went through my very heart.

Then Geraldi fired twice in rapid succession. One of the leaders pitched forward and hugged the neck of his horse, which began to slow down to a hand gallop, and then a trot, shaking off its loose-limbed rider at the same time. The other clutched his shoulder. Then one arm dangled weakly. With the other, he began to tug frantically at his reins. And so, all in a trice, they were gone.

I can't believe it, even now. But there it was before my eyes. At one moment, three desperate and dangerous men were spurring to cross our line, and the next moment there was one dead, and on the sands another man lay writhing in pain, and the third was helplessly out of the fight, with all of us rushing on past him.

We had won. Or, rather, Geraldi had won, and as for the other eight, they were far off and losing ground as we rushed for the town and safety — a short, short pair of miles from us.

Then it happened. Those riders with Winchelmere suddenly stopped galloping, halted their horses, and began to fire with steady hands. Geraldi had turned his horse toward us, and, as he did so, I heard the little gray pony snort. He put his head down with a stumble, then pitched head over heels and lay without a quiver. Geraldi was flung far. He turned in the air, struck the ground with frightful force, and lay there doubled, helpless.

I saw Winchelmere and the rest drive forward. I even heard their wild yells of victory, as though the fall of this one man meant far more than the three of them he had accounted for. Then Mary was sawing at the head of Peter. Why? I don't know. A mad impulse to turn and charge back — and, of course, be lost entirely with Geraldi. I swung my quirt with all my force. I brought it down like the slash of a sword on the rump of the stallion, and off he bolted for the town, quite out of Mary's control.

For, after all, what could we have done, had we been twenty women, instead of two?

# CHAPTER
# SIXTEEN

## "What of Geraldi?"

Peter pulled up at last in the middle of the town, and, as I came pumping up on the roan, Mary was slipping to the ground. She clutched Peter's mane with one hand, the stirrup with the other, and leaned her forehead against his shoulder. And he, as though he understood, turned his head around to her.

She had given up all hope, but not I. A sort of madness was in me. I could not tell myself that Geraldi was dead. I ran into the hotel — screaming, I'm afraid.

After a moment, there were men around me. Men in overalls, rough, unshaven fellows, and I blessed their roughness, and I caught at their hands and begged them to take their weapons and their horses and ride with me. I would show them the way. There were dead and wounded men not two miles away. A terrible murder had been committed. Heaven forbid that Geraldi had given his life for us. He must still be living. You cannot kill a panther with one fall.

They did not wait for explanations. They heard one burst of my appeal, and then they scattered. I head tramping of feet upstairs and down. Men were shouting in the distance.

"You'd better drink this," said a woman with a kind, anxious face, hurrying up to me.

I swallowed the glass of water that she offered to me. Then I took her by the hand and dragged her outside. I pointed to Mary, still motionless beside Peter. "Take her inside," I told the woman. "Be kind to her. Her heart is broken."

The woman of the hotel gave me one keen, understanding glance, and then ran to Mary. It was like taking charge of a child. I saw her lead Mary away by the hand, and then I scrambled back into the saddle. Not on the roan, for he was totally spent, but on Peter. There were already twenty mounted men in the street, their horses whirling in impatience, waiting for me to lead the way. Out we poured and rode to the place.

We found on the ground the first man whom Geraldi had shot down.

"That's that dago yegg, Strozzi," someone said. "He's the bird that done the big job in Denver last year. It's a good thing that he's gone."

But what of the others? What of Jimmy Geraldi? They were gone!

We found a back trail running through the sand, deeply imprinted. We even found a sprinkling of what the men declared to be blood at one place, but then the trail led into a gravel-bottomed draw.

After that the pursuit split up. A half dozen poured out into one sandy valley, and a half dozen in another direction, although I shouted at them that it was no good, because such small bands of fighters would

216

simply be overwhelmed, even if they *were* able to overtake the criminals in the desert.

However, they went their own way. I followed, blindly, hopeless, and for half the day we roamed back and forth, and at last we came back in silent gloom, for the trail had been hopelessly lost — hopelessly complicated by our own foolish milling about in the sand.

When we returned, I went into the hotel at once, carrying the saddlebag with its weight of gold and jewels. But I hated the very thought of the treasure that was inside it. It had cost the life of Geraldi, I told myself, and heaven alone could tell what it had cost Mary Ingall. Her love for me, at least, would be gone forever.

I found that kind woman had put Mary in bed, and, wonder of wonders, Mary was sound asleep. I looked at her with amazement. Her nurse put a finger on her lips, and there were tears in her eyes.

She led me out of the room and whispered to me in the hall. "We can't tell. When she wakes up . . . then we'll be able to know what's happened to her mind. But now it's like a child's. It's a blank. She'd better have a stranger with here, I think, when she opens her eyes again. I've been a nurse. I know a little about these things. What has happened?"

I could not answer.

She gave me a queer, suspicious look and then advised me to go into the next room and lie down to rest.

So I've come in here, but not to lie down. I've been sitting here thinking, going over again all that has happened since I left dear, safe, peaceful Boston, wondering all the time what the end is to be. I think of the past — I think of the future — and I know that I — I am to blame for everything. I never can forgive myself.

# Through Steel and Stone

# CHAPTER
# ONE

## "The Two Kings"

The *Casa* Oñate lived under a double sway, like a kingdom with two masters. One king was San Luis; one king was Pepillo. Pepillo was a young mountain lion, caught when he was a blind kitten, mothered by one of Oñate's cats, and then brought up to flourishing youth. He was wonderfully good-natured, even when a drunken man blundered into his silken flank as he slept in the sun. But he was a thoughtful cat. Sometimes he would sit for a long time in a corner, lashing his sides with his three-foot tail, and glaring wickedly. But, as a rule, Pepillo was the quietest of domestic pets, with a wonderfully large vocabulary, and clean beyond belief in all of his ways. Pepillo was the king of the household.

The other was San Luis, and San Luis was a tall billy goat, with long wool of the creamiest, and a patriarchal white beard that fell deeply from his chin. His horns curved back from a brow that was continually wrinkled with a frown of impatience, and, even while he was eating, San Luis's little bright eyes went forever from side to side, looking for trouble. He was ready to leave off everything for the sake of a fight. They called him San Luis because he was so spotlessly white and cream, and because he was so brave in battle. He was the second king of the household of Oñate. Pepillo reigned indoors. San Luis reigned outdoors, as far as the bars of the corral where the horses were kept.

They met, as today, in the neutral ground, the no-man's land, of the patio. The rest of the house was falling rapidly to ruin. The stars looked through many a section of the fallen roof, and the floors groaned underfoot. When Pedro Oñate stamped in anger, he was sure to strike up a cloud of the dust of rotten wood. But the patio was very much as it always had been. It was horseshoe-shaped, with ten columns and eleven arches enclosing a cloistered walk and giving upon the patio open court that was closed in, on the remaining side, by an adobe wall. All the pillars were intact. None of the arches had broken down. Standing there in the patio, no one could have guessed that the house was going to ruin except that one chimney had fallen and, in its fall, had beaten a hole in the roof. But that was a detail. It would be repaired tomorrow.

For the rest, it looked like a piece of the grand old days, when Spain had newly found an empire in the West and filled it with a few masters and many slaves. The vine that covered the patio wall and hung thick over the arched entrance was rich with yellow roses. In the sun they looked like tufts of fire; in the shadow they were like tarnished metal. Other vines climbed everywhere over the house. No matter where the sun stood in the sky, the patio swayed and drifted with shadows, like water, except at the single hour of noon. Then the sun descended a little from the central sky and burned the patio and shriveled the leaves of all the vines with white heat and made the very winds shrink back into the hollow ravines, so that nothing could be seen to stir.

Even San Luis, who scorned all things, respected the sun at this moment and kept to the shadow. Even Pepillo, who luxuriated in a bath of fire, exposed to the white shafts no more than the tip of his tail and his forepaws, with the talons unsheathed, sunk in the rain-moistened floor of the court. The two guards gave up their walk, to and fro, and stood in the shade of the arched entrance, with the hanging tendrils brushing about their heads. They leaned on their rifles and looked askance with awe at the motionless prisoner.

For Geraldi lay in a deep rustic chair in the exact center of the court, exposed to the falling torrents of sunshine with only a cap upon his head. The waves of light were reflected from him. He seemed to tremble and quiver with the heat waves that were cast up from his body. He had turned his hands palm up to take the sun. Of his face, only the eyes were shielded by the narrow visor of his cap, and his lips were seen smiling faintly in enjoyment of the blasting sun.

Little Giovanni came out to him. Giovanni was ten, but he looked older in face and younger in body. He had the olive skin of Italy, a sallow, unhealthy skin, and eyes of polished black.

"You'll be sick," he said to Geraldi. "You'll be sick in the head and afterwards in the stomach if you keep lying out here in the sun at this time of day. My mother said so."

"Your mother is kind to trouble about warning me," Geraldi said.

"She isn't kind," Giovanni shouted, "because she hopes that you *will* get sick!"

"But you don't want me to be sick," Geraldi contradicted, still without opening his eyes.

"If you get sick," said Giovanni logically, "you wouldn't be able to teach me to whittle, or to sing, or to throw a knife. But," said Giovanni, "my mother says that I am to talk to you no more."

"Then you shouldn't be out here talking to me now."

"I'm not," Giovanni responded. "I came out here to talk to San Luis and Pepillo. Luis, come here!" He snapped his fingers. San Luis, his mouth filled with soft green tendrils that he had just torn from a vine, stopped his busy munching long enough to cast an impatient glance of contempt at Giovanni, and then went on eating.

"My mother," Giovanni said in his bright, high voice, "says that I should hate you and try to kill you, because you killed my father."

"And what do you say to your mother?"

"I say to her that you are teaching me how to shoot and how to throw a knife. After you have taught me enough, then perhaps I could kill you."

"Yes, that is true," Geraldi said, nodding.

"But," argued the boy, "you didn't kill my father from behind, did you?" He added: "Come here, Luis!"

"No, I didn't kill him from behind."

"He was shooting at you when you shot him?"

"He was."

224

"Then it was just a fight," Giovanni reasoned, "and that's fair. Besides, I'm only a little boy. I don't have to worry about killing people when they teach me how to fight and how to use a knife. Afterwards, when I grow up . . . well, that's another thing. Then I might have to fight with you, even."

"I hope not," said Geraldi.

"But nobody could beat you," Giovanni said.

"And why not?"

"Because you could dodge a bullet. Because you could dodge a knife, even."

Geraldi sighed, out of pure contentment with the dreadful heat of the sun.

"Come here, Luis!" commanded the boy.

"He'll never come when you call him like that," Geraldi said.

"Why not? He knows me very well."

"Yes, perhaps he does. But he doesn't think it's respectful to call him by one name. He's a saint, isn't he?"

The boy laughed a little. "He's only a goat," he said.

"He's San Luis," Geraldi persisted. "You'd better call him that way."

"San Luis, San Luis!" called Giovanni. "You see, he doesn't come. San Luis, you fool of a goat, come when I call you. Come here to me! Look at him," went on the boy. "He says that he doesn't care what pleases me. What would you do if you were me?"

"I'd teach him to follow me."

"How would you teach him?"

"By being kind to him."

"Kindness takes a great deal of time."

"It lasts longer, however," Geraldi advised the boy.

"You'll see that I can make him come," said Giovanni.

He went to San Luis and took him by the reverend, snowy beard. The goat got up at the first tug and butted at the boy, but Giovanni smote him with his little fist between the eyes. "I'll teach you!" Giovanni scolded.

Geraldi opened his eyes and saw San Luis being led toward him, blinking, obedient in fear.

"You see that I didn't need to be kind," Giovanni said in triumph.

"I see that," Geraldi said. "But this means that he'll never come to you unless you take him by the beard."

"Yes, it means that, perhaps. San Luis is a fool. He ought to come when I call him."

"Let him alone."

Giovanni relaxed his grip.

"Come to me, boy," Geraldi said softly.

The big goat walked to him and butted at the arm of the chair — but gently, gently.

"He loves you," said the boy with wonder. "And you've only had a few days with him. My mother says that you use magic to make things love you. That's the reason why she hates you so much. You ought not to do such things, you see?"

"No?" Geraldi answered. "But how about Pepillo? Will he come when you call him?"

"Pepillo is a devil," declared the child. "But I can make him do things. You watch him now." He called: "Pepillo!" Pepillo crouched. "He won't come,"

226

Giovanni said. "But I'll show him that I can master him." He ran to Pepillo and caught him by the tail. "Get up!" Giovanni shouted. Pepillo sat up on his haunches and caught Giovanni by the shoulders between his armed forepaws. His lips grinned back terribly over his needle-sharp teeth. His head moved forward trembling — trembling with eagerness as if to drive those fangs into the throat of the boy. "Down!" Giovanni said fearlessly, and smote the great cat on the nose. Pepillo sank slowly to the ground and remained there, lashing his tail, but blinking in fear beneath the raised hand of the child.

# CHAPTER
# TWO

## "Taming Wild Things"

To watch this performance, Geraldi had deigned to open his eyes — shadows among shadows — and now he said: "Come here, Giovanni."

The boy came.

"Someday," said Geraldi, "Pepillo will want to tear your throat."

"He wants to everyday," laughed Giovanni, "but he's afraid." He added: "Just the way that my mother wants to tear your throat everyday, but she's afraid, too. So Pepillo is afraid of me."

"But you can't always be sure," Geraldi cautioned. "Any day Pepillo might forget the whip and stroke you across the face with one of his paws, which has four sharp knives. And he might leave the knives out of their sheaths. Even your mother never would be glad to see you after that."

"I don't care," said the boy. "I'd rather be terrible to look at than beautiful. I've been practicing for hours," he went on, "and now I can hit a target with my knife one time in three."

"Let me see," said Geraldi.

The youngster ran into the house and came back at once with a block of soft pine that he put at a distance of a few steps. He took in his hand a small knife, short of hilt, narrow of blade. It lay flat on his palm. He threw the knife, and it stuck in a corner of the block.

"You're learning," Geraldi confirmed. "But you're learning wrong. You must always throw with just a flick of the wrist. If you fling back your arm as far as that, everyone will see what you are about to do. When a knife is to be thrown, Giovanni, it must be thrown in an instant of surprise when another man, say, is reaching for a gun to kill you. Suddenly a ray of light leaves your hand and runs into his heart. He falls down without any sound. Give me the knife."

The two men at the patio archway turned and held their rifles at the ready. One of them even raised his gun still higher and took aim at Geraldi.

He paid no attention to this. The knife glanced carelessly from his hand and stood fixed and quivering in the center of the block.

Giovanni began to groan and complain. "I shall never grow up. I shall never be able to learn to do that," he said.

"On the other hand," Geraldi contradicted, "you may grow up quickly enough . . . in one day. One day, one hour, one second even, may make the difference between a boy and a man. It made such a difference to me."

"Ah," Giovanni sighed, drawing in his breath as though he were drinking. "When you killed for the first time?"

There was no chance for Geraldi to answer. A woman ran out onto the patio. She reached for

Giovanni and clipped him loudly upon the cheek. He backed away from her, his face wry with pain, his eyes fixed maliciously upon her.

"Go into the house!" she shrilled at him.

"You have no right to cuff me," said the boy. "You're not strong enough to do it. I can throw a knife now."

She turned on Geraldi. She was a fine young woman, still under thirty, but she did not look entirely healthy. There were dark shadows beneath her eyes, which made them seem larger, to be sure, but also made them sad. Now they flashed and blazed. Her lips trembled with emotion.

"You are putting a devil in him!" she shouted. "You never will stop until you have ruined my family . . . all of it."

"Giovanni, go into the house." Geraldi said. "Take your knife and go into the house. And if I ever again hear you speak to your mother as you have spoken now, I'll give you no more lessons."

The boy tugged the knife from the block of wood; the two guards lowered their rifles and grinned a little to one another as they marked the black look that Giovanni cast at his mother. But he retreated without another word into the porch and disappeared through the first door. Bianca Strozzi remained before Geraldi. He had raised himself from the chair and stood languidly before her.

"May I smoke?" Geraldi asked.

"Ah, bah!" she gasped. "Why are you always trying to play the grand gentleman?"

"I beg your pardon."

"Why are you always acting as though every woman is a princess and you a prince?"

He remained silent; he looked down to the ground as though abashed.

"You want me to think that you are paying attention to me," she said, "but I know that you are despising me. But not as much as I despise you, you *gringo*. You . . . you murderer!" Her voice broke on the word. Even the two guards grew a little excited and looked savagely at Geraldi.

He, however, gave no answer.

"Now you want to steal away my boy. But I am watching you. Heaven help me to punish you. Heaven help me to make you as miserable as you have made me." At the thought of her own sorrows, tears of self-pity rushed into her eyes, but she dashed them away and shook her head. "I am waiting. I shall find a time," she added, and ran back into the house.

Geraldi then rolled a cigarette. He felt in his pockets. "A match, please . . . one of you fellows?" he asked.

They consulted each other.

"Is it a trick?" one asked.

"I dunno," said another.

"You go, Dick. You gotta give him a light, anyway."

"You go yourself, Joe. I ain't gonna. It ain't my job."

"All right. I don't welsh on a little thing like that."

So Joe approached and handed over a box of matches. Geraldi lighted the match, and, as he waited for the sulphur to burn away and the flame to clear, he looked up through the shadow of his visor at the face of

Joe. The latter grew uneasy. He even gave back half a step.

"Thanks," Geraldi said, and returned the matches. "Smoke yourself?" he invited.

"Thanks," said Joe. "But not on this job."

"You boys have a hard time," Geraldi said in his usual soft voice. "I'm sorry for you."

"We get double pay," explained Joe. "And we don't get paid for talking to you," he added by way of rough apology.

After that he withdrew hurriedly to the archway, and, once there, he threw a glance of triumph at his companion, as one who has dared a vast peril and come from it unscathed.

"He looks pretty small when you get right up close to him," Joe confided to Dick.

"Does he? He's big enough," Dick responded. "Suppose," he added, "when you was standing there he'd made a dive for you and snatched one of your guns?"

"I give him the matches with my left hand. I had my right hand on my gun, and the gun tipped up, coverin' him. But what would *you* have done if he'd gone at me?"

"I'd have put a bullet right through your back, hopin' to drop him."

Joe shuddered. "Would you've done that?"

"Would I eat ham an' eggs?" snarled Dick.

They glared at one another, but, after all, there was a certain understanding in the face of Joe, and he admitted: "Sure, it was a fool thing I done. I could've thrown him the matches. But I was sort of showing off, I guess."

"I guess you was," Dick agreed.

Geraldi had been standing, smoking his cigarette, and now slipped back into his chair, but, having been roused, he sat more upright and fastened his glance on the big cat in the shadow. He watched it for a long time with such a fixed gaze that Pepillo snarled with yellow-burning eyes. When Geraldi whistled, the big cat stood up, shook himself, and walked away. He went as far as the archway. A second whistle stopped him, and he began to stalk toward Geraldi, sinking almost to his belly.

"You'd better look out, Geraldi," Dick warned. "That hellion'll jump you some day and tear your innards out."

Geraldi did not answer. He whistled again, more softly. Pepillo came and crouched at his feet, looking ready to spring at his throat, but then, as though subdued by Geraldi's outstretched hand, he finally thrust forward his big round head and rubbed it against the finger of the man. After that, he curled himself across the feet of Geraldi and, basing his head on his paws, stared fixedly at the two guards.

"How the dickens did you do that, Geraldi?" asked one of them.

"I don't know. Power of understanding," Geraldi answered.

"Power of something," Dick said. "I wish I could make the brute act that way. I'm scared of it every time that I turn my back. Why don't they shoot it and take the hide before it rips somebody up?"

"I'll tell you why," Geraldi answered, leaning a little to stroke the silken fur of the back of Pepillo. "Men like to have danger around them, you know. Something that'll kill others and purr for them."

"That's why they want women, maybe?" Joe suggested, who had been married and to whom the subject was a bitter one.

"Maybe it is," Geraldi said pleasantly.

Dick said suddenly: "You're gonna get an answer now, Geraldi. Here comes Rompier back, and the Frenchy looks like he's been riding hard."

Hoof beats came up to the patio gate, paused, and then a small, lean man appeared. He walked quickly onto the patio, cast a gloomy side glance at Geraldi, and then walked on without a word into the house.

"You're out of luck, Geraldi, I guess," Dick announced. "I'm sorry for you, old-timer."

# CHAPTER
# THREE

## "Rompier Reports"

Having passed Geraldi without a glance, Rompier entered the house and went up a shattered stairway to the upper floor. There he found a room with goatskins on the floor and a couch covered with similar hides.

On the couch was stretched a big man with blond hair and pale-blue eyes, reading and smoking cigarettes. He put down the book and raised himself on one elbow as Rompier entered.

The latter remained near the door, hat in hand.

"Sit down, Lucien," said the big man.

"We've let ourselves in for trouble, my lord," Rompier said, taking a chair.

But even then he sat respectfully erect, his eyes continually on the other. His lordship nodded.

"Of course, there's trouble," he said cheerfully, "as long as Geraldi is living and breathing. He's born to cause trouble all over the world. He always has. He always will. Go on, Rompier. Tell me what happened. You went down to San Felice?"

"Yes. Not straight down. I drifted from place to place where I could hear a little talk."

"Of course. You wanted to know what people were saying. If we're not subjects to public opinion," he added with a smile, "at least we have to consider it."

"I don't like the work, and I don't like the place or the people," broke out Rompier. "I almost wish I'd never left Europe for this game."

"Almost," noticed the big man. "But not quite, Lucien."

"There's a chance of making a great winning," admitted Rompier. "But the proper place to work is in big cities. The people are sheep there. Out here, every man is a wolf. One man is nearly as good a fighter as another . . . every man has a horse as tough as leather . . . every man knows the country . . . and every man would risk his life for a hundred dollars . . . for nothing but the fun. I like fox hunting, Winchelmere, but I don't like to be the fox."

"These hunters had no good news for you, Lucien?"

"They want us," said the Frenchman, snapping his fingers. "They've been stirred up by that demon of a woman."

"Mary Ingall?"

"The old one, I mean."

"Ah, her aunt."

"She's gone everywhere," Rompier said. "She's cabled even to England. Everybody in the world knows that Lord Winchelmere has turned bandit in the West."

His lordship sat erect. But instead of answering, he made another cigarette.

"And you'd think," complained Rompier, "that an English peer is the natural enemy of all these people.

236

They actually thirst for your blood. She's drawn up long descriptions of you. She's guessed your weight to a pound. She's even drawn a picture of you that's an excellent likeness, while waiting for the real photographs of you to come over from England."

Winchelmere rose and went to the window. He parted the hanging vines that partially curtained it in a green shower, and looked through them down upon the court. There he could see Geraldi, with the mountain lion stretched at his feet. He said at last: "I knew that I would have to pay for it when I stepped in against Geraldi. Oh, I'd heard of him enough. But I didn't think that it would necessarily mean the end of my old life." He turned on Rompier cheerfully. "But let the old life go. Now I'm a citizen of no country. I'm free. And if perfect freedom hurts, it's only for a time. Prisoners miss their cells, but they don't miss them for long. Go on, Rompier. I understand this much. I'm a proved outlaw. I'm disgraced in my home country. So much the more reason for making this a rich haul. Now, exactly what did you do?"

"After I'd picked up what information I could . . . and stolen one of the posters that the woman published from her drawings of you . . . I went on down to San Felice. I entered the town by night. I thought it would be the most interesting way of going in," he added with a wry smile.

"They have your description, too?"

"They have. Along with it, they have that of Kalam, of course. And, also, Pedro Oñate's ugly face."

"We are all marked down," said his lordship calmly. "Which simply means that we shall all have to stay by the ship that much more closely. We'll have to be good shipmates, Rompier. Go on."

"I went into the town by a side lane and made for the hotel."

"A grand opportunity we missed in that hotel, Rompier."

"I know it. It was Geraldi again. The devil is in him."

"He *is* the devil," his lordship said with a good deal of feeling. "You got to the hotel and there you found the two women?"

"Of course. I stopped long enough to make myself up as a *peon* in good circumstances. I put on the ragged beard and mustache. I wrapped my neck in a gaudy strip of silk and put a gun and a knife in another scarf at my belt. Then I went into the hotel and asked for a room. They weren't too anxious to have me as a guest, but I finally got an attic room. It was good enough for me. I only wanted to be under that roof. I didn't intend to spend too much time in my bed."

"Of course not. You spotted the rooms of the two Misses Ingall?"

"That was easy. I was going to search those rooms the first chance I had, but then I learned that they had made a deposit in the safe of the town's new bank. After that, I wasted two whole days finding out all about the bank and its safe."

"And what did you find?" asked Winchelmere with keen interest.

"I found nothing to make me any happier. The bank had put in one of the newest contrivances. It has a lock that would defy the expert. And it's guarded day and night by men who know how to shoot straight and who can't be bought off."

"Did you try that, even?"

"No," said the other. "But I had a look at them. Simply cowpunchers straight off the range, and that breed doesn't know how to be crooked."

"Of course, they don't," said his lordship. "One would think that every ragged 'puncher was a millionaire, only interested in supporting the law. Except for a few gunfights, here and there. Go on, Rompier. Your story is dragging a little."

"There's enough to say when I come to it," Rompier assured the other. "After I found out that it was no use trying the bank, I saw that we'd have to fall back on Geraldi to buy the box, the diamond, and the emerald. I noticed that the two ladies walked out in the little garden of the hotel every evening, and that no one else ever did the same thing. When I was sure of that, I put myself in their way. The very next evening, when they turned the corner of the pine trees, I was in front of them. I took off my hat and bowed to them. The older woman wanted to know if I had something to say to them, or if they knew me.

"I said . . . 'You only know me by name and reputation. I am Lucien Rompier.'"

"Rompier, Rompier," chuckled his lordship, "you always were very keen after a dramatic effect."

"Not a bit," Rompier said, "I simply wanted to make that conversation as short as possible. Besides, I'd had a little shock of my own."

"What was that?"

"The older woman looked about as usual. Hard as nails and as keen as a fox. But the younger woman looked as if she'd just got out of a sick bed. And got out too soon, at that. Hollow-eyed, my lord. And she used to be a beauty."

"She's been grieving for Geraldi, of course," said his lordship. "I'm almost sorry for her. Her father killed . . . and then her lover dropped under her eyes"

"Almost sorry?" asked the Frenchman sharply.

"In these affairs," Winchelmere explained, "it doesn't do to let your heart soften. Go on."

Rompier stared at him for a moment. "I come from a warmer climate than yours," he said at last, and then continued. "The moment Mary Ingall saw me she cried out . . . 'Jimmy! Jimmy!' . . . and she clasped her hands at me.

"I said at once . . . 'He's alive, Miss Ingall.'

"She reached for her aunt and held onto her arm. Even that hard-faced woman said . . . 'Thank heaven!'

"Then she asked me why I had come. I said that I wanted to make a bargain. I didn't have a chance to say any more. Mary Ingall broke in . . . 'You'll give us Geraldi alive, and well . . . for the golden box and the diamond?'

"'And the emerald,' I added, losing no tricks.

"'Yes, yes. Everything,' she said. 'And you shall have everything. Oh, willingly, willingly.'

240

"I was a little touched, Winchelmere. She spoke from the heart. Only two people in the world could have heard her without being stirred."

"One of the two is myself," his lordship stated. "And the other?"

"Geraldi! However, it was quickly arranged after that."

"They are to give us everything for Geraldi?"

"Everything!"

"I told you," Winchelmere said, "that the game was worth the price. It will be done with in no time, and we'll be started back across the Atlantic."

"With Geraldi alive and after us," Rompier said bitterly. "By gad, Winchelmere, if he goes back to them, he must go with a slow poison working in him."

Winchelmere looked fixedly at the speaker. "Like Cromwell," he said, "you're thorough, old fellow. Nevertheless, that's an idea. What do we do next?"

"Simply get a note from Geraldi that he's alive and well. They'll pay for that note with the emerald. Then we can arrange the rest of the transfer."

# CHAPTER
# FOUR

## "The Henchman of Horus"

They went down together to find Geraldi, and they found him seated with Pedro Oñate at a little table in a corner of the patio, playing two-handed poker. Geraldi was dealing. The whisper of the cards, for one second, was like the noise of a soft wind.

"An artist, an artist," Lord Winchelmere stated as he looked on. "Geraldi, if I could have you with me, we would lead the lives of two emperors."

"As I remember," Geraldi said, looking up with a smile, "if two men claimed the empire, one of them had to be put underground. Is that right?"

Winchelmere and Rompier drew up chairs.

"Lucien has arranged everything," Winchelmere explained. "We simply begin by getting a note from you that you're alive and well treated, Geraldi. That begins things."

Geraldi nodded.

"After that," Winchelmere continued, "inside a week, we'll be able to hand you over to them as safe and as sound as you are now."

The widow of Strozzi came out into the patio, saw them, and cried out: "There's blood on the hand of every man of you, if you make him a friend. Do you hear, Lucien? There is blood on your hand!" She screamed at them in such a terrible voice that the Frenchman started halfway from the table and then slowly lowered himself back into his place.

"You're talking like a great fool!" he said roughly. "We're bargaining now for your widow's portion."

"I don't want money!" she cried. She ran at them with a clenched hand above her head. "I don't want blood money. I want that he should die, as my poor Giovanni died! I want . . ."

Lord Winchelmere raised his hand. "You'd better go back to your work," he said. "We're very busy here, *signora*"

She gave him the blackest of bitter looks, but he prevailed upon her, and she went back slowly under the arches, stopping now and then to stab them with her glance of hatred.

"What would your first payment be?" asked Geraldi.

"The emerald," Lord Winchelmere replied frankly.

"You get the emerald for a note written by me?"

"Yes."

"Then you return me to them safe and sound, and for that, I suppose, you get the box of golden Horus and the yellow diamond? Is that it?"

"Of course."

"Good people, aren't they?" Geraldi commented heartily. "What am I to them? But they'll give up a fortune to ransom me.

"Aye," said Winchelmere, "and so we've brought this little squabble to an end. But before we go any further,

Geraldi, I want to know if you can't come to terms of truce with the rest of us?"

"To give up the trail, you mean?"

"You see how it has come out before," insisted the Englishman. "Very heavy odds against you, old fellow, and, though I know you're as gritty as steel, you see what happens when the odds are so long?"

Geraldi nodded.

"Then we'll make a double bargain, Geraldi."

"For what purpose, Winchelmere?"

"That you and I come to an end of this argument, my dear fellow. It never can bring any good to either of us. I don't want your blood. Why should you want mine?"

"I want to remind you," Geraldi said cheerfully, "of a little picture that I once saw."

"Ah!" his lordship whispered. He seemed enormously pleased by the turn that the talk had taken. For that matter, Oñate and Rompier were not a whit less happy and looked at each other with every indication of enormous relief.

"It was the picture of a rather oldish fellow . . . forty-five or fifty, say. With all the lines of work and brains in his face, you know. The sight of him running forward through the evening, with his hands thrown out before him like a happy soul about to rush into the gates of heaven. And before him a nearly naked man with a loincloth about his hips, and a headdress of a sham Egyptian style over his head, and his whole body glowing like burning gold. I remember that picture, your lordship. I suppose that you were the one who painted it?"

Winchelmere thrust his chair back from the table, intensely disappointed. "You're as bitter as a starved dog, Geraldi," he declared.

"You did the trick, of course," insisted Geraldi. "What was it? A sort of phosphorus that you rubbed on him? And the man it was rubbed on was Kalam, of course."

"We'll talk no more about it," Winchelmere stated emphatically.

"Certainly not," Geraldi agreed bitterly. "We'll simply speak of another thing . . . that same man, an honorable, kind, and upright fellow, lying flat in the dark of the trees with a knife wound . . . in his back. In his back, Winchelmere! In his back!" He repeated it over and over, hardly above a whisper, and his dark eyes drifted softly from face to face.

They grew dreadfully uncomfortable. They shifted in their places and stared at him, at the ground, at the sky. Winchelmere sat with lips stiffened to a straight line.

"That man," persisted Geraldi, "was my friend. He was with me. He had saved my life that same day. And I've registered a little oath between me and whatever gods there are, that I'll have satisfaction for that death. Five times over, Winchelmere."

"You talk," the Englishman said, "rather like a braggart. I won't be broad enough to say like a fool."

"Look," Geraldi said, leaning back in his chair. "You are confident now. You have me. Well, we shall see in the end."

"Forget all this argument," Winchelmere declared. "You can be as vindictive as you please. As for Ingall, after all, he stole the thing in Egypt."

"It's not true," answered Geraldi. "He found it. He took it away, we have reason to believe, simply because he wanted to restore it to what it ought to be, before he offered the proper share to the government of Egypt."

"Very well," Rompier interjected. "Why the dickens do we have to argue about it still? Finish the bargain, Winchelmere, and then let Geraldi do his worst. We won't be sitting with our hands folded in the meantime. We'll be up and stirring a bit in the interim, I expect. Is that right, friends?"

"It's right," Oñate answered, who had remained quiet until now. He was a Mexican, but he looked rather Japanese. He was always smiling, his face rising to a lump over either cheek bone, compelled by the smile, and his eyes lost except for slant glints of obscure light that came out now and then. At this point, he was looking fixedly at Geraldi.

"Coming back to the present business, then," Winchelmere said, white with anger, "I ask you simply to write a note telling Miss Mary Ingall, or Miss Emily Ingall, that you are alive and that you are well. I don't suppose that you grudge starting the ball rolling? Not if you're as keen to be free and start on our trail, knife in hand, as I think you are."

He spoke half sneeringly, and Geraldi answered: "You show the defect of greatness, Lord Winchelmere. The defect of greatness is too much logic. Open your

246

mind a little, my lord. Open your mind, and then you will see why I can't do this."

"You can't do this?" Winchelmere echoed, breathing hard.

"You can't do this?" Oñate, too, repeated, his smile beginning to have a terrible significance.

"How could I?" Geraldi asked.

"Suppose you try to explain?" requested Rompier, his face discolored with his fury.

"Why, my friend, I am in the hands of a god," Geraldi explained. "How could I betray him?"

"He's out of his head," suggested Oñate.

"I suppose I understand," Winchelmere said. "You mean to say that you're in the service of old Horus, and that you can't betray him, and help to lure one of his jewels back to us . . . to say nothing of the whole box . . . and the yellow diamond. Is that what you mean?"

"You *have* an imagination," Geraldi said, "once it has been properly stimulated."

"I don't believe that this is your real answer," Rompier insisted. "You're not going to force us to cut your throat like a pig in a slaughterhouse."

"No, no," said Geraldi. "I never shall die like that."

"What assures you of that?" Winchelmere asked curiously.

"I'm glad to tell you. The protection of the god, Lord Winchelmere. Horus, golden Horus of the two horizons, the creator of life, who shines in the double forehead of the night and the morning . . ."

"Rubbish!" cried his lordship. "Do you expect us to listen to such frightful rot?"

"Ah, Winchelmere, is that all you call it?"

"I'm going to be short with you, Geraldi. I'll ask you to say yes or no. Will you let Miss Ingall know that you're safe with us?"

"By no means!"

"Then," Rompier hissed through his teeth, "I think I'll have the cutting of that throat!"

"Shall I tell you, Rompier, what the god reveals to me?" Geraldi asked.

"Tell me, then. By heaven, I *do* think that his brain is gone."

"Simply this . . . that one by one they are going down. Not all at one stroke. Giovanni Strozzi is dead. The rest will only go by degrees. I am sorry for you. By one and one you go down. Oñate, Rompier, Kalam, the thief . . . and finally his lordship, Winchelmere. One by one, as sacrifices, shall I say, to golden Horus, Horus of the double sun . . ." He smiled faintly as he spoke.

The others rose and left the table in horror.

"I've a mind to finish him, madman that he is," the savage Rompier snarled.

"Hush, hush," Oñate ordered. "See him laugh. See him laugh."

For Geraldi lolled in his chair and silently laughed.

"As if he were in heaven," Rompier said, grinding his teeth.

"He *is* in heaven," Winchelmere stated slowly. "He's in a paradise of swords."

# CHAPTER
# FIVE

## "Four Men Plan"

They convened in the room of Winchelmere — Oñate, Rompier, his lordship, and Kalam, the Egyptian.

"He refuses to send the note," Winchelmere began. "He probably would refuse to go with us and be saved. Seyf, suppose you speak first and tell us what we'll have to do?"

Seyf Kalam made a gesture with both hands, palms out. His sallow face was not altered as he spoke, except that the strange, archaic smile of old Egypt always was on it.

"I have no voice," Seyf stated. "I lost it when I was taken by Geraldi, and my life bought off for the price of an emerald. A high price for a man like me. But whatever the rest of you decide, I am ready to do. I now have a double price to pay." Seyf Kalam smiled.

Lord Winchelmere listened attentively. "We've agreed to that," he said. "If this consummate demon Geraldi manages to take one of us, we are to ransom the lost man, if we can, at the price of one of the stones. We began with the four emeralds and the golden box. Strozzi is dead. Seyf has been captured and has lost his right to one stone. There remain three emeralds. I have one," Winchelmere said, fondling his pipe with stronger fingers, "and Oñate has another."

The Mexican sat with crossed legs. He nodded dreamily, and stroked with absent-minded unconcern the spurred heel of his left shoe.

"Rompier has the third," said his lordship. "Our fat friend is now off on scouting business for all of us, and, when he comes back, no doubt he'll want to have one of the stones in his own keeping."

"He can whistle for it, if you mean Edgar," Rompier said.

"When he comes back," insisted Winchelmere, "we'll have to match to see who gives a stone to Edgar. He's earned it, I should say. But, mind you, these emeralds are only in our keeping, individually, and, when they're sold, the profits are divided equally among all hands."

"Five shares," Oñate grumbled, "out of three stones."

"If we had the yellow diamond," Rompier remarked, "I tell you that we'd have a fat share for each of the five of us that are left. But there is no hope of getting the diamond."

"We'll have it," Winchelmere insisted, "before three days are out."

"By turning in Geraldi for the stone?"

"And the box," Winchelmere added. "We'll have a clean sweep or nothing at all. The box, the fourth emerald, and the diamond are the ransoms for Geraldi. And she'll pay it."

"And how are we to get Geraldi down to San Felice?"

**250**

"Tied in a sack in the tail of a buckboard, if necessary," said his lordship. "Rompier, suppose you go down to the village and try to get us a buckboard there, and a span of horses."

"Is there no other way of persuading him?" Kalam asked.

"It is hard to make him do things. I have been in his hands, my friends."

"He'll consent to nothing to save his own hide," answered Oñate.

"He's touched with madness . . . more than touched," Rompier declared. "Who could understand a brain like his?"

"I think I understand him perfectly," answered Winchelmere. "It is simply this way with Geraldi. He needs sensation . . . a great sensation. After all, there are millions of sensationalists in the world, and they all abuse themselves. They extract pleasure out of their nerves by putting a strain on them. There's the drunkard. He drinks not the pleasure of the liquor, but to drug his brain with the fumes of alcohol. He loves to feel his reason tottering. There is the glutton who stuffs himself to bursting for the mere pleasure of feeling that he has overburdened his stomach to the point of nausea . . . and still he can eat more than a normal man. There is the drug fiend. He has to have his breath of snuff now and then . . . or opium and a sleep full of good dreams."

"And Geraldi's like that?" sneered Rompier. "He eats no more than a greyhound. He hardly touches liquor. Certainly he never touches drugs."

"Geraldi is like the others," Winchelmere insisted. "He is a glutton, and what he eats is danger. To be under cover of a loaded gun is an exquisite pleasure to him. I know a man who hunted with Geraldi, and he said that Geraldi's one great delight was in pushing into thick brush after a wounded lion. Once, in the twilight, they gave up a lion that had slipped into a deep cave. Afterward, they missed Geraldi. Common sense had told him to give up the hunt, just as it had warned the others. But the picture grew up in his brain, clearer and more clear . . . to slip into that cave, to crawl along, feeling his way. At last to flash an electric torch and try to finish the big beast . . ." The speaker paused. The others were watching with large eyes. "He didn't take his heavy rifle. It would have been too clumsy. He went back armed with a single-action Colt, such as he uses here. He worked into that cave, and the lion winded him and charged. Geraldi was half drowned by the roar of the brute, but he flashed on his light and fanned six shots into the king of beasts in a second or so. When the others arrived, having heard the uproar, they found that all six of those shots were in the head of the lion. But he wouldn't have been killed if it hadn't been that one bullet by luck crashed through an eye and found the brain. Otherwise, we'd be having no Geraldi to bother us here. And that, you see, is Geraldi.

"For my part, I wouldn't be in his boots for all the wealth of Midas. He never knows when he may be over-mastered by some strong impulse to attempt the impossible. Danger is the air he breathes and the food he eats. But just as the drunkard wakes up some night

252

and feels the craving in his blood, and fights against it, and prays that he can resist but at last finds himself getting out of bed to dress . . . so Geraldi must wake up in the night and feel the spur and fight against it, and at last get up to try some terrible, some impossible adventure."

"I think that's true," Rompier agreed. "For instance, he's essentially an honest man. But he's equipped himself to cheat at cards, at dice, and to fight like a tiger with any weapon. Simply so that he may be where danger is. I can see that in him."

"They tell a tale of him in Cairo," Kalam began. "He had a great enemy there . . . a jealous man . . . a gambler, who decided to get Geraldi out of the way. So he laid his plot, hired his killers, and sent an invitation to Geraldi to come and sit in at a friendly game of cards. One of the hired men played double . . . went to Geraldi and warned him. And what did Geraldi do?"

"He would go to the place, anyway," Winchelmere said.

Kalam opened his slant eyes wider. "You've heard the story before, then?"

"No, never before."

"But that was what happened. He did actually go to the place. He sat down at the table. While they were playing, he won a good deal of money. And then, quietly, he told the story of how the man had brought the warning to him."

"It must have been a glorious fight," suggested his lordship with a nod.

"It was a great fight," Kalam affirmed. "I was there." He said no more. Perhaps he was one of the hired killers; perhaps he was the jealous man. At any rate, he knew Geraldi.

"Get the buckboard, by all means," Winchelmere said. "Go down and get it right away, Rompier. We'll start tonight or tomorrow morning. Geraldi will have to go with us, even if we have to chloroform him to take him along."

They agreed to that.

"I'll get a pair of horses to travel in harness, too?" Rompier suggested.

"Yes."

"What should I pay for a buckboard and a pair of ponies?"

"You ought to get a good buckboard for a hundred dollars, if it isn't new," said Oñate. "And ponies? Two hundred dollars for a good span. A really good brace of mustangs."

Rompier stood up. "After we get Geraldi down to San Felice," he said, ". . . and he's a long distance from San Felice now . . . how are we going to get the girl to come to him?"

"We might," Winchelmere proposed, "carry Geraldi in a sack straight into the hotel and leave him there in her room. She'd pay over the goods to us . . . she's already promised."

"Trust the word of a woman?" the Mexican asked sharply.

"Of that woman . . . yes," his lordship replied.

254

"I," Oñate said, "never would do it. Still, I think that this is going to be an adventure that we will all remember."

"Not all of us," put in Kalam softly.

"Now, what do you mean by that?" Lucien Rompier asked.

"Ah, well," Kalam said, "it is only a thought that came over my mind, and there is no good in making my friends unhappy because of it."

"We'll hear it," Winchelmere coaxed.

"Well, then," Kalam continued, "it occurred to me that some of us will die before the golden box and the diamond are in our hands."

Shoulders were shrugged uneasily.

"What the hell put that into your mind?" asked Winchelmere with a frown.

"Your own words," Kalam answered.

"What words?"

"I can tell you that, too. When Geraldi laughed in the patio, did you not say as you came away that Geraldi was living in a paradise of swords?"

"I may have said something like that . . . with a figurative meaning, of course."

"Ah, of course. But in a paradise of swords, men must die, must they not?"

# CHAPTER
# SIX

## "Pepillo Grows Up"

Many strands began to be woven into the fate of James Geraldi, so that it is necessary to take them up one by one, and to begin at this point with San Luis, that noble goat whose courage was so resistless, whose strength was, indeed, as the strength of ten.

It has been said that the precinct of Pepillo, the mountain lion, was limited to the house, and that the patio was the neutral ground on which the two rivals met upon amicable terms. But surely it could not be said that fear of Pepillo for a single moment kept San Luis from the interior of the house. It was rather a series of kicks and whacks that he had received on his ribs and back during the period of his more sensitive youth that had convinced him, unwillingly, that it was not wise to pass the threshold of the house. Convinced of this, he philosophically gave up that whole region.

But if he had to give up the house, he tried to make sure that Pepillo had given up the great outdoors. His superiority over Pepillo had been established during the kittenhood of the lion. And, as size and strength came to Pepillo, a few times he had used his claws on the goat — always with terrible results to himself. For the goat could charge with the suddenness and almost the inescapable speed of a cannonball, and at the first sign of anger on the part of Pepillo, San Luis's head went down — that head of iron, armed almost unnecessarily with two huge, backward-bending horns — and the goat drove himself in a compact ball of combative courage straight at the enemy.

Once he had cornered Pepillo and almost smashed his ribs. Once, really horrible to relate, he had butted Pepillo full upon the end of his sensitive nose, and caused it to bleed for endless hours, and made it swell up to gigantic proportions. From that moment, Pepillo surrendered all thought of fighting with the white streak of danger. When San Luis put down his head and pawed the ground like an angry bull, Pepillo glanced around with wild, yellow eyes and sought a means of retreat.

All cats, great and small, are cowards at heart. Perhaps the leopard or the black panther are exceptions. But in no cat is there the glorious desire of combat for the sake of combat, such as stirs in the heart of a fighting dog, say — or of a goat.

Despite his growing bulk, therefore, despite the fact that he now had sufficient power in his supple paw and forearm to smash the skull of San Luis or to rip out his ribs at a stroke, Pepillo never forgot those first two lessons, and he cringed when he saw the enemy. Nevertheless, it was hard for him to be cooped up in the house. There was much to be gained by venturing out into the nearby fields and the hills. He knew, for instance, all the arts of catching field mice — scraping up their habitations, buried shallowly under the surface of the ground. He was beginning to know the runs of the rabbits, and he had acquired the patience of his kind in waiting for a kill. For he had learned that one mouthful of wild-caught game is better than pounds and pounds of the butcher's choicest cuts. Rich in this knowledge, Pepillo began patiently to work up the possibilities of the territory around the house, full of squirrels, rabbits, mice, and — now and then — a chance-caught dog, as it strayed up from the village and went sniffing through the brush.

So Pepillo grew stronger and warier and more intelligent. For he was entering upon that business of life for which instinct and a million generations of his ancestors had fitted him.

But there were embarrassing moments. Once, when he was returning to the house, licking his whiskers, terrible San Luis had come upon him and bumped him so heartily that every one of Pepillo's ribs gave under the pressure, and he rolled over and over. Before he could gain his feet there was another back-breaking thud, and Pepillo leaped up with a howl and fled screeching up a tree. There he lay on a branch for hours, his eyes burning green with fear and yellow with rage, while San Luis insolently grazed beneath the tree, or lay down to chew his reflective cud. It was not until Bianca Strozzi came out and drove San Luis away, with shouts of laughter, that Pepillo ventured down to the ground and then fled away for the house with gigantic leaps.

Now, on this fatal day of days, Pepillo had watched San Luis leave the patio. Afterward, a scent of distant game came faintly to the nostrils of the great cat, and in his heart stirred the love of hunting. He would not go out the patio gate. That would be inviting danger at once. Instead, he sneaked through the house and, through a lower window, sprang out onto the bank beneath, and so off through the brush until he came out into the open at the rear of the barn. There he crouched a moment, turning his big round head from side to side, searching everywhere with his yellow eyes. But there was no sight of San Luis, and there was no scent of him.

At last, contented, Pepillo ventured perilously forth. He always had been interested in the bottom rim of the barn, where the moisture of the earth had rotted the boards. But at this particular spot, there was a sort of blind alley. That is to say, the harness shed jutted out on the one side and the tangled and dangerous mass of a heap of ruined thorns arose on the other. Between the two, there was a narrow entrance, and this opening spread out generously along the base of the barn.

To this spot Pepillo came and hesitated, lashing his sides with his long tail, and cursing San Luis as only a cat can curse. Delightful fragrance, at that moment, assailed him from the barn. With all his heart he yearned to investigate carefully that lower rim of decayed wood with his sharp, steel-hard, and steel-bright claws. But, once entered into the natural trap, what if terrible San Luis should come in pursuit and block up all means of escape? The heart of Pepillo failed within him. He turned and hastened back to the brush, but, once there, he was haunted by the memory of that fragrance that meant meat, not plentiful, but young and tender.

At last all the hair of his back bristling, he started up and went boldly forward. The thing should be finished quickly. One stroke or two. And then he would spring back out of the trap . . . With beating heart he slunk to the edge of the barn, and a single stroke, as of half a dozen strong chisels, ripped the rotten wood away. Two nests of mice were revealed, and their squeals were extinguished first under the paw and then in the teeth of Pepillo. There was still a frantic squeaking of fear — music to the cruel ears of Pepillo. He sniffed; he strove to look. Somewhere, in a crevice between two beams, a full-sized mouse was trembling in an attempt to get at more perfect cover. With tentative paw, Pepillo reached under, fumbled, failed. He tried again, and this time one of his natural knives touched something incredibly soft and yielding. There was a pitiful shriek of fear, another of mortal agony as the knife blade was driven through the body of the mouse. Then Pepillo drew out his paw carefully and looked down with pleasure at the small impaled body, still writhing. He licked it off with relish, and then turned to flee.

Behold, blocking the entrance, was San Luis! With dread malice, the goat pretended not to see, and, half turned away, he was cropping the grass. But his eyes were blood-red, and Pepillo knew in every thrilling fiber of his body what that meant. He shrank back against the wall of the barn. At that, San Luis advanced a step or two. Innocent interest was in his bearing. But he shook his head a little, as though feeling with pleasure the weight of his horns.

Pepillo frantically turned and leaped up against the wall of the barn. His huge claws sank into the wood, but this was too old and weak to bear the weight, and down he slid, spitting with fear and fury. He turned about, his tail swishing from side to side, desperation in his eyes. There was no escape, and the courage of the frightened arose in the frozen heart of Pepillo. He would fight, because instinct said that it was better to fight and die than to surrender weakly.

San Luis advanced still farther, lowered his head, crouched a little. The strong muscles of his legs quivered with preparedness for the sudden, furious charge. And up the nose of Pepillo to his very eyes sharp pains of reminiscence were darting. San Luis charged! Like a white arrow from the bow he drove at the big cat, and Pepillo stood up on his hind legs with a cry of fear and struck out like a pugilist.

The blow landed on the side of San Luis's head. It came with a little less force than a grizzly could have used, but it was sufficient to fling the goat upon his side, utterly stunned, and with his cheek torn to shreds. Pepillo looked down as upon a miracle. He could not believe that the terrible, hard head of San Luis had proved as soft as this. But there was blood on his paw, blood on San Luis — and the goat lay helplessly upon his side, making faint, vague movements of his legs as though striving in vain, instinctively, to regain his feet.

It was enough for the big cat. Instantly, its teeth were in the throat of San Luis, and one brave life was ended.

No sense of guilt oppressed this murderer. He ate as never he had eaten before. Then he lay in the sun and cleaned himself. Finally he crept off into the brush and found a cool shadowy nook, and slept. But all through his sleep his ears were twitching. He would drive his claws suddenly into the earth and his yellow eyes would open, hungry in his dreams for another such kill. At last Pepillo had grown up.

# CHAPTER
# SEVEN

## "A Precious Pair"

While Pepillo slept in the woods with crimson stains on his velvet breast, Lucien Rompier at last had left the house. Hardly had he mounted a horse and started down the road toward the village than he was aware of a fat man riding up the slope toward him, mounted on a stout mule, and playing a guitar with considerable skill while he sang in a rich, baritone voice.

Rompier grinned with pleasure as he watched him, and, concealing himself in some high brush, he rode out suddenly with a shout when the fat man was a few yards away.

The latter at the first stir had dropped the guitar, allowing it to be supported by the sling that ran around his neck, and slipping down behind the neck of his horse with a wonderful agility — considering his bulk and his years — he covered Rompier with a Colt.

The Frenchman merely laughed and threw up his hands in mock surrender. "You've beaten me, Edgar," he confessed.

The fat man heaved himself up in the saddle again with a groan of effort. "You nearly laughed yourself into a bullet through the heart," he said. "I've been practicing, Lucien, and must admit that I shoot a little straighter than I used to."

That possibility Rompier admitted with a smile. "What have you done on your trip, and how are things in San Felice?" he asked.

"Sweeter than honey." Asprey grinned, shifting the guitar into his hands again, and fingering it softly as he spoke. "Everything goes well. I go up to report to General Winchelmere."

"Will you tell me what you found, Edgar?"

"I had to go cautiously," the fat man said. "The day has come when I can mask my face, but I can't mask my stomach. However, I managed to get fairly close to San Felice and finally into it. I saw both the women, and I was satisfied. The older one is as hard as steel, still. She would fight things out to the bitter end, you can be sure. But the younger one is tired of life. She's in love, Rompier. It's like seeing a woman in love with a tiger in the jungles. Why should the pretty little fool fall in love with Geraldi? But she's in love. She's grown pale. Her eyes are hollow. She starts at every shadow. Only," he added, "on the last day before I started, she seemed to have regained a little life. I actually heard her singing."

"Because she had seen me," Rompier stated.

"You?"

"I'd been there before you, Edgar," the Frenchman said with satisfaction. "Do you think that a clever fellow like our Winchelmere would have given such a job as that to one man only? Certainly not. He sent the pair of us. You looked at the ladies. I talked to them."

264

"I congratulate you," Asprey said with no apparent jealousy. "I couldn't try the same thing. They both know me. My voice would be a poison in their ears. You, old fellow, you arranged everything?"

"I did my best," Rompier confirmed. "I'm going down to the village now to buy a buckboard and a pair of horses. Geraldi refuses to be fairly exchanged against the box and the diamond and the emerald. We have to bundle him up and take him down by force."

"I'll go with you," Asprey said. "Tell me everything as we go along."

They journeyed down the hillside, and Rompier told the details of the singular conversation between Geraldi and the rest, and the conclusion of the argument with Geraldi's derision of them all and of their plans.

"If I were Winchelmere," said the fat man with much earnestness, "even if I had to give up the golden box and the jewels, I'd put a bullet through the head of Geraldi and think that the richest day's work that I'd ever done."

"You've double-crossed Geraldi," the Frenchman said rather brutally, "and he may be out for your scalp. But we can manage to keep away from him afterwards."

"I double-crossed Geraldi," Asprey admitted frankly and without shame. "But I'm the last one that he'll go after. First, he has to settle the account of the man who lured poor Ingall into the woods . . . that's the Egyptian . . . then the man that knifed Ingall from behind, and that man is . . ."

"Be quiet," Lucien Rompier hissed. "You talk like a fool . . . or a woman."

265

The fat man smiled. "You agree with me in your heart," he observed. "And you're right, Lucien. He'll have you in the end for letting your knife run into Ingall. And, of course, when that's done, he'll want Oñate on general principles, and he'll be sure to take after Winchelmere as the choicest morsel of all, because Winchelmere engineered the general scheme of things. After I hear that the last of you is dead, Lucien, then I'll begin to worry about the security of my own head."

Rompier regarded him with a savage silence. Suddenly he said: "You're right, Edgar. We ought to do it. We really ought to do away with Geraldi now that we have our hands on him. But Winchelmere never would consent to that. And you hardly can blame him. The price of Geraldi is the golden box, man, and the diamond and the emerald. Winchelmere reckons that the price of the diamond alone would be a hundred thousand pounds."

The fat man whistled, until his brown cheeks distended, and his fat chin quivered with emotion.

They rode on in the sun. Before them the village appeared, one winding street, partially fenced in with houses on either side.

"How are you people keeping Geraldi?"

"Like a king. Giving him everything."

"You'll be giving him the keys of the house, too," the fat man said in alarm.

"No fear of that. There was no killing him with confinement in the cellar. We keep him there from dark to dawn. But when the day begins, we turn him loose and let him walk about the patio."

**266**

"Damn!" Asprey cried, shaken quite from his philosophy. "You let him go free in the patio?"

"Not exactly free. We keep a pair of riflemen watching him, a pair of trusty men who'd as soon shoot out the whites of his eyes as not."

"He'll cut their throats . . . he'll cut their throats!" exclaimed the fat man, actually stopping his horse, so strongly had consternation seized on him. "He'll kill them and take their horses to ride away on."

The Frenchman nodded. "Possible, but not likely," he said. "We're guarding him in another way. We made a bargain with him. Every day he's to sit out there, but only if he'll give us his word of honor that he won't attempt to escape during the day."

Asprey mopped his red, streaming forehead. "You gave me a frightful shock," he said. "Damn, Rompier, you've shortened my life ten years with the shock that you gave me. I tell you, man . . . it was terrible! But this is better. If you have his word, of course, that will do." He paused and looked up to the pale, sun-whitened blue of the sky. "Because," he continued, "I know that man, and I know that he'll never break his word of honor. And isn't it strange, Rompier, that a man no better than you or I will keep his promise like a priest . . . while we would break an oath for the sale of picking a beggar's pocket?"

"You speak for yourself," Rompier ordered.

"Ah, well," — smiled Asprey — "there's always a limit to French honesty, as I've found before. Even a French thief feels, in his heart of hearts, that he's a noble fellow." He laughed, and went on playing the guitar, while his sides shook with contented mirth at his own thought.

Rompier favored him with the most savage side glance, and so they rode into the town in a far from amiable humor. They inquired where they could find a buckboard and a few horses for sale, and the blacksmith, whom they asked, left his forge and came out, wiping his hands futilely on his leather apron.

"You want a bang-up, good-as-new buckboard?" he asked.

"We want a sound rig," Asprey stated, "and it doesn't have to be new-painted, as far as that goes."

"What's paint?" asked the blacksmith with generous emotion. "Paint don't count. You want the good hickory . . . that's the main thing."

"And a spring or two?" Asprey added cheerfully.

"Springs?" the blacksmith repeated. "I never went in for them none. They don't save nothin' but wear on the seat of the pants, and, if your pants wear out there, you can put a patch on 'em, can't you?"

His grin made Asprey chuckle in a deep, cheerful voice. "Of course, we can. Let's go over and have a look at this buckboard that you're talking about. Who owns it?"

"I do myself, you'd be surprised to hear," said the blacksmith.

"I am surprised," Asprey declared.

"I'll show you the way," said the other. "Ride down the street and turn in at the first lane on the right. The first pasture gate is my place. I'll be waitin' for you there."

"Leave everything to me," Asprey said, as the two rode on. "I understand these people. I'll get it for half the price, and I'll have the fun of beating him down. I tell you what . . . even a Scotchman can't make money out of a Yankee." He struck a loud chord on his guitar, and he began to sing in his strong, clear voice, full of unction, rich with rhythm.

"You do the talking and the bargaining, then," Rompier said. "I was told I could pay a hundred for the buckboard and a hundred for each of the two ponies."

"Robbery," Asprey spit.

"All right," said the Frenchman. "Get them as cheap as you can. But mind that you don't talk more than you have to. That's *your* weakness, Edgar."

# CHAPTER
# EIGHT

## "A Horse Deal"

The blacksmith did not go straight to his little farm or to the gate that opened onto it. He went on the run, to be sure, for he stopped at the side of a house not far away — a modest little house, screened behind a few young poplars.

"Hey!" called the blacksmith.

A woman put her head out the window. She rested her sewing on the sill.

"How are you, Billy?"

"I'm fine," he replied. "Where's the sheriff?"

"He's in the back room, havin' a bit of a snooze."

"Wake him up, will you? One of them fellers is come down from the Oñate place. The sheriff said that he wanted to have us let him know the next time that some of 'em come around."

"I'll fetch him right away," the sheriff's wife said. "But he's sure enjoyin' a good enough snooze. Listen, would you, how he's snorin'."

The blacksmith, uninterested in the heartless manner of men, simply added: "Tell him to hurry. There's a pair of 'em come to buy my buckboard. Maybe I can sell them the buckboard and then use it for cartin' them off to the jail." He chuckled in appreciation of this brilliant possibility, and so he turned and struck off at a run again, covering the ground rapidly, for his legs were both strong and long. He took a pair offences in full stride, and he came to the pasture gate and already was opening it when Rompier and Asprey walked their horses into view.

"Look at him panting," Rompier laughed, as they rode through the gate. "You'll have an easy job to make a bargain out of him, Edgar. He's keen to sell . . . very sharp to sell."

Billy, the blacksmith, closed the gate and ran the bolt home into the guard. He remarked cheerfully that the weather was turning hot even for this season of the year, and then he hurried ahead to get to the wagon shed before them.

"We're not as hot as he is," Asprey said, a little more sober. "He hasn't run all the way simply to come here. Where has the fellow gone?

"Nonsense," Rompier said, "you'd suspect a shadow in the clouds."

"I would if there were no sun in sight," said the fat man. "I don't like the look of that fellow. But we've got to have a buckboard."

The door of the wagon shed was pushed open, and the blacksmith pulled the buckboard out. It was, as he had said in the first place, not at all distinguished for its appearance. The paint had been boiled off its wheels and its body by the bitter strength of the summer suns, and, in addition, at least half the top of the leather cushion on the driver's seat was gone, and the horsehair stuffing protruded.

Asprey and his companion dismounted, and Asprey took the wheels one by one and shook them — violently, and then with care. All of them rattled.

"The nuts, they need to be screwed up a little," Billy suggested, gone anxious in a moment.

"Yes," Asprey agreed dryly, "they need to be screwed up a little. It might be quicker to put on new wheels, though." He finished his survey of the running gear, the shafts — marked with long cracks in the withered surface of the hickory — and even the bottom of the bed of the buckboard.

"Well, sir," Billy said with a rather forced good cheer, "what do you think of her?"

"I should say," Asprey replied, "that a man never would be lonely in the buckboard."

"No?" Billy said, willing to be pleased by every favorable comment. "And Why do you say that?"

"Because it would always be talking to the driver."

"A little rattling, what does that matter?" Billy asked. "The kind of roads that we got around here, how could a buggy help but rattle pretty quick? Joe Shaw, he got a swell rubber-tired buggy two years ago. It's all gone now. The kind of roads that we got, they're something awful. But this here . . . you take my word for it, she'll hang together. Look at her . . . strong, she is." He illustrated his words with a bit of proof, giving the near forewheel a tremendous jerk. The buckboard groaned and stirred, but the wheel remained upright. "Look here, those wheels they all track as straight as a string,"

Billy argued. He pulled the buckboard farther out as he did so, and demonstrated that what he said was true. The wheels, indeed, traveled in straight lines, with little wobbling.

"What would you want for that?" Asprey asked.

"Want for it? She cost a hundred and eighty-five, new," Billy lied thoughtfully.

"Listed at ninety-eight fifty, brand new!" Asprey retorted.

"Ninety-eight, your hat!" Billy shouted, red with honest indignation. "If I didn't pay a hundred eighteen . . ." He stopped. He saw he had been trapped. He despised himself and hated the smiling fat man. "And then I had a lot of extras that come to the hundred and eighty-five," he added, biting his lip and turning sullen.

"I could throw away twenty-five dollars on the old rattletrap," Asprey said. "Not a penny more."

"Twenty . . . ?" began the blacksmith. And then he broke into bitterly satirical laughter. "Well, good bye, gents," he said, and picked up the shafts, preparatory to backing it into the shed. "Ninety dollars for to be givin' this here away," he declared.

"I might raise to thirty," Asprey offered, "but that's all!"

"You been raised in a hoss country. It's plain that you don't know rigs," Billy said. "Ask anybody . . . ask anybody in town if this ain't a good rig. They've all rode in it."

"Thirty dollars," Asprey repeated stubbornly.

The blacksmith seemed furiously endeavoring to back the buckboard into the shed, but he seemed too blind with anger to succeed. "I tell you, it would be a gift at seventy," he mumbled.

"Well, we'll make it half of that. Call it an even thirty-five."

"Whatcha wastin' my time for?" Billy asked. "I'm a busy man, even if you ain't." He added: "I'd be robbin' myself, if I took a penny under fifty dollars for it. But for needin' money, I wouldn't think of that."

"Forty dollars," Asprey stated.

"For the sake of ma kin' a trade and bein' friendly," Billy said, "make it forty-five, and I'll give the wagon away to you."

"Come along," Asprey said to his companion. "We're wasting our time, as he says."

Suddenly Billy capitulated. "Forty it is!" he exclaimed. Then he added with a childish smile of pleasure: "I raised you fifteen, anyway."

"You would have sold it for the twenty-five," Rompier declared suspiciously.

"Sure. Or for twenty," Billy said. "It ain't been used for two years. But it's a good one. It'll never break down on you."

"And now a pair of horses?" asked the fat man.

"They're lookin' you in the eye right now," said the other, pointing toward the corral fence. "They like you, and they've sort of got an idea that you'd be wanting to take them home."

"How much for those bays?"

"You mean that fine pair over there? I was offered three hundred and twenty-five for that span last week, but I refused. But I'm in need of money, I don't mind sayin'. Seein' that you and me already have done some business, I would favor you by sellin' that pair for three hundred, partner."

Asprey rode up close to the corral fence, Rompier beside him.

The tall, gaunt figure of the sheriff emerged from behind the shed and advanced toward Billy.

"You want 'em, Sheriff?" Billy asked quietly. "For heaven's sake, wait till I sell that pair of bays, will you? They're a pair of suckers."

"That pair you bought in for seventy-five bucks?"

"They was dead pore, then. I've got 'em fatted up, them ponies." He added again, sharp with vindictive curiosity: "You want 'em, Sheriff?"

"Shut up," the impolite sheriff said. "Go on with your robbery. I'll listen."

"A hundred and a quarter for the pair," Asprey said, as the other came up.

Billy halted, shocked and hurt. "I used up all my arguing on the buckboard," he sighed. "I've given you a bottom price, stranger."

Asprey yawned. "What are they good for?"

"Look at 'em," said the blacksmith. "You never seen a finer, prettier pair of hosses in your life."

"Or jack rabbits," Asprey added. "They'd never need a stable at night. You could just cover them by throwing a coat over the span of them."

"You can have your joke," Billy said. "But quality is what counts in this here world. Besides, you look at a big hoss. He tires himself out carryin' his own weight up a hill, and he breaks his shoulders to pieces braking his own weight going down a hill. Ain't that right?"

"I suppose it is," Asprey agreed. "I wouldn't mind paying a hundred and fifty for that pair of ponies, though."

"I'm always willing to meet a friend," declared Billy. "We could make it two hundred and fifty."

"Might I?" Asprey said. "I tell you, man, that span is not worth more than a hundred and seventy-five at the outside. Ask your long, skinny friend if I'm not right. You probably picked them up from Gypsies for fifty dollars the pair. But I'm willing to be liberal."

He had motioned toward the sheriff, and the latter now stood up and removed from his mouth the straw that he had been chewing with blank, bovine eyes. "I got no very good ideas about hosses," he said. "And I wouldn't know within a hundred dollars."

"Hold on," Billy protested in a panic. "I'll take a hundred and seventy-five."

"And harness?"

"For fifty more . . ."

"Two hundred for horses and harness?"

"You're grinding me down," Billy said, a grin of pleasure, nevertheless, breaking through in spite of himself. "I'll close with you, though."

"But about men," the sheriff said, "I'm kind of curious. Some of them have a price on 'em, you know."

# CHAPTER
# NINE

## "On the Subject of Fishing"

Up to this point, the fat man had been relishing the bargaining. Now, as he heard this ominous speech from the lean, uncouth stranger, he did not turn his head, but he looked straight at Rompier, and the Frenchman looked back at him. There was much meaning in that exchange of glances.

"Some come cheap," went on the man of the law, "and some are high-priced. If you can get the cheap ones whole-sale, it's pretty good. But if you got a chance to catch even one of the high-priced ones, it's worth a gross of the small fry."

"Are you a manhunter?" Rompier asked.

"A fisher, you might say," corrected the sheriff. "I angle for 'em. Sometimes I catch a few." He was looking over the distant hill, his eyes gentle with meditation, puckering to see his own thoughts.

"And what sort of bait do you use?" Asprey asked, having finished paying the blacksmith for the wagon, horses, and harness.

"It ain't the bait that counts," the sheriff replied. "It's the way that you handle it."

"There's a best way, of course," Asprey said.

"Of course, there is," replied the sheriff. "Sometimes you lower into the water without raisin' a ripple, and sometimes you gotta throw the hook in with a splash. It all depends upon the kind of fish, and what it'll rise to."

"I can understand that, in a way," said Asprey. "But what sort of fish do you mostly go after?"

"Oh, any kind," the sheriff replied. "So long as they got a name. A fish that's got a name for being hard to catch is the kind that I like to try. Sometimes they're lean. Sometimes they're fat. Sometimes little and sometimes big. You never can tell what'll interest me, as long as there's a name attached."

"You never go after suckers, I suppose?" the fat man pursued, still wonderfully genial.

"Why, I wouldn't have 'em," said the sheriff. "If I get one of 'em, I pick it off the hook and chuck it back into the water. You never can tell. The sort of streams that I fish, sometimes the softest sucker in the world will turn into the hardest-boiled kind of game fish." He shook his head in innocent wonder.

Rompier began to back his horse, and so reached a position at a little distance and on the farther side of the sheriff. At that, the latter squared himself on the fence. He looked straight before him, but it was plain that he was keeping both men covered from the tail of his eye. At this moment, if either of the criminals had had any doubt as to the character of the gaunt stranger, it was removed by a little gust of wind that opened the sheriff's coat and allowed them to see a tarnished steel shield attached inside the lapel.

278

"All right, all right," said Asprey. "I'd like to see you fishing one of these days."

"And maybe you will," the sheriff replied, "because, as I was sayin', sometimes I play for lean fish, and sometimes I play for fat ones."

Here he let his glance flash toward the fat Asprey, and the latter could not help changing color a trifle.

"We'll have to get on," Rompier announced.

"We will," Asprey agreed. He could not help adding for the sheriff: "I hope you have luck with your fishing, stranger. Big or little, lean or fat, I hope that you're able to fill your hamper. What sort of fish do you want today?"

"I want the bribery an' corruption fish," the sheriff responded innocently.

"That's sort of speckled, isn't it? Like a trout?" asked Asprey.

"It is, but it ain't fit for no white man's table."

"Well," the fat man said, "what do you do with it when it's caught?"

"Cut the head off and feed it to the dogs," the sheriff replied with a strange little undertone of metallic hardness in his voice.

"Feed it to the dogs . . . but not the head?" Asprey murmured, now pale, indeed.

"That's it. Because the head of it would poison even a dog."

"Well," Asprey said, "so long!"

"So long," said the sheriff.

Asprey drove the buckboard. Rompier went beside it, leading the extra horse, and so they jogged through the gate, which was held open for them by Billy, the blacksmith, his face disturbed by a leering, evil smile.

They jogged through the village.

"What does it mean?" asked Rompier.

"Is he following?"

"No."

"No sign of him?"

"Not a sign."

"Nevertheless, he's coming after us . . . drifting along through the trees, perhaps."

"What was it all about, Edgar?"

"Couldn't you hear for yourself?" he replied gruffly.

"I don't understand all the dialect. It isn't the sort of English that I've studied and lived by."

"Maybe it'll be the kind of English that you'll worry and hang by, in the finish," Asprey declared darkly. "He was working me up, Rompier. Dash him!"

"What do you mean by working up?"

"I mean to say that he wanted to make sure that I was the man he wanted, and, when he was sure of that, he decided that he would wait for a better chance to take me."

"What better chance? What do you mean, Edgar?"

"This," said the fat man. His face suddenly convulsing with rage and savagery, so that it became like a terrible mask, he caught out a revolver with wonderful speed and fired into the air. A low-flying crow wheeled barely in time. A tuft of feathers was detached and floated slowly down, and the bird flapped heavily away with a frightened cry. "I mean that," said Asprey, his teeth set.

280

"You mean," Rompier said, "that the sheriff would have arrested you if he had not been afraid that you were a quicker man with a gun and a straighter shot than he?"

"I always give even the devil his due," Asprey stated. "The man isn't alive that the old fool wouldn't tackle. It's part of his principle to make himself fight anyone in the world. But you were there, Rompier, and he knew about you, too."

"What?"

"Oh, you have a reputation, my son. And you can place your money on the fact that fisher never foolishly risks his life. One man . . . yes. Two men . . . no. Not unless he can play safe. Courage . . . but not folly. That would be his motto."

"He seems," Rompier suggested, more worried, "to be a mixture of wise man and fool."

"And why not?" Asprey asked.

"Because he threw out enough warnings to drive us both out of the country."

"Did he? You don't consider, Rompier, that he wasn't at all sure of me. He wanted to talk to me a little . . . and *make* sure."

"*Did* he make sure?"

"How could I keep my face?" asked the fat man indignantly. "A country lout, a miserable loafer, sits on a fence and begins to talk nonsense. How can I guess that fellow is the sheriff, or the deputy, at least? I had no warning. He saw in my face all that he wanted to read."

Rompier nodded. "In France they do things in a different way. They arrest a suspect first, and they question him afterwards."

"They tie the hands of the law in this country," admitted Asprey. "And a good thing for me, today, that they do. But it's time for me to move along."

"It is . . . that's plain. What did he mean about corruption and bribery?"

"It's an old story," Asprey explained. "Once I had my hand on a fortune. I could have been a very rich man. In order to play the cards correctly, I had to work the governor, and the governor happened to be an honest fool who was in the hands of his secretary. The secretary was open to reason, of course. Well . . . and there you are."

"What beat you?" asked Rompier.

Asprey turned ashen with emotion. "The Frigate Bird," he snapped.

"Ah, Geraldi."

"The same."

"That's why you hate him so thoroughly, eh?"

"I'll be the end of him, too," declared the fat man. "Stop talking, Rompier. I want to have a chance to think." His thoughts were of such a nature that Asprey was purple in the face by the time he drove the buckboard up to the patio gate of Oñate's house.

There the two riflemen nodded at the fat man.

"You've got a pair of lucky-lookin' cayuses there," one of them remarked.

"Luck?" Asprey snapped. "There's no luck bred or born in this county." He strode onto the patio, where

Pepillo lay in the sun, eyes closed, fur ruffling to let the heat soak down to his skin. His white breast was now stainless and so were his paws, which were crossed one above the other, in absurdly human fashion.

Geraldi sat in another corner, half in sun and half in shadow, invincibly idle and luxurious. The fat man smoothed his face and approached the prisoner.

# CHAPTER
# TEN

## "A Sporting Idea"

It was very close and stifling hot on the patio at this hour. The wind could not stir. It was benumbed with the sheer golden weight of the sun. From Asprey the moisture distilled into little rivulets that coursed steadily down his face.

But Geraldi, immune from the effects of temperature, was stretched in pallid coolness in his chair.

The big man lingered by him. "What do you think of, Jimmy?" he asked. "While you lie there, hour after hour, what do you think of?"

"Rats and mice and such small deer," Geraldi said, smiling.

Asprey looked at him with undisguised wonder. "You're not worried, Jimmy? They're treating you well, here?"

"Thanks to you, no doubt," Geraldi responded, still genial. "You must have put in a few good words for me."

Asprey went on into the house, whispering to himself: "Thanks to me. What's in his mind? Does he really hate me less? Who can understand him?" He climbed up the stairs to the room where Winchelmere

**284**

still lounged with his book. Asprey paused in the doorway to consider the big, handsome fellow. He recognized in him, at least, one quality like that of Geraldi — this ability to relax utterly and so, no doubt, to be prepared for every crisis as it arose. He walked in, locked the door behind him, and sat down in the window.

"You shut out the light, Asprey," Winchelmere said.

"I do," the fat man stated. "I shut out the hope, too."

"Bad news?"

"The worst. A long, lean hound of a sheriff has recognized me, and he's probably drumming up a posse at this moment to surround Oñate's place and comb it from top to bottom."

"That would make a haul for a country sheriff, wouldn't it?" murmured Winchelmere. He thumbed the pages of his book, as though anxious for Asprey to be gone.

"You understand what I say," Asprey stated. "He spotted me, and he wants me. No doubt he wants some more of you."

"What are we to do, then?" Winchelmere said.

"You won't take my advice. In fact, you don't want my advice. You've made up your mind already."

"Come, come, my dear fellow," said the younger man. "Don't think that I fail to appreciate you, Edgar. I know that you're worth all the rest of then rolled together. Of course, I want to hear what you have to say."

"Mind you, then, I mean this. I've weighed the facts. Let's get ourselves together. You already have three stones that are worth having . . . enough to reward you for your work and leave something over for us smaller fry . . ."

"Not at all," Winchelmere protested. "We split everything in equal parts."

This generosity made Asprey stare. "That's broad-minded, to say the least," he commented. "But now suppose we go a little further. Suppose we become strictly logical, old fellow. You have the jewels. Almost half the value of the whole haul from Ingall."

"A good deal less than that," corrected his lordship.

"Also, you have Geraldi, the price of the rest of the stuff."

"I love to hear a precise mind at work," Winchelmere stated, and smiled.

"Now, let me tell you what I seriously propose," Asprey continued. "Geraldi is more dangerous than poison gas. Move him down into the sub-cellar. There is one, you know, dug under this old place."

"I know it. They used to keep wine in there . . . in the palmy days of the Oñate family."

"Take him there, and quietly brain him."

"A cold-blooded business," said his lordship.

"I'd gladly do it" Asprey assured the Englishman.

"Would you?" murmured Winchelmere, and closed his eyes. Whether in horror or in mere thought, Asprey could not quite guess.

"And now let me tell you a little more."

"By all means, Edgar."

"The thing for us to do, seriously, is to thank heaven that Geraldi is a dead man. Take what we have. And leave at once for far fields."

"In short," said the other, "you take this country sheriff very seriously?"

Asprey frowned and collected his thoughts, like a man who does not wish to exaggerate. "There aren't many natural officers of the law," he said. "But this fellow is, I think, as patient as a snake and as dangerous as a rattler."

His lordship opened his eyes wider and looked straight up to the ceiling with a faint smile. "Ah, ah," he said. "And that's what we have to deal with now? Asprey, I see that you're right in every respect."

"You agree, then?"

"Yes, that the sensible thing is for us to put Geraldi out of the way and make off at once with what we have."

The fat man smiled with sinister pleasure.

"But," Winchelmere went on, "I'm held back. Not by the usual scruples that a man might feel about such a business, but because it would give me an enormous amount of pleasure to use Geraldi as a sort of bill of exchange. It would be a blow . . . to his vanity . . . from which he would never recover. I enjoyed looking at him when I first made the suggestion. His face wrinkled as though he suddenly had grown old."

Asprey was silent, but intent. "You like him, too," he remarked sarcastically.

"I hate him," Winchelmere sneered, "with a magnificent hatred. He has wrecked my old life, split me away from the chance of an honorable pretense at existence in England, and forced my hand in every respect. Besides that, he has been in my hands and has slipped out. He has taken a treasure out of my pocket, as you might say. And the result is, Edgar, that I can't be contented with an ordinary revenge. To lead him into a cellar and smash his skull! That would be quite sufficient for most men. But not in this case. I want to use him, as I said. And then I want to have him at full liberty to come on my trail again. I want to encourage him to match wits, craft, and strength against me, and then see what comes of it."

"That," Asprey declared, "is sporting."

"Thank you," said his lordship.

"But," Asprey continued, "there was a speech that the gladiators used to make to the emperors before they fought. You remember? 'We, who are about to die, salute thee!' You might wind up with that speech yourself, my friend."

"True," said the other calmly. "If I were alone against him. But I don't intend to be alone. I intend to employ the strength and the craft of Oñate, and Rompier, and that yellow rascal, Kalam, and above all my most valued friend, Asprey, from whom I am learning something every day."

The fat man pressed the plump, soft tips of his fingers together. Then he nodded. "Pride makes a man foolish," he said, "but also it makes him wise. I wish you luck. But I think that this decision of yours is going to break your neck . . . and mine, also." He got up.

As he reached the door, Winchelmere came to his feet in turn. "Do you agree with me, Edgar, that it might be a great game?"

288

"There's only one thing that turns the balance in your favor," Asprey said, "and that is that I want to have you for a friend. For the sake of that, I'll stick with you to the end." So said Edgar Asprey, with a hand suddenly pressed against his heart, as though the last words had come with a sudden rush from that seat of the emotions.

He lied. Winchelmere knew it. Asprey was perfectly sure that the other understood. And still that lie came off with a certain grace.

To a degree, we are all children watching a play. Even when we know that the spoken words are unreal and rarely in earnest, still, we cannot help but applaud them and let our hearts be warmed by them. Moreover, the acting of Asprey was so very good that Winchelmere was vastly pleased as a professional critic. He saw that the veil he penetrated might be far too thick for another person to see through.

So he bowed to Asprey. "I'll never forget this moment," he said with a simple heartiness.

When Asprey was through the door, Winchelmere broke into silent laughter, and that was a mistake. For no sooner was he outside in the hall than the eye of Asprey was clapped to the keyhole, and he saw the laughter with perfect clearness.

Asprey went on his way down the hall, moving with a wonderfully silent step in spite of his bulk. As he walked, he rubbed his soft, thick chin with the moist tips of his fingers and wondered if all was well.

"Jimmy," he said in the gentlest of voices, "I have something to tell you."

"Fat men never can bring good news," Geraldi stated.

"No, Jimmy, I cannot. After all the things that have passed between us, you'll be surprised to hear that I cannot help being fond of you."

"You have a big heart," Geraldi said.

"Jimmy, don't laugh at me. I want to tell you, now, that you have just passed a great danger. Your life has been in the balance. And now . . . you may thank your gods that the balance has turned the right way. You are safe. Your life is not in danger."

"On which side of the balance did you throw your weight?" asked Geraldi.

"Jimmy," the fat man said in a soft voice, "can you ask?"

"Shall I thank you?" Geraldi asked. "Or shall I thank Horus? Golden Horus. Horus of the two horizons, of the evening and the dawn, Horus of the . . ."

"Damnation!" Asprey exploded, and walked hurriedly away. He turned at the pillars of the patio. Geraldi was smiling after him like a great, sleepy cat.

# CHAPTER
# ELEVEN

## "Pepillo Passes"

Little Giovanni, earnest and eager, sat on the arm of the chair of Geraldi. "They are going to take you away tonight," he said.

"Have you heard that?"

"I have heard them talking. From the room above them. It was just as you thought. I can crawl in there, and no one knows that I am there. There is a great crack in the ceiling. I can hear everything they say. Sometimes I can see them, too."

"You are my ears and my eyes, Giovanni," Geraldi said.

"But why have you let them keep you here?" asked the youngster, eyeing Geraldi with an almost impersonal interest. "Why don't you kill the two men at the gate of the patio and go away?"

"How shall I kill them, Giovanni?" Geraldi asked gravely.

"That can be done easily. I shall first get the best horse from the stable. The great black stallion which *Señor* Winchelmere says is his horse, but which I know is yours."

"How do you know that?"

"When you call him, he will come . . . even to the gate of the patio . . . and put his head under the arch and whinny to you."

Geraldi nodded. "There would be a horse for me. You'd saddle him and . . . ?"

"And open the gate of the corral. Then, when you called, he could come."

"Of course. But still there would be the two men standing at the patio gate with their rifles."

"Sometimes you sit just in the center of the patio," said the boy. "Move out your chair there, now. I give you, then, some of the little knives that I practice with. First, I have sharpened them until they are too sharp to see. And then I pass them to you. At the right time, you throw them. One sticks in the heart of the pale man. And you run through the entrance, calling to Peter. He comes. You are away, and you catch me up behind your saddle . . . what could we not do together, señor."

"So," Geraldi began. "Still, all of this is for nothing, because I can't break my word. And I have given my word that I shall not try to escape if they let me sit here in the sun."

The boy snorted with disgust. "They have no right to keep you."

"Perhaps not."

"Then you have a right to get away."

"Besides," Geraldi tried to explain, "I don't want to kill those two men, even if I could. They never have harmed me."

"They stand here with guns."

"That is true. But one must be reasonable. Every life that a man takes is a burden of lead, Giovanni, bent around your shoulders, to carry the rest of your days."

Giovanni was not too young to realize that this was a metaphor; certainly he was old enough to appreciate the solemnity of Geraldi. Finally the latter said: "Also, you could not leave your mother. Could you?"

"Perhaps not," admitted the boy. "I'm no use to her."

"You will be in a few years. If you can't do her any good now, you could break her heart by going away from her."

Giovanni, pouting sullenly, scowled at the world and at all these new thoughts. "It is very hard," he said. "It is very hard for a man to be free. Is it not? You, however, are free. You are the only man in the world who is free."

"Why am I freer than others?"

"Because," the boy said with a sudden inspiration, "you are brave enough to live by yourself. All the other men . . . they must have wives and friends and children. You are by yourself. That is why you are free."

Geraldi contemplated this thought in silence, and it seemed to him so true that he did not attempt to argue about it.

"What else did you hear in the room?" Geraldi asked, bringing the talk back to its starting point.

"I heard the fat man say that you should be killed. There was no safety for the rest of them if you remained alive."

"I thank him for that."

"Why do you smile?"

"Because I am thinking. Go on, Giovanni. What else did you hear?"

"I heard the big man . . ."

"His lordship . . . Winchelmere?"

"Yes. He said that you must not die. He wants to trade you for something. As if you were a horse or a cow. Afterwards, he wants to fight with you."

For the first time, Geraldi showed real interest and sat up in his chair. "Did he say that? I'm surprised, Giovanni. I'm surprised. I see that there are good points about his lordship. I shall have to remember him a little longer than I thought."

"That is all that I remember. That is all that was important," said the boy. "Look at Pepillo sleeping in the sun. He's a lazy beast, isn't he?"

"Do you know why?"

"Because everybody pets him and nobody ever makes him do things . . . except you and me. I kick him in the belly or the ribs. That makes him move."

"You'd better stop that. Someday he'll be grown up."

"What do you mean?"

"The reason he's so lazy, Giovanni, is because he's saving his strength for the day when he'll break away from this place. He wants to have fat on his ribs before he goes off into the mountains to live."

"Do you think that?"

"I do."

"He'll never leave. He doesn't dare. He's too afraid of San Luis."

"One day," Geraldi assured the boy, "he'll turn and slit the throat of San Luis from ear to ear."

294

"How do you know that?"

"Pepillo whispered it in my ear, one day not long ago."

The boy laughed, and he flung an arm around the shoulders of Geraldi. "I wish they would not take you away," he cried. "Afterwards, what will I do?"

"Away from my chair," whispered Geraldi. "Your mother . . ."

Although Giovanni jumped fast, he was too late. Bianca Strozzi came running to them from the doorway, and swooped at Giovanni. He evaded her with ease.

"Come here to me," she commanded.

"I won't!" Giovanni yelled. "I don't have to come . . . and you can't catch me!"

"You . . . you ungrateful . . . ," she began. Emotion choked her.

"Go to your mother," Geraldi said sternly.

"She will beat me," whined Giovanni.

"What if she does? Are you a man or a baby?" Geraldi asked.

Reluctantly the boy went toward Bianca, but her passion had altered its object in that instant. For she whirled upon Geraldi with a veritable devil in her eyes.

"*You* can make him do what you please . . . murderer!" screamed the widow. "You've made him despise everything and everyone except yourself. I . . . I . . ." She ceased again, impotent with rage under the calm and steady eyes of Geraldi. They were not unkindly eyes.

He said gently: "I know that you have to hate me. But remember that it was in the middle of a fight. It was at a distance. Bullets were flying everywhere . . ."

"A fight!" she shouted. "You never would have dared to stand before my husband. You would have turned and run like a beaten dog! He was a man that . . ." Her voice broke.

At that moment little Giovanni called: "Look, Mother!"

She turned her head instinctively and saw the boy standing beside the big cat.

"Look, Mother! I can make Pepillo curl up into a ball."

It was, doubtless, to do anything to distract the attention of his mother from Geraldi. The boy rapped Pepillo in the ribs with his shoe.

Pepillo turned, indeed. But one paw was raised high in the air. Silently he snarled, furious, his face contorted, his white fangs glistening. And his tail began to lash with rage.

"Giovanni . . . darling . . . you little fool! Come here quickly!" screamed the frightened mother.

"Bah!" Giovanni replied. "There's nothing to be afraid of." And he kicked Pepillo again, and this time straight in the unprotected stomach.

The reaction of Pepillo was swift and surprising. He had learned the force of his blow that same day. His muscles were fairly tingling with the electric consciousness of his powers, and he wanted to use them again. Can a millionaire let his money rest idle in a bank? He struck as he had struck at the goat. But on that occasion his claws had been bared, and now the last vestige of fear and respect for human beings caused Pepillo to keep the claws buried in the velvet. It was only the soft inside of the paw that struck. Even so, there was enough force to have broken the shoulder of a grown man. It was Giovanni's very lightness of body that, in part, saved him. As it was, he was hurled through the air against the nearest pillar of the patio, and he fell limp from that. Pepillo was on him at once. There was no remaining reverence in his furious heart now. He wanted his second kill, and his wicked eyes were on the throat of the boy as he sprang.

Now all of this had happened with dreadful suddenness. The two guards, with their ears filled by the wild shriek of the mother, had barely time to catch up their rifles and turn about. No hand was ready, save the hand of Geraldi. From somewhere in his clothes he brought out one of those little slender-bladed knives, heavy in the haft, with the steel drawing out to a mere ray of light. It flicked from his hand, aimed at the exposed side of Pepillo just behind the shoulder. Even then chance was all against Geraldi, for, if the little blade struck a rib, it would snap off and do little harm. Chance, however, flew with the flying knife. It found the tender surface between two ribs and slid home to the hilt.

Pepillo, with a death shriek, leaped on past little Giovanni and clutched the top of the pillar, clawing wildly to get up. In an instant, his hold relaxed and he fell with a loose thud against the ground. A small puff of dust arose from the spot. Pepillo did not move. His mask still gaped, his lips still grinned back from his teeth. But even this ended. His head rolled a bit to one side, and his beautiful and dangerous life was ended.

The two guardsmen, grunting with excitement, came charging in and found Bianca Strozzi bent over the limp form of her boy. She swept him into her arms. There was a streak of blood across his forehead. Bianca crushed the limp body in her arms against her breast, crying — "Giovanni! Giovanni! Giovanni!" — again and again with more heartbreak in every cry.

"Is he hurt bad?" asked one of the men humbly.

"He's killed!" Bianca Strozzi moaned. "And you've let him die . . . under your eyes . . . under your guns!"

# CHAPTER
# TWELVE

## "A. Prisoner, Indeed"

Geraldi had risen from his chair to throw the knife. Now he sank back in it again. "You'll stifle Giovanni!" he cautioned the woman.

She ran to him suddenly and laid the limp body across his knees. "Save him, *maestro!*" sobbed Bianca. "You can! I saw you strike for him! Heaven bless you!" She knelt beside him in the dust; she caught his hand and kissed it.

The two riflemen stood agape, helpless, willing to assist, but clumsy-handed.

"Hush!" Geraldi murmured. "He's not badly hurt . . . I think. Stunned. We'll see to his head. Look! Only a cut in the skin. His shoulder . . . you see, the arm works freely. His legs are not broken. I think his ribs are sound, too."

Bianca Strozzi hung upon these words, as though by each separate declaration Geraldi endowed another portion of the child with life and soundness.

Giovanni's eyes fluttered.

"Be quiet," Geraldi said to the woman. "Don't make any outcry. You see he's doing very well."

The eyes opened wide. Giovanni looked up with unclouded gaze at Geraldi.

"You see, you were right," Giovanni muttered, and laughed a little.

Bianca Strozzi raised her eyes and her clasped hands. But whether she adored Providence or Geraldi, it would have been hard to say.

Giovanni sat up with a little gasp. "What happened?" he asked. "Things are sort of a blue, as I remember them."

Bianca picked him from the knees of Geraldi. "Come to see!" she said, and half carried and half dragged him to the limp, dead body of Pepiilo. "Look!" she said, pointing.

The boy drew out the stained knife, and his eyes turned slowly to Geraldi.

"I told you!" cried Bianca Strozzi. "I called to you. I warned you. Little rascal!" She struck Giovanni, but very, very softly.

"*He* threw it!" Giovanni said.

"He did," Bianca confirmed, catching her breath. "*He* gave you your life. Heaven bring him safe through danger. Heaven watch over him."

The eyes of the child filled with tears, and his mother, seeing this, caught him again in her arms and carried him from the patio, sobbing as she went. Over her shoulder, with dim eyes, Giovanni watched the face of Geraldi to the last moment.

"A proper job you done," one of the guards said to Geraldi. "A finer or a slicker or a smoother thing *I* never seen!"

"Nor me," said the other.

The two went back to the entrance to take up their posts. Then Geraldi saw Lord Winchelmere loitering in the doorway of the house. He came slowly out and paused beside Geraldi's chair.

"At your clever tricks again, I see," he said. "Corrupting the guards. Corrupting the women and the children, Geraldi. Up to today, I thought that I need only worry for fear she'd put poison in your food. Ah, Geraldi," he went on, "I admit that you have a certain way about you."

"Thank you," Geraldi stated, but the slightest of shadows passed over his eyes.

The hope that had risen in him had been extinguished at its source.

"And so we go," said his lordship, who seemed to have interpreted even that passing emotion perfectly. "The window no sooner is opened to us than it is slammed and locked and shuttered again. However, it was a neat bit of work, Geraldi. Did you plan the whole thing? Did you put it in the mind of Pepillo?" He smiled at his own preposterous question. "It's time for you to turn in for the evening," he continued. "Before morning, I hope to have you on the way down to San Felice. There, Geraldi, I expect to exchange you for certain articles of value in the hands of Miss Ingall and her aunt. I know," he continued, "that you have a romantic notion that your life should not be had for such a price. But, my dear fellow, you'll understand my viewpoint. I can't very well put a knife in your back. Neither can I afford to give you away for nothing. Will you go with us, or do we have to . . . take you?" He asked the question with a little lift of the eyebrows.

Geraldi replied with silence and the faintest of smiles, allowing just a white glimpse of his teeth.

Winchelmere, waiting no longer for a reply he knew he would not get, sauntered on to the gate, looked out, and then back to the house. He called to one of the men: "Joe, catch Peter for me this evening and put my saddle on him. I may need him before the morning." He turned to Geraldi as he said this and chuckled a little. For between them there was almost more rivalry over the subject of Peter than about all else put together. Then the big Englishman went into the house.

Shortly after this, Geraldi was escorted from the patio. It was dusk, and the vines along the walls began to look like long streaks and overlaid masses of shadow, so that the world seemed a soft and restful place to all but Geraldi. He was conducted through the house, and then down a steep flight of stairs into the first cellar of the place. During the day he was allowed a vast deal of liberty, and it might be said that the two guards who watched over him were not so much actual preventatives of an escape, but simply to keep an eye on him as a matter of form.

At night, however, he refused to be bound by any parole. As he had said to Winchelmere, when the Englishman had proposed such an engagement: "One never can tell. If I give you a complete parole, then it means, of course, that I either have to give up all hope for my life or for my honor."

302

"Between those two," Winchelmere had said with a caustic smile, "I'm sure the latter would be your choice."

Geraldi had said nothing. He rarely spoke to Winchelmere. There was too great a gap between them, a void that neither could overleap.

Winchelmere had said with a cold laugh that he feared he could not assure his prisoner of comfortable nights, and he set out to fulfill his promise. So, each night, they fastened Geraldi securely, as they had done on this occasion. Around his wrists they wove a long piece of soft, strong baling wire, such as is laid on the middle of a bale, where the strain is the greatest. And, having secured the wrists behind his back in this fashion, they made security doubly sure by fastening another piece of wire from his elbows across his breast. After that, more wire secured his ankles together, and his knees were bound fast. Still this was not enough, and a final strand ran down from his wrists, and across his knees, and so to his heels. This system was adopted because Lord Winchelmere in person devised and installed it. He declared that he would have no patent locks and irons put on Geraldi. Because, as all men knew, Geraldi could read the secret of any lock, and open it with a breath. More than that, he would not trust even a dog to ropes. A dog would gnaw them through, and so would Geraldi — like a fire. But this tough iron wire was another matter. Soft and pliable, it could be worked well into the flesh above the wrists of the prisoner. It gripped to the very bone of the man.

So Geraldi was forced to lie all night upon his face. His hands were behind him. If he ventured to try to lie on either side, very soon it was as though his arms were breaking. So the nights were very long, indeed, and Winchelmere chose, with unnecessary cruelty, to confine his prisoner early in the evening and release him to his parole late in the morning. To the last of these long agonies, therefore, Geraldi was now taken, and the load of wire bent upon him with the harsh haste of people who forget what pain they can give. Winchelmere came in person to oversee the work. When it was done, he said quietly to Geraldi: "Your last night, my friend. Tomorrow we take you to market. Good night."

# CHAPTER
# THIRTEEN

## " 'Tis Well to Have a File"

There was a plain pallet of straw. It was not aired during the day, and, therefore, the moisture from the floor of the cellar had soaked through the mattress and gave Geraldi a moldy scent in his nostrils all the night long. He soon was disturbed on this evening. The door of his cell was of the heaviest oak, and outside it two men spent the entire night, one sleeping and the other waking, alternately in two-hour shifts.

This door now opened, and, although he was turned away toward the wall at the moment and, therefore, could see nothing, he heard one of his guards rumble: "Be short and quick. The old man would take our heads off, if he knew that we'd even let you speak to him."

Then the troubled, broken voice of Bianca Strozzi called to Geraldi: "Giovanni sleeps, and all is well with him. I have come to tell you that I pray for you, dear friend. Farewell, and heaven help you more than I can help."

"There, that's enough," broke in the man's voice roughly. And the door slammed before Geraldi could make any answer.

He was instantly at work, however. For, when Bianca Strozzi had raised her voice, it seemed to Geraldi that his quick ear had caught the slightest sound of metal against stone, a smaller sound than the tinkle of water falling for an instant into a stone basin. He could only move upon his side, wriggling like a seal deprived of flippers. But in this manner he worked himself across the damp floor until he was close to the entrance. There he began to move his face as another would have moved a hand, touching the skin lightly against the floor, here and there. For an hour he worked, and, during that hour, a thousand cramps came in the muscles of his neck, but he went on patiently, finally pressing his chin into the crevices near the wall. There, at last, he felt something cold as the back of a snake. But as he touched it again with his chin, he noticed the harshness of the surface.

It was his hope Bianca Strozzi had not left all to the power of prayer. She had committed some hope to this file she had managed to drop on the floor. But next, to use it. He turned his back to the wall and, with his groping fingers, found the treasure. Outside the door he heard one of his guards coughing. So perfectly did the wall fit and so thick was the wood that even at that close range the sound of the coughing was stifled to the quality of a sob.

He managed to stand up — a difficult task. Then he worked himself slowly down the wall that was composed of heaviest stone, laid up without mortar. The crevices between were what he searched with the tips of his fingers. At last he found one that suited him, and into this he wedged the file with all the iron strength of his hands.

It was of the finest steel. He knew that by the sharpness of the ridges on the face of the tool. He proved it an instant later as, standing with his back to the wall, swaying his body from side to side, he chafed through the wire that fastened wrists and knees and heel in a straight line. With that wire severed, his activity was doubled. He turned his attention to the strands that bound his elbows in place, and these, too, parted at a few touches. After that, he could thank a long gymnastic training for his next feat, which was to pass his bound wrists beneath his feet. This he contrived with many a snaky wriggle and writhing motion.

This achievement placed his hands in front of him, and he could work now with so much added surety that it was almost like passing from light to darkness. He began to chafe the right wrist bindings against the file, and it was a delicate process, which meant keeping the same line of cutting always on the edge of the tool. But he felt the wires give one by one. The file had to sink into his own flesh to tear through the last few wrappings, but he set his teeth and even smiled at this small pain as he worked. So, in another moment, his right hand was free. He paused in his work, but began again almost at once. In another instant his feet also were liberated.

But what had been gained, after all, by this liberation of his body? There was no grating through which he could cut with that same heaven-sent file. There was only a solid wall of stones and two keen-eared guards to listen to the first attempt he made to escape. However, he had made up his mind long before as to what he would do. He lighted a match and picked out on the floor the largest of the great flags that covered it. With the hilt of the file, at the edges of this flag he worked, and, since there was no mortar, the flag presently came up free, but heavily, in his hands. He lighted another match. Below him appeared earth. He thrust his foot into it, tentatively, and the foot went through into emptiness. It was as he had hoped — the sub-cellar opened directly underneath his cell.

The adjoining flag was soon up, using the ponderous first one as a lever, and, with the earth beneath them beaten down, two edges of strong stone arches were presented. Between the two, Geraldi dropped down to the floor of the room beneath.

By glimmers of match light he worked through the brief maze of the old wine rooms. He found what had once been a stairs, now an incline from which the steps had moldered and rotted away, and up this he passed to the level above. He saw the gleam of a pair of distant lanterns and distinctly heard a man singing very softly as he walked back and forth. Geraldi smiled brightly. There were his guards, seriously employed in their work. It was as though his ghost remained behind, imprisoned in the wire. He himself walked free, the file still in his hands.

He climbed to the floor above, and now he wasted invaluable time in going to the rear porch of the house where, as he knew, a bucket of water was standing. With that water he washed the mold and grime from his face and hands, and dried himself with the roller towel that hung against the wall, Western style. Still further he delayed, to brush his clothes as clean as possible, and, when this was done, he turned his attention back to the house, moving down the lower hall, and then stepping aside to the gun room.

Here all manner of tackle was kept, and his own equipment that had been taken from him at the time of his capture was among the rest. Scrupulously he took only his own — a bundle of oddly shaped keys, a thin case filled with slivers of steel of various sizes — more important to Geraldi than all the keys in the world — two single-action, old-style Colts, their sights and triggers filed away, and a pair of those slender knives of his that fitted into a double sheath. He took also his own electric lantern, for this he would need before his work was done. Last of all, he strapped on his wristwatch.

He smiled to himself to think that these professional thieves had not laid hand upon a single item of his property. What sense of delicacy was this? Or was it, by chance that not one of them wished to have the first owner call in person to redeem his goods? He thought grimly of that for a moment. Then he went into the hall and passed down to that room that was occupied by the lord and master of the household — Pedro Oñate.

Of that silent, evil face he knew less than he did about any of the others in the house, for Oñate scorned conversation, feeling, instead, that action was more his vein. The door of Oñate's room gave readily to the hand of Geraldi. He opened it softly and slowly, preventing a creak. Then he crouched low and slipped in. He saw the bed at once, with Oñate dimly outlined upon it against the starlight that entered by the window. He lay face down, sprawling, like a dead body.

Geraldi dropped the cold muzzle of a revolver on the back of the Mexican's neck. And he said in Spanish: "I come, señor, to relieve you of the thing which you have in trust."

Oñate lay perfectly still. Finally he whispered: "Afterwards, Señor Geraldi?"

"Afterwards, I put a safe and painless gag between your teeth. And I leave you here, unharmed."

"In the heel of the right shoe," Oñate said without further bargaining.

Geraldi secured him swiftly, deftly. He had experience in such business, and he used all his knowledge. In three minutes Oñate had less possibility of motion than a frozen snake in mid-winter.

Geraldi left him and went straight across the hall, carefully closing the door behind him. In the opposite compartment Rompier, he knew, was sleeping. That door in turn he opened with as much care as he had used before. Instantly there was a rustle of bedclothes.

"Who's there?" asked the guarded voice of the Frenchman. Then he muttered: "The draft of wind, I suppose."

His bare feet sounded instantly on the floor, and he advanced through the darkness until the iron hand of Geraldi caught him by the throat and the gun of Geraldi was clapped to his head.

"The emerald, Rompier," Geraldi whispered, and relaxed his grip on the throat of his man.

"Certainly," Rompier said. "With the greatest of pleasure, my dear friend. In the heel of the Colt that is under my pillow. And I, Geraldi?"

"A gag and a few ropes, and my regrets," Geraldi responded. "That is all that I can offer."

"I accept with thanks," said the Frenchman. "You've not the time, now, but will you write to me and tell me how you managed all this?"

# CHAPTER
# FOURTEEN

## "The Wind is Rising"

There remained the last and the greatest obstacle. Geraldi went down the hall and paused before the door of Lord Winchelmere. It was framed with a glistening line of golden light. Geraldi stooped and tried the keyhole, but the key was in it from the inside, and all vision was effectually blocked. So he rapped boldly.

"Come in," said the careless voice of his lordship.

Geraldi swung the door open and saw Winchelmere seated at a small table beside the window. A hooded lamp was near him, and he was writing busily.

"You're half an hour too early, Rompier," he said, without looking up. "You shouldn't have disturbed me so soon . . . but, since you're here . . ."

Geraldi closed the door. At the continued silence, Winchelmere turned his head. It brought it closer to the lamp. The blond locks seemed to turn to flaming gold. He looked for an instant from the brightness into the dimness, bewildered. Then he narrowed his eyes. His voice was perfectly calm.

"So, here you are at last, Geraldi."

"A little early, I fear," Geraldi said. "Earlier, even, than Rompier?"

"Even earlier than Rompier," the big man repeated, "but always welcome to me, old fellow." He waved to a chair.

Geraldi sat down with the slightest of bows. He held the revolver negligently in his hand, the muzzle resting across his knee.

"And what can I do for you?" Winchelmere asked, with a smile that seemed far from affected.

"Lower your voice, and give me a little information."

"You have sensitive ears, then?" asked his lordship courteously.

"They've bothered me from my childhood," Geraldi responded. "They've brought me all sorts of bad news."

"You want to know about what, then?"

"The emerald, my lord."

"That I am keeping?"

"Yes."

"You have the other pair?"

"Yes."

"Then I couldn't afford to embarrass such a patient collector," Winchelmere said, with the slightest quiver of his voice as he spoke. He opened a little drawer of the table and took out a twist of paper. This he undid and spilled the bright green gem upon the palm of his hand. "Is this it, Geraldi?"

"The very one," said the latter. There was a faint creaking in the hall, as Geraldi thought.

"The wind is rising again," Winchelmere stated.

"Suppose you put the emerald on the top of the table," Geraldi said, "and then face the wall."

"Certainly," his lordship said, and he rose from his chair, taking the lamp in his hand.

"Put the lamp down!" Geraldi commanded sharply.

"Willingly." Winchelmere, with an obedient nod, nevertheless, swung the lamp across the face of the window before he placed it again on the table.

"And that," Geraldi commented, "is a signal, I think?"

His lordship already stood with his face to the wall, in the corner of the room. He answered nothing as Geraldi scooped up the jewel, with one sharp glance to make sure that it was real and no sham. His second glance was for the patio, and clearly he made out two men running through the patio gate and the glimmer of their rifles. It had been a signal, indeed, and his time was very short. Exit by the window, certainly, was stopped already.

He remembered the faint creaking he had heard in the hall, and he gritted his teeth. Perhaps that way of exit was also crowded with silent fighting men, waiting for the word of Winchelmere. Desperately his glance swept the room. Through twenty chinks in those moldered walls, it might be that hostile eyes were now covertly watching him.

He gathered the three jewels in his hand, and, stepping back a little, his gun still leveled on Winchelmere, he thrust the emeralds into a deep crevice — far in, until his fingers gritted on the mortar.

"Winchelmere," he said, in hardly more than a whisper, "you've taken advantage of my generosity. If I'd known what was in you, a knife in the back might

314

have settled you. As it is, I trust to chance. Good night." He stepped to the door and jerked it quickly open, leaping at the same time through the gap.

It was his hope that the very speed of his actions might disconcert any watcher in the hall, but he sprang into the grip of many arms. They crushed him with their weight and with their force. They bore him straight back into the chamber and smashed him against the wall. He saw before him the contorted faces of Rompier and Oñate, and the expressionless eyes of Kalam. Lord Winchelmere loomed head and shoulders above this group.

"Tenderly, tenderly," his lordship advised. "There's no need to break him in bits . . . simply secure his hands, Lucien. You can help him, Seyf."

It was done with the speed of science. The weapons of Geraldi were removed from him again.

"Up again, down again," Winchelmere hummed. "How unlucky you've been in the last stages of the encounter."

"I trusted too much to you, Winchelmere," Geraldi replied, anger for once breaking through his self-possession. "If there is another time, I'll better know how to handle you."

"There'll be no other time," said Asprey, a huge bulk in the doorway. "Winchelmere, you've had a sufficient warning this time, I hope?"

"And here you are at last?" murmured his lordship. "Just when we need you, Asprey?"

The irony did not escape Asprey. "You trusted wire and walls to hold him," he said. "Have you lost anything?"

"Only what we'll quickly have again. But first, what happened to you, Rompier and Oñate?"

"A gun at the back of my neck," Oñate admitted. "That was all. Then Seyf came and passed a knife through the ropes. Bah! I have the taste of the gag still in my mouth!"

"It was practically the same for me," Rompier announced. "I thought that a wind opened the door of my room. *He* was the draft that budged it."

"Seyf," said the leader, "we write down in red what you've done tonight. We write it down in red," he repeated.

There was a single, flashing smile from Kalam, then his dark face was as gloomy as ever.

"And now," Winchelmere said, "in what pocket are the emeralds?"

"I haven't got them," Geraldi answered.

"That's childish," said his lordship. "Will you make us search you through to the skin?"

"Do you remember the creak in the hall . . . the rising of the wind, as you called it?" Geraldi asked. "And when I glanced out the window, I saw that two men were running for the house. I guessed that all ways might be blocked to me, and so I disposed of the emeralds, my lord."

"A pretty thin lie," Oñate stated. "We'll take him and . . ."

"Let him be," Winchelmere said curtly. "He's hidden them. That's obvious. Search the room, my boys. Search every crack in the walls."

He joined the search. A wall to a man, the floor to another, they went over the surface carefully and swiftly. Geraldi saw Asprey go past the crack into which he had thrust the gems. With a flashlight, the fat man probed the crack — and then went on, while Geraldi breathed more deeply with relief. It seemed impossible, unless perhaps a slight fall of mortar had powdered the emeralds over and so concealed them. But Asprey went on. Perhaps to return later, and try to steal the jewels for himself alone?

At last the search stopped.

"Not here," Winchelmere announced decidedly. "Then he threw them through the window. Rompier, search the court, will you? Kalam and Oñate will help you."

They left at once. The fat man remained with the Englishman and Geraldi.

"Was it the woman?" Winchelmere asked good-naturedly.

Geraldi waved his hand and smiled in turn. "Why do you ask me?" he said. "Is it impossible for a man to work even out of wire?"

"Yes," said his lordship. "Totally and absolutely impossible. But let it drop. Asprey, where's Bianca?"

"She and her boy have skipped out," he returned.

His lordship nodded. "I guessed that, long ago," he said. "What do you suggest now, Asprey? We're not going to find the three stones, I take it."

"Of course, we're not," Asprey said. "There's only one thing to do, of course, and that's to *persuade* Geraldi."

He put a singular emphasis upon the word persuade, so that Winchelmere frowned a little. "You have a tender heart, Asprey," he said coldly. "But," he went on, "we have to be practical people. Geraldi is now our only remaining bill of exchange. We must turn him in for gold and diamonds." He laughed as he spoke. "You mustn't singe a good bill of exchange, Edgar," he concluded.

The fat man unwillingly nodded.

# CHAPTER
# FIFTEEN

# "In the Name of the Law"

It was a little after midnight when they left the house. The order of their going was: Geraldi in the front seat of the buckboard, his feet lashed together, and his hands tied behind him, and fastened, in turn, to the iron rail that ran around the rear of the seat. Lord Winchelmere held the reins, sitting beside his captive. In the seat behind was Oñate, a rifle across his knees. Behind the wagon were tethered big black Peter, with Winchelmere's saddle on its back, and a tall, thin, gray mare, the favorite mount of the Mexican. Still farther to the rear rode Asprey, a very sure shot and a known fighter; he would keep the guard to the rear, while in front of the buckboard or to either side rode Lucien Rompier and Seyf Kalam, with eyes as keen as the eyes of eagles.

Asprey had advice to give. "Drive hard," he said to Lord Winchelmere, "until we get through the two patches of woods. I have that lean sheriff in my mind. He's been lying too low, too quiet this evening. So far as we can tell, Bianca may have slipped off and told him everything she knows, which is too much. Everything she guesses would be plenty to hang us all.

I have in mind that the sheriff is doing something tonight. He'd be a fool to wait for morning."

His lordship agreed with this advice perfectly, and, as he gathered the reins, he said quietly: "Oñate, in case we run into a pocket of danger . . . then we can make up our minds that Geraldi will be no further use to us. In that case, a bullet through the head, if you please."

Oñate grunted. There was no doubt about his willingness to execute that suggestion, and Winchelmere, sending the two ponies down the road at a brisk trot, added to Geraldi: "You understand my position, of course? I really hate brutality."

"I believe you." Geraldi smiled and looked away from his companion and up to the stars.

There was no more talk. They struck a twelve-mile-an-hour gait, the ponies stepping out freely in the chilly air of the mountain night, and in a moment they were in the thickness of the woods. The road was quite out of sight, most of the time. The trees were simply an added tower of blackness on either side of the way, and the road itself could barely be guessed at, the ponies finding their own footing. Still Winchelmere drove as boldly as though full daylight showed him the ruts.

With a great noise the buckboard crashed on. Every board in it seemed loose, and the wheels rattled like snare drums. Still their choice was made, and Winchelmere, although he set his teeth, did not make a single objection. He was very alert. A great part of the time, as they whistled through the darkness, he kept the span in check with one hand, while the other rested lightly on a short-barreled carbine of large caliber that lay between him and the outside of the seat.

They had gone a full mile through the first stretch of the woods, and beyond these they were somewhat heartened to see the pale flush of the rising moon in the east, and then the rim of her disk pushing up. Lord Winchelmere looked toward it with a nod. Rapidly it sailed up, first like a wheel, rolling up the side of the mountain, and then detaching itself like a great, golden bubble and floating up through the blackness of the sky.

Geraldi laughed softly.

"And why?" asked his lordship.

"Great Horus!" Geraldi answered in a voice of pretended emotion. "Golden Horus, Horus of the two horizons! You see that he has sent his sister out to look after me."

Lord Winchelmere, in spite of himself, shuddered a little.

"You have the nerve of a lion, Geraldi," he commented briefly.

"Thank you," said Geraldi.

"Listen to me," said Winchelmere, speaking low, without turning his head.

"I can hear you."

"Geraldi, you and I have been enemies, but not enemies of long standing. Now, my friend, I make a suggestion to you. The best that can happen to you is to make the end of this journey, be delivered like a dog to Miss Ingall, and let her pay your ransom. Most men wouldn't mind that. But I know that it's poison to your pride. The worst thing that can happen to you, on the other hand, is to have a bullet through your spinal column, fired by our attentive comrade, Oñate, on the seat behind us. But I have a suggestion to make to you."

"Very well," Geraldi said without warmth.

"I'll set you free, Geraldi. We'll tap Oñate on the head, take Peter and the gray mare . . . she's a sprinter . . . and bolt away from these fellows . . . drift a bit of lead into them, if necessary . . . and then we'll go back to the house and pick up the emeralds that you left there. Mind you, I don't want a share in them. They'd be all yours. You've worked hard enough to get them. Afterward, my profit will come out of having you with me in future deals. Will you think that over?"

Geraldi thought it over, accordingly, while they climbed a steep hill, at the very top of which the broad face of the moon flared down at them.

"I should thank you for that suggestion," he said at last, "but I'll tell you, Winchelmere, if I were starved for water, I wouldn't take a drop from you."

Winchelmere simply laughed at this bitterness. "After all," he declared, "I really expected some such retort. I don't know why I knew . . . but I did."

They gained the top of the hill. Before them stretched a long slope, flooded with pale silver. Halfway down a woods began, ran for not more than a furlong, and then the open country waited to receive them into its safety.

"That one little spot of danger . . . and then we are free," the English lord said. He gave the ponies the whip, and they jerked the buckboard down the road at an astonishing clip, the iron-rimmed wheels bounding from the rocks and knocking out great sparks. Oñate cursed violently in the rear seat, but made no direct protest.

"Too much stomach to Oñate," Winchelmere commented to Geraldi. "And yet . . . he's a beautiful man for a murder." The remark had its obvious point.

In a moment they were shooting into the thickness of the woods. The trees grew so close together that even the light of the full moon could only penetrate with dim streaks and rays, here and there. Their huge trunks stood like grotesque forms drawn out of a wild imagination, and the roots sprawled and coiled like serpents by the way.

"One more instant . . . then the open," murmured Winchelmere.

And straight before him a ringing nasal voice called: "Stop! In the name of the law!"

Winchelmere gasped, and, catching his carbine under his arm, he pumped two shots in the direction of the voice, at the same time loosing the reins to the eager horses. A flare and roar answered, and the ponies stopped, frightened by that outburst of noise and flame. There was a violent wrench at the rear — big Peter had flung himself back in terror and, snapping his lead rope, fled.

Geraldi saw Rompier plunging away for safety to one side of the trees, and Kalam racing in the opposite direction. Winchelmere, rising, leaped back over the rear of the buck-board. And why did Geraldi himself continue to live and breathe? He twisted his head in time to see Winchelmere swing onto the gray mare and lift her away into the trees with bullets singing around his head. But Oñate still remained in his place, slumped heavily to one side, his head hanging down upon his chest. He seemed to be slumbering deeply, but Geraldi knew that it was the sort of slumber from which men never waken.

In the meantime, there was a bold rush of men at the buck-board, and that high-pitched, nasal clangor overriding even the noise of guns as the sheriff yelled: "Hosses, hosses! Ride, men, ride!"

He drove up on a mustang himself, and cut the ropes that held Geraldi.

"The gal told me about you. Good luck. Git a hoss, if you can, and foller us!"

And he was gone, his men streaming after him, some on the trail of Winchelmere, and some riding hard after Kalam or Rompier.

But none, as Geraldi noticed, had turned back up the road. Fat Asprey had been allowed to slip away unpursued.

With that, Geraldi whistled loudly, and again, and again. A faint neigh answered him, then came a crashing through the shrubbery. Peter, the big black horse, came careening back. Hastily Geraldi snatched the rifle and the revolvers of Oñate. In another moment he was in the saddle, sending the stallion flying out of the woods.

He did not ride forward or to either side, as the sheriff had suggested. Instead, he held his course to the

324

rear. The road was not straight enough for Geraldi, it seemed. He went across country as a bird flies on its way. Fences rose — the stallion flew over them. He came to a wide gap of darkness, with a creek shimmering in the hollow heart of it. And big Peter flew over that, also, and so he drove on, and pitched headlong into a mighty forest of spruce, and wound among the trees, still at breakneck speed.

Running out from those shadows of danger, at the last he had the knot of buildings before him, of which the broken-backed roof of Oñate's deserted house formed the highest point. Toward this he rode, but more slowly now, checking the stallion not toward the patio but to a copse in the rear of the house. There he threw the reins, dismounted from the panting horse, and was instantly through a broken window. He ran swiftly, noiselessly, down the hall and up the stairs until he came to the chamber that Lord Winchelmere had occupied. There, with no other light than the broad shaft of the entering moon, he found the crevice in the wall, thrust in his fingers deeply — and brought out three glimmering bits of green.

# CHAPTER SIXTEEN

## "The Better Man"

He was very impatient, but he controlled that impatience and made himself sit still in the darkest corner. So still did he sit that presently a rat began to gnaw at the mopboard, making a great noise, and after a time it came out and brushed its whiskers and, with beady eyes, looked up into the face of Geraldi. But the latter did not move. He remained as still as the stones of the wall, and the rat continued toward the table, beneath which he found something of interest that kept him running to and fro.

At last Geraldi raised his head. The slightest of movements, but it sent the rat shooting like a shadow for its hole. The entrance was small. It stuck there for an instant with a pitiful, choked squeal of terror, then scraped its way through, its snaky tail flashed out of sight, and it was gone.

Still Geraldi listened. He heard the far-off beat of hoofs. He heard them pause near the patio entrance. The sheriff, coming to search the house? He leaned a little, and, through the open window, he saw a bulky form enter the patio and hurry toward the house, his feet making no noise upon the ground. Geraldi sat back

**326**

in his chair. Still listening, he heard the faintest murmur, as of hinges stiff with rust, on the floor below. Then a soft creak — as from the stair.

He rose and stood against the wall in the corner. At once a big form loomed in the doorway, hesitated, and then went swiftly to the wall and thrust a hand into the crevice where the emeralds had been concealed.

"They're gone," Geraldi said. "Safely in my hands again, Edgar."

The fat men turned with a gasp. "Geraldi . . . you!"

"It's the end," Geraldi announced sternly.

The fat man answered nothing.

"Ordinarily," continued Geraldi, "I never soil my hands if I can avoid it. But a sneak and a traitor . . . a liar and a murderer. By heaven, Edgar, you're long overdue in the next world, and I intend to send you there."

Asprey's trembling gray lips parted, but he could not speak.

"You have a gun. Fill your hand," Geraldi said suddenly.

Asprey did not move.

There was a muffled exclamation of disgust from Geraldi.

And then Asprey answered, panting: "I'll never go for a gun, Jimmy. I know you're my master."

"I'll shoot you down, then," Geraldi responded, "as I'd shoot a coyote . . . a sneaking, treacherous coyote." He added: "You see that I give you a fair break. I have no weapon in my hand."

Asprey laughed. The sound was a harsh rattle in his throat as he answered: "I've seen you juggle guns, Jimmy. I can't be tempted."

"I'll turn my right side away from you, Asprey. Will that tempt you?"

"If you mean to murder me, murder me," said the fat man. "But I'll never try to defend myself against you. I can't. I know that you're the better man, Jimmy."

Something like a snarl formed on the lips of Geraldi. He went across the room with one bound. "Why can't I do it?" he exclaimed in a whisper through set teeth. "I ought to . . . Heaven knows you're overdue. But I can't . . . I can only . . . mark you." The thin blade of a knife gleamed in his fingers. It made a lightning-like cross in the air.

Asprey, with a cry, covered his bleeding face with his fat hands and sank upon his knees. He cried out again, wiped the blood from his eyes, and looked forth.

But Geraldi was gone. Like a shadow he fled down the hall, through a rear room, and dropped lightly to the ground. He cast one glance back at the blank face of the house, and then entered the woods.

Black Peter waited for him, whinnying softly at his coming — then shrinking back with a snort of disgust. So Geraldi mounted and rode at last out of the copse and came into the full blaze of the yellow moon.

There was little superstition in him, and yet he shivered a little, and, putting his hand into his waistcoat pocket, he clutched with a convulsive grasp the three emeralds that belonged to the golden box of Horus, the hawk, the god of the two horizons.

Beneath the moon lay the mountains, veiled with moon mist, looking huger than by day. Beyond them was the desert. In the desert lay his goal.

He spoke softly to the stallion, and Peter stepped out with a long, easy stride, like the trot of a wolf, and headed across the mountainside.